The Scandal of It All

She caught a flash of Strickland's luminescent eyes, the blue reaching deep inside her. As she gazed down at him, everything else faded.

Blood rushed to her ears as his hands slid beneath the veil of her hair to hold her face, his broad palms rasping the tender skin of her cheeks, thumbs sliding back and forth.

He stared at her for the briefest moment. Just a fleeting clash of gazes and then he pulled her down to his face. She froze at the shocking sensation of his lips. There was the barest, infinitesimal moment when she considered pushing him away.

Then that thought died.

It had been so long since she kissed a man.

She felt like a green girl, her lips quivering and barely moving against him. Almost as though this were the first kiss she ever had. And in so many ways, it was.

By Sophie Jordan

The Rogue Files Series
THE SCANDAL OF IT ALL
WHILE THE DUKE WAS SLEEPING

The Devil's Rock Series
FURY ON FIRE
HELL BREAKS LOOSE
ALL CHAINED UP

Historical Romances
ALL THE WAYS TO RUIN A ROGUE
A GOOD DEBUTANTE'S GUIDE TO RUIN
HOW TO LOSE A BRIDE IN ONE NIGHT
LESSONS FROM A SCANDALOUS BRIDE
WICKED IN YOUR ARMS
WICKED NIGHTS WITH A LOVER
IN SCANDAL THEY WED
SINS OF A WICKED DUKE
SURRENDER TO ME
ONE NIGHT WITH YOU
TOO WICKED TO TAME
ONCE UPON A WEDDING NIGHT

The Scandal of It All

The Rogue Files

Sophie Jordan

AVONBOOKS

An Imprint of HarperCollins*Publishers*

HarperCollins
PUBLISHERS
Since 1817

This is a work of fiction. Names, characters, places, and incidents are products of the author's imagination or are used fictitiously and are not to be construed as real. Any resemblance to actual events, locales, organizations, or persons, living or dead, is entirely coincidental.

First Avon Books mass market printing: August 2017

Print Edition ISBN: 978-0-06-246362-3
Digital Edition ISBN: 978-0-06-246363-0

FIRST EDITION

17 18 19 20 21 QGM 10 9 8 7 6 5 4 3 2 1

For my Aunt Loretta, one of the first heroines I've ever known. Your strength, energy and infectious laugh forever inspire.

The Scandal of It All

Chapter 1

The black-garbed ladies mingled through the room like bobbing crows, pecking at the food on their tiny plates with the same vigor with which they prattled about the recent demise of Lady Vanderhall, now at eternal rest in the velvet-swathed coffin positioned against the far wall of the drawing room.

Black baize fully draped the room, hiding the floral wallpaper. The impenetrable fabric covered the windows, too, shutting out all light. Candles flickered atop every surface, casting dancing light and shadows in the shrouded space. Tomorrow family and friends would escort the coffin to the church for the funeral. Until then vigil was maintained. People came and went, never letting the candles burn out. Always the room remained illuminated. Always the body never left alone.

"So tragic," one beak-nosed lady pronounced, waving her ham sandwich about imperiously. As though she were the first to make such an observation on this most unhappy occasion.

"Do you think her daughters will have any memories of her?" another inquired, searching through the room for the small girls.

"Doubtful. They're but ten and eight, I believe. Still such infants. It's doubtless for the best, though."

Graciela, the Duchess of Autenberry, downed the rest of her lemonade in the hopes it would chase the sour taste from her mouth. She looked longingly in the direction of the door, ready to escape.

For the *best* they forget their mother? It would be as though she never existed, dust lost to the wind, and these gabsters deemed that for the best? She hoped they were wrong. Entirely wrong.

The recently departed Lady Vanderhall had been her friend, and Graciela had few enough of those to feel her loss most keenly.

As soon as word reached her of Evangeline's unexpected death in a riding accident, Graciela had quit the country and traveled back to Town to pay her respects, leaving her daughter and stepdaughter behind at Autenberry Manor. No need to drag them all this way for something as dismal as a funeral, and Lady Vanderhall had been only a vague acquaintance to them.

At any rate, her daughter and stepdaughter preferred to stay in the country. This time of year Town offered very little diversion. Building snowmen and sledding down hills and reading Byron before the fire whilst they sipped chocolate held more appeal to the girls. In truth, at this particular moment, it held more appeal to Graciela. This was simply unbearable. She was already saddened over her friend's death, but these mourners only made her grief worse with their unfeeling remarks.

She didn't think she could abide one more moment of poor Evangeline's vigil, and tomorrow—the funeral—would be even more difficult.

"Bunch of carrion." Mary Rebecca fell in beside her, perhaps the only true friend left to her.

Like Graciela, Lady Talbot was a young widow not entirely favored by the ton. From the very start, they were outsiders. She was Irish, whilst Graciela hailed from Spain. More than one lady had discreetly accused them of stealing a noble husband away from a more deserving *English* lady. Graciela had heard the quiet mutterings when she first arrived in England at the tender age of eighteen. And she still heard them now at the age of five and thirty. Some things never changed.

"Lud! I think they relish it," Mary Rebecca murmured. "The misfortune of others makes them feel better at their own bleak lives."

Graciela shot a glance at her friend, bringing her cup to her lips. "I think we've paid our respects enough for this day."

"Indeed." Mary Rebecca nodded in agreement and turned away. "Shall we take our leave?"

They departed the house with but a few snide glances cast their way.

"I've a house all to myself," Graciela announced, slipping on her gloves as their carriages were brought around. Stepping out onto the stoop, she nestled into her ermine-trimmed cloak. Faint flurries of snow shook down from the afternoon sky. "Why don't you join me for some refreshment? We can properly toast to the memory of Evangeline and you can recount your holiday with the children. I should like to hear of it all."

"A house to yourself? Whatever is such a thing? When I took my leave this afternoon, my boys were pummeling each other with wooden swords whilst my daughter pitched a tantrum because she couldn't find her favorite shawl." Mary Rebecca looked heavenward. "Somehow the fault was mine to bear."

Graciela chuckled, understanding perfectly. "Of course."

"Indeed, I am in no hurry to return home. Lead the way, dear friend."

Smiling, Graciela permitted a groom to assist her into her carriage. It was true. She usually never found herself alone. Her daughter, Clara, and her stepdaughter, Enid, were always underfoot. Graciela preferred it that way. She enjoyed being surrounded by family and friends. She dreaded the day her daughter married and left her. Certainly she wanted Clara to find happiness and marry a good man, and at ten and four that day would be here before she knew it.

Life passed quickly. It seemed only yesterday Graciela had been running through Papa's vineyard in her bare feet, a girl with tangled hair, giggling as she played games of chase with her siblings and cousins. And now she was the mother of a daughter half-grown.

It wasn't just Clara she dreaded losing. She would miss Enid, too. Her stepdaughter was, by all accounts, a spinster. And yet Graciela expected she would marry someday, too. She read the longing in her eyes for a home of her own, a husband and children. She'd observed this in her face, watching as other girls her age married and started their own families. Her stepdaughter was headstrong and clever with definite bluestocking tendencies—not precisely the most sought out characteristic in an English bride, but Graciela had no doubt she would eventually meet a gentleman comfortable with her distinct charms.

And then Graciela would truly be alone. A widow watching the seasons change as she waited for visits from her family.

When she arrived at her town house, she forced herself to shake off such maudlin thoughts, blaming them on the grim circumstances of the day. The house felt quiet without Clara and Enid . . . empty, even though a score of servants occupied it.

She and Mary Rebecca made their way to the drawing room. She slid off her gloves and rang for her favorite Madeira, grown from the lands that were once Papa's vineyard. Now some distant cousin held those lands as well as Papa's title, but one sip always took her to the home of her childhood and all its sweet memories.

Before Autenberry. Before life became so very . . . disappointing.

Mrs. Wakefield, the housekeeper, brought the decanter along with several cakes and biscuits. More than they could ever eat in one sitting, but Graciela and Mary Rebecca fell on them ravenously.

"Thank you, Mrs. Wakefield. I couldn't stomach food earlier today," Mary Rebecca declared, taking her first bite.

"Such a dreadful shame about Lady Vanderhall," Mrs. Wakefield opined. "You'll never see me atop anything with four legs."

Mary Rebecca exclaimed at the deliciousness of her first bite. "You really must send the recipe for these lemon biscuits along to my cook. They are delightful."

"I'll do that, my lady." Mrs. Wakefield nodded at Lady Talbot as she moved to the doors, pausing before taking her leave. "Will you be dining at home tonight, Your Grace?"

Dinner. She stifled a wince at the mental image of herself eating all alone at the great big dining table. "Yes. A tray in my rooms will be adequate though. Thank you." Eating alone in her room was far preferable.

The housekeeper nodded and departed.

After several more lemon-iced biscuits, Mary Rebecca fell back on the chaise with an utter lack of dignity, her hands palm-up at her sides. "What a terrible day."

Graciela nodded grimly. "I can't believe she's really gone."

"Only a month ago she was talking about joining me and the children in the Lake District before the season got under way." Mary Rebecca shook her head and released a small sound of disgust. "You never know when your end may come."

"She was almost our age," Graciela murmured.

"Aye, she would have been six and thirty in November."

Graciela paused midchew. The biscuit suddenly tasted like dirt on her tongue.

"What's wrong?" Mary Rebecca eyed her as she sat up and reached for another biscuit.

She shrugged, an uncomfortable nest of knots forming in her stomach. "I thought she was older."

"Evangeline? No, she only looked older. That wretched husband of hers put the years on her face."

Graciela moistened her lips. "I'll be six and thirty in September." Which meant that Graciela was *older* than Evangeline. Older than her friend who had just died. Her death was unanticipated, to be certain. A freak accident, but still a rather jarring realization.

"Well, then. I expect you're next." Mary Rebecca winked.

"Oh!" Graciela tossed a half-eaten biscuit at her friend. Trust Mary Rebecca to make such a poor jest. "That's a fine thing to say!"

"What?" Mary Rebecca swiped at bits of crumbs that dotted her skirts. "You think I like it any more than you do? I'm two years older than you. The truth is it can happen to any of us. Death does not discriminate. Evangeline was up and about, talking and laughing, one moment, and then . . ." Her voice faded away, but what was left unsaid hung heavily between them.

Graciela sighed.

Mary Rebecca added, "It does make you think. I, for one, intend to enjoy my life . . . however much there is left of it."

Graciela gazed into the crackling fire until she was forced to blink. It did, indeed, make one think.

She was a widow of ten years. She had lived the last seventeen years in England, first as a dutiful wife, then as a devoted mother and stepmother. There was little else to her identity.

Sweet Clara, so full of life, would be quick to cut strings and embrace her future. Soon Graciela would be alone with only the walls to stare back at her. She had no interest in remarrying. Once had been enough.

For all intents and purposes, she donned a happy mask when references were made to her late husband. As far as the outside world knew, she had been blissfully married to the late Duke of Autenberry. She maintained the ruse for her daughter. For her stepchildren. She would not taint the memory of their father with the reality of what was. She would keep the truth to herself. The past was best left buried. It did not account for anything anymore.

She had the present and future to occupy her.

Before today that had seemed like enough. More than enough.

Sitting here, though, beside Mary Rebecca, with the death of their friend hanging over them like a dark storm cloud, what she had in her life no longer felt like enough.

She felt a void. A desperate itching need for more. For more *now*. And more *tomorrow*.

"I better stop eating or I won't fit into the shameful dress I planned on wearing tonight to Sodom."

Graciela sat up a little straighter at the mention of the infamous club. Even if she herself had not stepped foot beneath its disreputable roof, Mary Rebecca had apprised her fully of all the delights and depravities to be had there. Anything to suit one's tastes. Dark or light. Fleeting or more permanent in nature. Lovers or strangers. All came together there. Admittedly, Mary Rebecca's tales had titillated and scandalized her in equal parts. "You're going to Sodom? Tonight?"

Mary Rebecca had invited Graciela to join her at the pleasure club countless times over the years. Graciela always declined. She'd had a man in her bed once. She felt no compulsion to recruit another.

"After a day like today a visit to Sodom is more necessary than ever. It will remind me that I'm alive." Mary Rebecca raised a fair eyebrow. "Perhaps you need the same reminder. Will you join me?"

It wasn't long after her husband passed that Mary Rebecca took her first lover. She and Lord Talbot had been a love match. Mary Rebecca had been a simple country girl he met while he was buying Thoroughbreds on her father's farm in Ireland. She claimed that once accustomed to the delights of the marriage bed, she couldn't live without a lover's caress again.

Graciela could not profess the same need.

She had been fond of her husband in the beginning. He had doted on her then. Even if older than herself, he had been a handsome man, and yet she had not enjoyed the marriage bed. It had been a disappointment. *She* had been a disappointment to him in that regard. He'd told her as much on their wedding night. *Given your fiery disposition, Graciela, I had thought you would be more exciting than this.*

He'd uttered this as he climbed from their bed and donned his robe, belting it rather savagely at his waist, his gaze cutting her to the quick. He'd left her that night—their wedding night. Alone. A girl no more in a cold bed, yearning for comfort. It was the first night of many where she would swallow disappointment and contend with the vagaries of a husband swollen with his own sense of entitlement.

Autenberry's disappointment in her only made her tense and more self-conscious. Hardly conducive to becoming proficient in the art of love-making. She knew her husband had strayed from their marital bed. In the last years of her marriage, he'd spent more time in the beds of other women than in hers. It stung only a little. Mostly it was a relief—and she supposed that was a testament to the poor state of her union.

Perhaps it was time, at last, to move on and see what it might be like with another man. The act itself couldn't be so unsatisfying all the time or why would so many people make such a fuss about it?

She swallowed against the sudden dryness in her mouth. "Mary Rebecca . . . tell me a little more about Sodom. What's it like there?" She had never pried, never pressed to know anything about the place beyond what Mary Rebecca volunteered (which had been ample), but now she was curious to know . . . willing to learn. "Going there doesn't mean you *have* to . . ."

"Oh, no!" Mary Rebecca waved her hands in a flurry of movement. "Your mere presence is not a binding contract into wicked deeds." She released a huff of laughter. "Trust me, there are plenty of voyeurs. There are also those who only drink and play cards. They don't partake in any of the activities above stairs." Mary Rebecca winked. "Pity, though. That's where all the fun happens."

"Hm," Graciela murmured, not yet ready to commit.

"You can go there to simply play and be admired . . . no one says you have to bed anyone. Nothing is more exciting and flattering than snaring a man's attention. Even if it's only flirtatious banter, it feeds a woman's ego and can make you feel . . . alive."

With a start, Graciela realized it had been years since she felt alive. Perhaps never. There had never been sparks with her husband, after all. Almost immediately upon their marriage she had erected walls to protect herself. On the surface she was a happy, biddable wife. But inside she was numb and hollow, forcing herself to forgo all her dreams of love and passion for her reality.

She stared at her friend for a long, thoughtful moment. "Indeed," she murmured. "It would be exciting to feel alive. Again." She added the last word lest her friend sense how truly deprived she was. Mary Rebecca would only pity her if she knew her heart and body had been deprived not only the years since her marriage but all the years during her marriage, too. Graciela didn't want that.

"We can don masks. Many do," she offered.

Graciela snorted. "With my accent? And coloring? They'll know at once it's me." Enough ton ladies had muttered within her hearing that she was as swarthy as a field hand. She harbored no misconceptions on that score. She was too recognizable.

Mary Rebecca shrugged. "The lighting is dim.

And who said you need to speak at all?" She waggled her delicate eyebrows. "You can do other things with your mouth. If you wish."

"You're a wicked woman, Lady Talbot." Graciela shook her head and laughed. "But what of the banter you mentioned?"

"Then speak. Talk." She shrugged. "Truly. It's really no concern. If anyone guesses at your identity, so what? I've been going for years and everyone knows it is me behind the mask. I've endured no adverse consequences. My children have not suffered. Ladies of the ton still glare at me . . . as they have always done. It matters naught what I do with my spare time. That will never change. I'll always be that Irish upstart who snared the Earl of Talbot. We're widows, Ela. We're allowed a great deal more latitude." She reached across the space separating them and clasped Graciela's hand. "It's been ten years. You're overdue for some pleasure. It's time." Her friend gave her hand a hard squeeze as though imbuing her with a dose of confidence. "Live a little."

Live a little.

She glanced down at her black mourning dress and was reminded of Evangeline, cold and dead in a coffin.

She lifted her chin. "What time are we leaving?"

Chapter 2

"Dipping rather deep tonight, aren't you, Autenberry? Is it your intention to get foxed?" The Earl of Strickland stared across the table at his longtime friend.

"Perhaps," the Duke of Autenberry grumbled with a shrug. "Is it your intention to *not*?"

Colin blew out a breath. "There was mention of cards and women. Any chance we'll get to that tonight?" The rate Autenberry was guzzling brandy, the only place he was headed was face-down on the floor, and then it would fall to Colin to pick him up and carry him home.

Autenberry's response was to slam back another glass.

"Is this because of your brother? Are you still annoyed with him?"

Autenberry's gaze shot to Colin at that question. "Half brother," he snapped. "And he's not my brother. He'll never *be* my brother."

Colin nodded slowly. *Annoyed* might be an understatement.

"I'm not annoyed," Autenberry added. "I'd have to give a bloody damn about him to feel annoyance." His fingertips circled the rim of his glass. "I feel nothing at all for that Scot bastard. Struan Mackenzie is nothing to me." Autenberry's mouth flattened into a hard line at this pronouncement.

Colin nodded but held his tongue, not believing him for a moment.

Autenberry's bastard half brother had won over everyone in his family, and there was no denying he was bitter at the recent development—no matter what he claimed.

Struan Mackenzie had even won Poppy Fairchurch—stole the tempting little shopgirl right out from under Autenberry. It didn't matter that Autenberry hadn't known he had the chit in the first place, as he was in a coma at the time. She was married to Struan Mackenzie now and that fact did not sit well with Autenberry.

"Very well. You're not annoyed. Just surly and

poor company." Colin gave up on his friend and lifted his gaze to scan the room. Just because Autenberry was in a sour mood didn't mean the entire night had to be a waste.

Even though most everyone was in the country for the remaining winter, Sodom was packed tonight. There were several scantily clad ladies, clearly indifferent to the wicked cold outside, masked and unmasked, circuiting the room. All manner of women to suit every taste and distract any man from his most foul of moods.

"You like redheads," Colin remarked, feeling like an adult trying to coax a child into eating his supper. "How about that bird?" He motioned to a likely prospect heading up the broad staircase to the private rooms above stairs. She had a nice, inviting sway to her hips.

Autenberry shrugged, evidently not tempted.

"Should we move upstairs, then?" Colin prodded, hoping to uproot Autenberry from his position in front of the bottle. "Perhaps we might find something to interest you." Ever since Autenberry woke from his coma, he had spent a good amount of time soused. Colin was hoping to break him of the habit.

"Go on. I'll be along once I finish my drink."

Colin sighed, rather doubting Autenberry would budge from his spot.

Shaking his head, he left Autenberry to drown himself in his brandy, no longer willing to stand witness as his friend spiraled deeper into whatever dark mire held him hostage.

He knew a brush with death could affect a person. Autenberry had just come out of a coma to find his world altered. That could affect a man's perception. Colin would give him space. Besides, he had his own demons chasing him this night.

He'd promised his grandmother that he would take a bride this season.

The old bat had ignored him for most of his life, but recently demanded an audience with him to inform him that he owed an heir and spare to the family line. He couldn't argue the point. It was time. He was nine and twenty.

His days of bachelorhood were fast dwindling. He'd always planned to honor his vows, so that meant nights like tonight, when he was free to cavort with light-skirts, were in short supply. Of course, he had hoped to harbor enough affection for his wife that honoring his vows would be no real trial. He had not met any debutante to tempt him, however. He couldn't even profess fondness for a particular chit. Not that he had spent any time searching among the proper drawing rooms, routs and balls of the ton. He had avoided matchmaking mamas, sticking to gaming hells and clubs such as Sodom.

Clearly it was time to take note of eligible young ladies. Or at least take heed of his grandmother's directives, as she did pay attention to such things. She had already sent him a list of debutantes she had personally vetted. All from impeccable families. All breeders. This, he'd learned, was the most essential criterion for his grandmother.

His mother had died bringing him into the world, and his grandmother blamed her for being too weak. From her chaise longue, drowning in pashmina shawls and surrounded by her cats, the old dame had proclaimed his late mother fragile and a poor breeder. She stabbed a gnarled finger in Colin's direction.

Your father should have married a hardier female. One that did not break so easily. Instead he was a fool, gulled by beauty. Not you, lad. I'll see to that. You'll be smarter than my Charles. You'll marry a fine young breeder.

If his grandmother spoke of his future bride as though she were a prize sow, he didn't bother to object. At nine and seventy, there was no changing her ways.

Colin's father died when he was a boy, but he did recall the large shadow of the man invading his nursery. With drink in hand, the imposing earl would stare out from red-rimmed eyes at Colin. *You've her look to you, lad.* Then, as though it was more than he could bear to observe, he would turn and leave Colin alone with his nursemaid.

That was the extent of his memories of his sire. The earl's passing was scarcely a hiccup along the stretch of his days. One morning the housekeeper informed him that he had died and then in her next breath inquired if Colin would like honey for his porridge.

His life went about its usual lonely course until he was sent away to school and met Autenberry. Marcus's family, in a sense, became a surrogate to him. Suddenly he wasn't so alone anymore.

Despite his lack of family bonds, he did feel an obligation to keep the Strickland line going. Or perhaps it was because of that very thing. His own lack of family. A pack, a clan to call his own. He wanted children . . . the family he never had. He'd spent most of his life imposing on the Autenberrys. Anytime he wasn't at school, he could be found with them. It was preferable to idling his time away at a deserted school or staying at his empty mausoleum with only servants for company.

His estate would no longer be empty once he married and filled it with his progeny. The thought provided some comfort and spoke to the secret longings in his heart. He wanted half a score of children, at least. He snorted. His grandmother would be thrilled to hear such hopes from him. Now he need only find the girl to give him those offspring.

But not tonight. Tonight he would not spend another moment thinking on marriage or the begetting of heirs.

He ascended the stairs. The second floor was quieter, darker. The kind of shady surroundings that invited trysts. He'd engaged in more than a few assignations at Sodom over the years. Tonight seemed ideal for another one.

He blinked, acclimating to the sudden gloom as he strolled down the corridor, passing open doors beyond which all manner of illicit activity took place. He strolled in and out of a few rooms. Perhaps he would spot that redhead and persuade her to go visit Autenberry and tempt him from his drink.

And that's when he noticed her.

Her utter stillness amid a room of voices and laughter and twisting motion snared his gaze.

He entered the spacious salon. Red-hooded lanterns cast the space afire, giving it an otherworldly ambiance. One could almost forget they were smack in the middle of London and not in some decadent den of iniquity far off in the Mediterranean.

The room had been thoughtfully devised. Alcoves were tucked into every corner and along the edges of the chamber, offering privacy for those who desired it. Cries and moans carried from the curtained nooks.

He angled his head, studying the female across the expanse of the red-tinged drawing salon, singular in her aloneness. She wore a domino like so many of the women present. Her gown was a deep burgundy and low cut, revealing a daring amount of cleavage. Nothing shocking about that. In this establishment she was rather modestly attired.

He walked deeper into the salon. Several people kissed and fondled each other on the couches. Laughter and chatter buzzed through the air. He inhaled the smell of want and sex and unleashed desires.

On a settee in the far corner, a man delved his

hand beneath a lady's skirts, working her into a fine frenzy. A few people watched, permitting themselves the titillation. One gentleman groped himself in a chair, opening his trousers and massaging his erection as the female panted, dragging her skirts higher so that her lover could work his fingers deeper and faster within her.

Colin knew the scene. He'd observed it before but never lingered long in such scenarios. He preferred privacy when engaged with a woman. He didn't like voyeurs arousing themselves at his or his partner's expense. When he was with a woman, he wanted no distractions.

Normally, at this point, he would turn and set about his own pursuits, but there was the woman in the corner still holding his curiosity. She reminded him of a rabbit frozen, caught in the sights of a predator. He smiled wryly. In this case, she had landed herself in a room full of predators.

Bright flags of color marked her cheeks. She was a novice to this scene and he felt a strange prickle of emotion. Pity? Protectiveness? The crazy urge to grab her and throw her in a carriage before the wolves got to her overcame him.

Shaking his head, he started to turn away. She was a grown woman who obviously knew where she was and what she was about. No one came to Sodom without an inkling of what they were about. She wasn't looking to be rescued no matter how intensely she blushed.

Then he noticed the pair of men descending on her. The Botsams were brothers, only a year apart and grandsons to the late Archbishop of Canterbury, and known all about Town for their depraved inclinations. Yes, the irony wasn't lost on him. No man let a daughter or sister anywhere near the pair of blackguards.

He'd attended Eton with them and observed their behavior firsthand. They had been cruel boys, delighting in crushing birds or torturing cats that loitered about the grounds. Once he and Autenberry had happened on them with the groundskeeper's daughter. They'd stripped the girl out of her knickers and were in the process of switching her backside raw. He and Autenberry stopped the brothers, but not without a fight. Colin still bore a scar above his eyebrow from where one of them had struck him with a rock.

According to talk, their conduct hadn't improved over the years. They were still sick bastards and he wouldn't wish them on his worst enemy.

His chest tightened as he watched them descend

on her. Even through the domino, he noticed her widening eyes as they backed her toward one of the alcoves.

He cursed beneath his breath, willing her not to be pushed into one of the nooks with them. The last thing she needed was to be dragged off where no one could see her or where her cries for help could be muffled.

His hands clenched as all three of them disappeared from sight in one of the darkened nooks. He was probably overreacting. It was Sodom, after all.

"Christ," he muttered and strode forward.

Chapter 3

One moment she was gawking at the most sordid display she had ever witnessed, wondering where Mary Rebecca had disappeared to and how she might take her leave from this place, and then two men were before her, suggesting filthy and lewd things that made her ears burn and her stomach lurch.

"What are you doing? Unhand me." Her gasped words and slapping hands went unheeded as they shoved her back down on a well-padded couch.

They moved in accord, like they had done this countless times. Their hands fell roughly on her. She was spun around, her face pushed down onto the couch as if she were some rag doll to be flipped about unceremoniously, without thought or care.

"Stop!" she choked as hands grabbed the hem of her skirts. She reached down to seize their groping fingers. Arching her back, she lashed out, kicking behind her. Her heeled slipper made contact with something. Pain radiated up her leg as one of them cursed.

The other laughed. "She's a fighter. This will be fun. Haven't had one of those in a while."

"You want to fight, eh?" A hard hand tangled in the back of her hair, straining her neck on her shoulders, forcing her head down and scattering her pins, sending the mass of her hair sprawling around her. "Go ahead. Fight. We rather enjoy that."

This wasn't happening.

She only wanted a night out . . . and to live a little. To feel alive and not like her poor friend, dead in a box. Now this was happening and all she wished for was the safety of her home. To be back in her drawing room before her crackling fire with Clara and Enid beside her. Not this. Anything but this. Clearly the thrill and excitement she had been looking for didn't exist. Not for her.

She struggled against the rock hard grip, and then suddenly the pressure at the back of her head was gone. She rolled to her side, twisting around to watch as a third man appeared, yanking one of her accosters off her. Her attacker lost his balance and fell to the floor. The new arrival, a shadowy figure in the alcove, pressed his booted foot against the neck of the man on the floor and grabbed the other one by the cravat.

She watched, frozen on the couch. Never had she witnessed such a brutal scene before.

"Botsam, I believe you and your brother heard the lady refuse your company. I'm sure you can find someone else receptive to your attentions. It is Sodom, after all . . . and there is no accounting for taste."

"You make it a habit of interfering, Strickland. First at Eton . . . now here. What? Are you following us about Town?"

Strickland?

Her heart lurched at the familiar name, knowing she was safe, even if it was regrettable for Lord Strickland to find her in such an undignified manner. The earl would never let a lady come to harm. Her stepson's friend was as honorable a gentleman as they came.

"As I recall, you both were trounced for your transgressions at Eton," Lord Strickland said. "Care for a repeat performance, Botsam?"

"It's just you here. I don't see Autenberry at your side this time. Might be difficult to deliver a beating without your friend. One against two are not the best of odds."

"Oh, Autenberry is not far. I'm certain he would be happy to deliver another thrashing on you worthless swine."

Panic swamped her and her heart thrummed in her ears. Her stepson was here?

Oh, no.

He couldn't see her here.

The earl continued, "Not that I'll be needing him tonight. I have this well in hand." He ground his boot deeper into the man's neck on the floor as though to drive home his point. The man cried out and whimpered.

"You don't really want to cause difficulties here, do you? You know Mrs. Bancroft has no tolerance for violence on the premises. I'm sure you wouldn't want your memberships revoked. Permanently."

There was a long moment of silence as the earl stared the man down. She didn't breathe as she watched them, her hand clutching her throat as she tried to decipher the silent exchange occurring between them.

Finally Botsam cleared his throat. "As you said.

There are more accommodating females present. We'll leave this one to your gentle care," he sneered.

Strickland uncurled his fingers from Botsam's cravat. "Wise decision."

Botsam's gaze flicked to her as he straightened his mussed cravat, assessing in a way that made her feel suddenly like dirt beneath his boot. "I confess I don't have much affinity for dark meat at any rate."

She sucked in a stinging breath. It wasn't the first time she overheard a scathing, indiscreet remark about her coloring. Her dark hair and eyes and less than milky complexion put her in marked contrast to other English ladies. Some men found her attractive—her deceased husband had once upon the time. Others, however, did very little to hide their distaste.

"You can have her, Strickland," he continued, waving his hand toward his brother still beneath his boot. "Mind letting my brother go?"

Colin took his time as though considering that. "If I ever see you mistreating a lady again, there won't be a next time." He lifted his foot and the Botsam brother on the floor scurried to his feet, holding his injured neck. He treated Strickland to one final glare and slunk away.

His brother followed at a slower pace, leaving them alone in the alcove.

She was aware of a rushing noise in her ears then. Her heart pounded hard, a dove desperate to take wind and escape. Before she could consider her actions, she crossed the space separating them and hugged him, her fingers clutching deeply into his shoulder. Her other hand dropped to his chest, trapped between their two bodies. He was a familiar shore amid the dark sea in which she found herself.

He stiffened with surprise against her. She opened her mouth to express her gratitude and relief that he arrived when he did and saved her from the most terrifying moment of her life—but then his voice rumbled out from his chest.

"You're very welcome, Miss . . ."

She started to thank him again, to explain, but then she closed her mouth with a snap.

Her mind raced.

He didn't know her. *Of course.* She was masked. It was dark. She had not yet used her voice.

This knowledge rushed through her, and it was a different kind of relief but relief nonetheless. He would identify her at once if she spoke. So it seemed obvious then that she shouldn't speak. She couldn't. There was a chance she could yet extricate herself from this situation without Lord Strickland or her stepson ever knowing of her blunder in coming here.

She pulled back from the embrace, biting her lip as though that could stop her from speaking. Her fingers fluttered lightly where they still rested against his chest. He was firm and solid, his chest broader than she had ever realized.

She glanced up and felt snared by his eyes. He had the loveliest eyes. She fought their pull and looked beyond his shoulder, half-afraid that her stepson might suddenly appear.

"They're not coming back," Colin assured her, lifting his hands to give her shoulders a comforting squeeze, misinterpreting her trepidation.

She returned her gaze to him. He thought she was still afraid of the Botsam brothers? He'd allayed that fear for her. She shook her head slightly. The only thing that would allay her other fear was being snug inside her house across Town.

He looked down at her, his silvery eyes peering at her through the gloom. She had always thought those eyes extraordinary. Always imagined they could see more . . . cut through everything.

Her stepson was impulsive, even hotheaded. He'd worried her more than a few times over the years. She had judged Colin to be a calming influence. Wise and thoughtful and circumspect. A good friend to Marcus. Precisely the kind of friend he needed. He'd even been a friend to her tonight, stepping in and saving her—and as far as he knew, she was a stranger to him.

He patted her shoulders. "Come. Let us get you from here."

By *here*, she did not know if he meant this room or this house. Whatever the case, she let him lead her away since away was where she wanted to be. It didn't require speaking and that seemed fortuitous.

He clasped her arm and tugged her behind him. Once in the corridor, his hand slid down her arm. Neither one of them were wearing gloves. His warm fingers wrapped around her hand and her heart beat harder in her chest.

A lifetime had passed since a man held her hand in anything more than a fleeting grip. Those touches were perfunctory. Just a quick assist from her mount or into a carriage. This was different. It was intimate and slightly possessive.

She slid a look at his profile. The strong line of his nose. The square cut of his jaw. She saw him as she always did . . . except she didn't. He looked different somehow now. Here, in this setting, he made her breath fall a fraction too quickly.

He was indisputably handsome. She had always thought this, of course, but with detachment. As one observes a beautiful piece of art. Or simply a handsome man—a handsome young man a matron such as herself might consider as a marriage prospect for her stepdaughter. How could she not? It was difficult not to notice when her stepdaughter stared after Lord Strickland with longing. Years ago she had thought perhaps they might make a match, but after watching their interaction, she was certain that Colin viewed Enid only as a younger sister.

Tonight, however, in this moment, Graciela was achingly aware of him . . . and that was unpardonable. She gave herself a swift internal shake and blamed it on her surroundings. Once she was free of this outrageous place, all would return to normal. *She* would return to her senses. She would again be a proper dowager duchess and Lord Strickland would be her stepson's friend. Much younger and much too forbidden.

He led her down a hallway, past couples so engrossed with each other they did not cast them a glance.

"I'm assuming you wish to leave?"

She nodded.

"I'll escort you out and hail a hack for you."

She smiled and nodded again. Perhaps she could leave word with a doorman for Mary Rebecca without Lord Strickland overhearing her. She didn't want her friend to fret, but neither could she stay another moment in this pleasure club whilst her stepson was on the premises. Mary Rebecca would understand when she explained the situation.

Graciela looked ahead, noting they were nearing the top of the stairs, where several corridors converged.

A gentleman crested the top, ascending the stairs to stand in the hub of corridors. She tensed, recognizing him at once.

His great height and bearing were as familiar to her as the memory of his father, her late husband.

A sour taste coated her mouth.

She froze, her heart a desperate hammering in her chest. It was too late. Her stepson was here. She was here. They would come face-to-face. She couldn't hide from him. Mortification loomed ahead.

Air stirred beside her and she sensed Lord Strickland close. His larger body stopping alongside her. She felt his breath on the side of her face.

Marcus faced them down the long length of hallway, a dark shape etched against the light from well-lit sconces. That same light cast his features into stark relief. There was no mistaking his identity.

She pressed a hand over her racing heart as though that would keep it from bursting free from her bodice.

Marcus lifted his hand in a two-fingered wave. "Strickland," he called, listing to the side. Clearly his balance was hard-won. "What'd you find there? Something to play with?"

There was the slightest slur to his speech. Evidently he'd been dipping deep tonight. It wasn't like him. At least not like him before the accident.

Things had changed since he woke from the coma. Since his father's bastard son had surfaced, he'd been different. He was no longer carefree. Perhaps she should have taken Marcus's feelings on the matter into account before she welcomed Struan Mackenzie into the fold, but she knew what it was like to be an outsider. She pitied Mr. Mackenzie, abandoned by his father, denied by his half brother. As the duke's widow, she felt responsible to right the wrongs done to him by the father who never acknowledged him.

She was certain that encountering *her* in a pleasure club wouldn't improve Marcus's bad humor. What had she been thinking? She should have simply ignored the foolish longing seizing her like some vicious malady. Never again.

If she escaped this unscathed and without discovery, she would never do anything so reckless again.

She and Marcus had always had a good relationship. She'd been fortunate in that regard. Her husband had not seen fit to provide her with a widow's portion—whether an oversight or a direct slight, she did not know. It mattered naught, she supposed. He was gone. Dead for years and she had forged ahead, putting all her energies into being a good mother and stepmother.

Marcus was generous with her, giving her free rein over the Autenberry properties, never questioning her choices of how she spent money, where she lived, where she spent her holidays, or how she raised her daughter, his own half sister. She had no wish to test the limits of that generosity. She knew better than to take the goodwill of her stepson for granted.

There were widows left in extremely precarious situations. For her daughter's sake, she did not intend to put herself in a similar predicament. England was home now and she dared not risk losing all that she had here.

There was nothing left for her in Spain. Her

parents had passed on and the family lands had gone to some distant relation. Her sisters had married and moved away. Even if she wanted to go back, there was nothing to return to.

Marcus took a step toward them and the hammering of her heart became a painful pounding.

"Well, let's see what you have there. She's not a redhead, but I won't hold that against her."

She backed up and collided with a warm male body. Strickland had moved behind her at some point. His hands came up to grip her arms. His scent assailed her. An underlying aroma of soap and sandalwood. Clean, virile male. If she had noticed it before, it had never affected her. Not as it did now.

As Marcus barreled toward them, she caught a flash of his eyes and her stomach sank. He was so close.

She couldn't face him. Not here. Not in this place.

As the distance between them closed, panic welled up in her. Even with a mask on, she felt exposed. She was certain he would know her. Perhaps not right away, but the moment she opened her mouth, he would know her. And how much longer could she play mute? The situation was dire. She felt like prey caught in a predator's sights.

Sucking in a sharp breath, she spun on her heels but didn't make it very far. Lord Strickland was still standing behind her. Still waiting. Still wearing a questioning expression.

"Don't worry. He might look like a raging ogre, but he's my friend," he reassured, clearly reading her distress even if not understanding the reason for it. "He's harmless, but even were he not, I would not let him touch you."

Warmth curled through her at his husky avowal.

She swallowed and nodded even as she sensed Marcus's approach from behind.

Her ever-increasing sense of urgency had her parting her lips and preparing to speak. She was out of choices.

Words fell, dropping like great boulders in the scant space between them. "Help me," she uttered quietly.

Lifting her chin, she gazed at him beseechingly, anxiously waiting for his reaction. Lord Strickland was her only chance right now in helping her avoid Marcus.

She strained her neck to look up at him. Had he always been this tall? This broad of shoulders? This imposing.

She stifled a wince. Not when she first met him. He'd been just a lad then, on the cusp of manhood. Pretty faced and gangly with a voice given to cracking. With only ten and eight years to her credit, she had been scarcely more than a child herself at the time.

That felt a lifetime ago. She took a soldiering breath. Neither one of them were children now.

Brushing aside the memory, she moistened her lips as her stepson called out from behind them. "Well, if the lady is so inclined, I wouldn't mind a go with her, Strickland."

Chapter 4

Querido Dios.

Her pulse fired against the skin of her throat at her stepson's shocking words. It was all the prompting needed.

She stepped forward, gripping Strickland by the jacket. "Help me," she repeated, her words a mere scratch on the air, practically inaudible. But audible enough.

He looked down at her white-knuckled hands on him and then back to her face. He angled his head, his eyes narrowing as he studied her. "Your voice . . ."

Exhaling, she nodded resolutely. She would

reveal the truth of her identity to him. So be it. Better him than Autenberry. "*He* can't see me here, Lord Strickland."

All doubt and wonder fled from his face. His eyes flared wide in full recognition. He took a step closer, bringing their chests flush. "Lady Autenberry?" he whispered, his breath warm on her face. "Graciela? What are you doing here?"

"Please. Get me out of here." Desperation edged her voice. "He cannot see me," she repeated, spacing each word with heavy emphasis, debating whether to lift her skirts and run if he shouldn't offer his assistance. Irrational maybe, but panic pounded through her, shoving out all reason.

His gaze scanned her face and then down the length of her. Those eyes gleamed brightly in the murky corridor, sparking with something she had never seen from him before.

His hand seized hers. Before she quite realized what he was about, he thrust her into the nearest room. The door snicked shut after them.

They stood in this new space, silent, still gazing at each other. He looked down at her, his back against the door as though to bar Marcus from entering. It was some comfort.

Slowly, he shook his head. "What are you doing

here?" She had never heard such a demanding tone from him before. In fact, nothing about him was typical right now. Not the way he spoke or looked. Not the accusation cutting from his eyes. "This is no place for you."

She bristled. She imagined he would not say the same thing to a man her age. Was she so very *old* and *matronly* that he did not think she had any right to be here?

Undoubtedly he consigned her to a certain category in his mind. A certain *sexless* category tantamount to nuns and grandmothers.

"I've every right to be here—"

"Oh, do you? Well, if you feel so very entitled to be here, then by all means, step out into that corridor and greet your *stepson*."

His words struck her like a slap.

He moved away from the door, grasped the latch and started to pull it open.

She squeaked and threw herself against him, flattening him into the door and shutting it again with a swift thud.

"No! Don't do that." Her breath escaped in hard pants that got lost somewhere in the vicinity of his chest. That's how tall he was. Her nose was directly level with his throat. Even in the shadows she could detect the thrumming pulse at his throat. Taller than average herself, she had always appreciated a tall man.

Her gaze flicked up to his eyes. He watched her, holding himself utterly still. Against her. Bodies flush. Hearts beating in cadence.

It was unnerving to say the least . . . and yet for the life of her she couldn't step back and peel herself off him. She couldn't stop staring into those pale gray-blue eyes that looked at her with angry emotion—another first. He'd always been so polite and proper with her. A perfectly circumspect gentleman.

His fierce expression and intense eyes mesmerized her. She moistened her lips and his gaze followed the movement. The blue of his eyes seemed to darken a shade—or maybe it was simply the dim lighting of the room? His stare dropped even lower.

A quick glance down reminded her of the indecent cut of her gown. Pressed against him like this, the tops of her breasts swelled above the neckline. She felt the heat of her blush start in her face and then watched as red crept downward over her dusky mounds.

Involuntarily, her nipples pebbled inside her corset.

She gasped. Even though he couldn't know

and he couldn't possibly feel her body's betrayal (*with him of all men!*), she lurched back.

Now, with a few feet of space between them, their gazes locked for an interminable moment. Her heart beat harder and faster in her too-tight chest. A chest that only seconds ago pressed intimately against him. Her nipples still throbbed, as though she still felt the pressure of his body against her.

At the thought of his body, she raked him with a quick glance, imagining that hard body of his . . . the pressure of it covering her—

She reined in her scandalous imagination with a firm yank.

The heat scoring her cheeks burned hotter.

She inhaled. It was simply being here, in this house of iniquity, that made her think such wholly unacceptable thoughts. About Lord Strickland, of all people. He was her stepson's best friend—a longtime family friend. Even if he weren't too young for her (*and he was!*), he was absolutely inappropriate as a candidate for dalliances. It was not only unseemly . . . It was perverse of her to even entertain such notions. He would likely be horrified if he knew.

He finally glanced from her to the door she blocked. At least it appeared Marcus was not following them. He likely thought Strickland wanted to be alone with her for a private liaison.

"You had to realize your stepson could be here." His tone was the height of reasonableness—and blast it all if that did not infuriate her. She was an adult. Six years his senior. She did not need to be taken to task by him.

"As a matter of fact, it did *not* cross my mind." She squared her shoulders. "It was a spontaneous decision. Besides, it's not as though Marcus confides his proclivities to me."

His lips twitched. "No, because that would be unsuitable."

Again, his tone and words had a way of making her feel foolish. She knew he considered her coming here unsuitable.

The latch on the door suddenly clicked behind her.

Time slowed as it cracked open.

She choked back a sound, her hand flying to cover her mouth as she backed away. If it was Marcus, there would be no hiding. She would have to confront her stepson and offer some explanation about her presence here. Although what explanation could she give? She was here . . . in this place where pleasure and depravity came together. What more need be explained except that she had become *that* woman? A free-spirited widow bent on pursuing her own pleasures with no thought to reputation or the strict moral teachings of her youth and Society.

Strickland reacted, moving hastily. He gave a swift shake of his head at her that reminded her of Sister Esperanza from her childhood. The old nun instructed Graciela and her sisters in their studies until the age of seventeen. The steel-eyed dragon conveyed much with a single sharp look. A lift of her thick eyebrow and a shake of her veil-covered head were the only things needed to keep Graciela in check.

Seizing her shaking fingers, he dragged her deeper into the gloom of the chamber. "Play along," he advised.

She followed without protest. They hurried forward, descending steps where the room sank into a wider chamber—with a bed at the center. A bed that was *occupied*.

She'd failed to assess her surroundings before, too caught up in Strickland and the threat of coming face-to-face with her stepson.

She gawked about her now as the young earl guided her through the chamber. A plush couch bumped at the backs of her knees. She twisted, looking down at it as she fell upon the comfortable seat.

Strickland sat directly beside her. So close he was practically an appendage.

She strained for a glimpse of the door, to verify if Marcus had in fact entered the room, but that bed and its occupants continued to snare her attention. The bed was *enormous*. A couple writhed together on the vast expanse. Soft sighs and moans were punctuated with the steady smacks of their bodies coming together.

She gasped and attempted to rise, to escape.

"Don't be alarmed." The earl grabbed hold of her hand and pulled her back down beside him. "It's not just us. Voyeurs are welcome. See." She followed the direction of his nod. A few other individuals were seated on the other side of the room across from them, watching as though they were observing a Vauxhall performance.

A man, too, stood near the hearth, one hand tucked in his jacket pocket, his eyes heavy lidded as he watched the lovers. She continued her perusal of the room, noting with some astonishment a pair of ladies seated very properly on a settee, their spines ramrod straight, as they sipped from teacups. They watched raptly at the scene, their eyes as hungry as the men in the room, and this gave her some start—that women could benefit as much as men from the carnal act.

She knew, in theory, that Mary Rebecca enjoyed her lovers. But seeing this display firsthand was a jolt. She felt awakened to the notion that women could voluntarily and willingly be sexual creatures—that they could revel in the deed every bit as much as men. It was strangely inspiring. Her skin felt feverish and too small for her frame, as though it were pulled tight across her bones. She fidgeted and adjusted her weight, painfully conscious of the strong male body beside her.

"Some people like to watch," he added in way of an explanation, the deep drawl of his voice serving to produce a throb low in her belly.

Realizing her mouth was sagging open, she closed it with a snap. Of course he would know about such things. He wasn't some novice to Sodom like her, awkward and requiring rescue on her first encounter.

It was both disappointing and embarrassing that she could not better cope with her present environment. It compelled her to flee, but there was still the matter of avoiding her stepson.

Marcus.

Her gaze flew from the fornicating couple on

the bed. She peered over Lord Strickland's shoulder and there he was, strolling into the room without the slightest hesitation, hands clasped behind him. The earl ducking in here with her had not deterred him. He had still followed.

"Look away from him," Strickland breathed beside her ear. "Unless you want him to recognize you."

She nodded once but could do little more than cast her eyes away for a scant heartbeat before looking back again.

"Strickland!" Marcus called.

"Shhh." The ladies on the settee glared at her stepson.

He shot them a cheeky grin.

She sank deeper into the couch, hoping to use the earl for a shield as Marcus made his way over toward them.

She leaned sideways into Strickland to whisper, "He's coming."

He turned his body, pressing closer, backing her deeper still into the sofa so that she was not so very noticeable. His gaze locked on hers as his arms came up around her, very neatly entrapping them. "Say nothing."

She flattened her lips even though she doubted she could speak further. It felt as though a boulder had settled itself on her chest, robbing her of air. Any possibility of speech vanished with his body against hers.

She'd been physically close to him before. Even danced with him on occasion. But this was undeniably different. It felt as though they were caught within a bubble. Just the two of them. And he was everywhere. Impossible as that seemed. His chest and arms caging her in, hovering over her. His body radiated warmth. She inhaled. *Dios ayúdame.* He smelled so good.

She knew this closeness was a necessity. He was attempting to hide her from her stepson. She was ever grateful. Truly. Even if she felt she might come apart at any moment.

"Trying to keep what you've found to yourself, are you?" The familiar sound of her stepson's voice, even slightly slurred from drink, stabbed panic through her. She glimpsed his face as he came to a stop behind Strickland, looming above them.

Swallowing back a whimper, she dropped her head on the earl's shoulder, burying her face and wishing that this entire moment were not happening.

She rolled her face slightly against the slope

of his shoulder, appreciating his presence all the more with her stepson a few feet away. And appreciating other things, too. Unlike so many gentlemen of the ton, he wore an unpadded jacket and she was permitted to feel the full solidness of his shoulder beneath her forehead. His body was well constructed and the fleeting thought crossed her mind: What did he look like beneath his clothing?

It was abhorrent for her to think of him in such a fashion, but the thought flashed through her mind nonetheless. *It must be this house.* The things she had seen and heard within this room. *Still* heard. The smell of sex ripe on the air.

It should have disgusted her. It *should*. Instead her body pulsed and ached hotly. Almost as though she were beset with fever.

The earl's breath fanned her temple and she felt his lips there, moving as he spoke in response to Marcus. "That was the plan in coming here, was it not? To achieve our own pleasures." His low voice brushed her skin, and yet it was loud enough for her stepson to hear.

Even so, in that moment it felt as though he were speaking directly to her.

Her lips parted on a raspy sigh against the fine fabric of his jacket. A shiver skated down her skin, traveling to her breasts. The peaks tightened, desperate for satisfaction.

"Indeed," Marcus replied, his disembodied voice so very similar to her late husband's that an acrid taste grew on her tongue.

Without looking at Marcus talking, she could almost imagine it was the late duke. The thought should have been a cold, quelling dose on her unwelcome ardor, but just then Strickland's hand came up to the back of her head. Long fingers speared through her half-tumbled hair, roughly shaking the mass fully loose so that it fell all around her. She knew he did it only to offer her further concealment, but it felt erotic and possessive and her stomach muscles quivered as his hard fingers buried in the strands and massaged the back of her skull.

Not even her husband had bothered to touch her hair. When it came to carnal relations, he'd always been quick about the task. Minimal touching and mostly below the waist. She knew it had been her fault because he told her so. Countless times he said she wasn't adventurous enough. Not inspiring enough. Not exciting. *You bring to mind a corpse, Graciela.* It was difficult to get into the spirit of the act after such a remark.

She closed her eyes as the pads of Strickland's

fingers worked into her scalp, stroking, pressing until her muscles relaxed.

The solid weight of a body dropped down on the other side of her, jostling the sofa cushions. Not just any body either. *Marcus.* She needn't look at him to know. The sickly twist of her stomach told her. She stiffened. For a moment she had lost herself to sensation, to Strickland's delicious smell and form.

Her fingers dug into Strickland's arms as though she needed support.

No, no, no. Please. This is not happening. Don't let it happen.

The couple on the bed grew frenzied in their movements, their sounds intensifying.

Suddenly she felt dizzy. She was stuck. Physically stuck between Strickland and Marcus.

She shifted her face higher, burrowing her nose farther into the earl's neck. Her lips were still parted and she could taste the salt of his heated skin. She trembled, her lips grazing him. The skin at his neck was so warm and inviting. Even as alarmed as she felt . . . the strangest desire to taste him with her tongue surged within her.

Fingers brushed the bare skin of her right shoulder. Just a brush but she flinched. It wasn't Strickland's hands. Both his hands were already on her. No, this was Marcus. Bile rose in the back of her throat. Her stepson was touching her. She was going to be sick.

"Please," she mouthed against him even though she knew he couldn't possibly have heard her.

Marcus's fingers slid intimately, exploratory, down the curve of her shoulder.

A shudder racked her. She had to stop him. She knew he would be as revolted as she was if he knew he was touching his stepmother in such a manner.

She lifted her head, on the verge of revealing herself. At this point what choice did she have?

She could not let this continue. Next he would be touching more than just her shoulder.

Strickland's voice vibrated against her. "Sorry, Autenberry. This one is mine alone."

Then, before she realized what he was doing, he was lifting her, settling her on his lap, her gown billowing around them so that she straddled his hips. Her hands landed on his shoulders for balance.

From this position, her face was higher than his. Her hair cascaded around her bowed head, curtaining her features from Marcus sitting beside them.

She caught a flash of Strickland's luminescent

eyes, the blue reaching deep inside her. As she gazed down at him, everything else faded. The sounds of the trysting couple dulled.

Blood rushed to her ears as his hands slid beneath the veil of her hair to hold her face, his broad palms rasping the tender skin of her cheeks, thumbs sliding back and forth.

He stared at her for the briefest moment. Just a fleeting clash of gazes and then he pulled her down to his face. She froze at the shocking sensation of his lips. There was the barest, infinitesimal moment when she considered pushing him away.

Then that thought died.

It had been so long since she kissed a man.

She felt like a green girl, her lips quivering and barely moving against him. Almost as though this were the first kiss she ever had. And in so many ways, it was. It was nothing like the chaste kisses she shared with the baker's son before she married—or the kisses she shared later with her husband. Autenberry was never very keen on kissing.

And then there was the way she was sitting atop him. Her thighs splayed wide, hugging his hips, skirts bunched around her knees. Beyond personal. Beyond intimate. The heat of his body seeped into hers. She felt strangely empowered even though she knew with one snap of his fingers he could overpower her.

Her fingers flexed against his upper chest, unsure where to go, what to do. Apparently her hands had a will of their own, though. They didn't want to shove him away.

His lips were softer than she expected. Warmth and pressure and pure sweetness slanting over her mouth.

Her fingers slid upward, coasting over his shoulders.

In response, his fingers clenched tighter in her hair. He pulled back slightly, his lips moving with the soft words only she could hear: "Kiss me. Make it look real."

Make it look real.

Because this wasn't real. Not for him.

He didn't actually want to do this with her. That was both freeing and oddly disappointing. She shoved the disappointment aside and focused on the freeing part. If she needed to put on a convincing show, then so be it. She had come here tonight to live, to experience all she had been missing so that her life, present and future, wasn't a total stretch of dullness.

An exhale passed from her mouth and fluttered against his. She tightened her grip on his shoulders and pressed her mouth to his, finally kissing him back.

He responded, his hold on her head turning her at an angle that allowed him to deepen the kiss even more. He took over, kissing her with lips and tongue and faintly scraping teeth, and it was all she could do to keep up, to breathe through her nose and not faint from the riotous sensations bombarding her.

She released his shoulders and wrapped her arms around him, hanging on as she spiraled down into the abyss of whatever was happening.

They were moving slightly. Or rather, she was. She was faintly conscious of rocking against him. She was lost, reveling in his tongue in her mouth, his fingers diving into her hair. She didn't open her eyes. She was lost to everything but him.

She gave the barest gasp when he dropped a hand to her hip, dragging her so that the core of her aligned perfectly over the bulge of his manhood.

His mouth burned hot and aggressive, punishing on her lips. She'd never been kissed so hard. So thoroughly. She felt him everywhere and this was just a kiss. *Dios mío.* What would the rest of it . . . *all* of it . . . be like with him?

You'll never know, because this was just pretend.

It was hard to remember that, however, when he pushed his hips up against her. It was hard to recall this was all a sham as she moaned and pressed down on that prodding hardness.

His kiss deepened and she continued to rock and grind until she wanted to tear their clothes away. She wanted no barrier. Nothing between them. Relief to the ache he had stoked. An invisible coil squeezed in her belly. Wild little sounds escaped her, swallowed up by him. It was torture. Exquisite torture.

A chuckle scratched the air beside her. "If you're not up for sharing, then you best get a private room because damn if I'm not half-sprung watching the two of you."

English might not be her first language, but she had no difficulty understanding Marcus's meaning, even as incredible as it sounded coming from the stepson she had known for more than half his life. Almost half *her* life. He'd only ever been a gentleman in her company. Perhaps she didn't know him at all. Just as she hadn't really known his father. Not until it was too late and the marriage vows had been uttered.

She fully returned to her surroundings, pulling back with a gasp, still astride Lord Strickland. Her wide eyes found his equally wide eyes as her fingers flew to her tingling lips.

The spell was broken.

Chapter 5

Colin told himself there was nothing more to the kiss than subterfuge. In order for Autenberry to think he was seriously attached to this woman and unwilling to share her. Kissing her was protecting her. Shielding her.

Actually, it was to protect both the duchess and Autenberry. He knew his friend would not be happy to discover her here. Just as he knew she had no wish to be unveiled before her stepson. It was for *them*. To avoid a potentially unpleasant situation. Not for him.

Nothing about this kiss was genuine or affected him in the least.

Unfortunately, he'd never been a very good liar

and he was lying on all counts. He was affected. His raging erection could attest to that.

Certainly, he'd entertained his fair share of inappropriate thoughts about the Duchess of Autenberry over the years. He was a red-blooded male and she was exactly to his taste. Sultry dark eyes and hair. An unabashedly curvy body. And when she spoke, he felt her voice like a purr on his skin.

Of course, he hadn't allowed himself to think of her in such an unseemly way in years.

He'd been a boy when he first clapped eyes on her and she had filled his overactive imagination with fodder for many nights during his adolescence—a fact that he had felt sure would land him in the fiery grip of hell. She was his best friend's stepmother. A married lady and far out of the realm of possibility. The older he'd grown, the more adept he'd been at turning those feelings off.

And yet now, a lifetime later, here she was straddling his lap. No longer married.

Fair-haired females with milk skin and cornflower blue eyes might be deemed the diamonds of the ton and all the rage, but he preferred a different breed of lady. One not precisely in abundance in London Society. The Duchess of Autenberry fit his tastes perfectly.

He'd always kept his attraction to Lady Autenberry in check, of course. Naturally, he would never dream of acting on any of his impulses. He had his honor, and dallying with his best friend's stepmother would definitely be in grave breach of that.

And yet the moment his lips touched hers tonight, it was no longer possible to keep things between them circumspect. He doubted that would ever be possible again. Any thought to honoring his gentleman's code flew out of his head. He'd been unable to think about the wrongness of his actions when she felt, when she *tasted*, so right. Her lips were the perfect degree of softness and they quivered against his so sweetly. The self-control he had mastered all those years ago suddenly didn't feel so . . . necessary.

He'd tasted her and now he could never go back. Things could never go back. He wanted *her*.

"Never took you for an exhibitionist, Strickland, and I've known you for years," Autenberry chimed, reminding him of why they had stopped kissing to begin with. She had heard his voice. Forget the fact that Autenberry was the reason they had even kissed in the first place. He was the reason they stopped. A fact that made Colin want to commit violence.

Colin tore his gaze from the woman on his lap to his friend. Autenberry cocked a dark eyebrow at him.

"I'm not," he replied, not lying.

Autenberry motioned with his hand around them. "And yet you chose this room."

Colin glanced around, his gaze taking in the man and woman on the bed, very zealously doing the act he ached to do with the woman atop his lap. His body didn't care who she was. It only longed to sink inside her.

He turned his gaze back to his friend only to find Autenberry staring at Ela again. Her face was, fortunately, still obscured by her dark nimbus of hair, but Autenberry was stretching out a hand as though to sweep it back from her shoulder.

He locked his hands on her waist and lifted her off him, putting her out of reach as he stood, blocking her with his body and also keeping her turned away from Autenberry's prying eyes.

"If you'll excuse us."

Autenberry's eyes glittered knowingly and then surveyed the room. "I suppose I'll find my own diversions, then."

"You do that." Colin didn't wait around to chat any more. With one hand on her arm, he felt her shaking. He needed to get her out of here. This entire situation was fraught with problems he couldn't even begin to wrap his head around.

Guiding her by the arm, he led her from the room. She followed eagerly. Together they stepped out in the hall. The door shut softly after them, muffling the sounds within.

She lifted her face to look up at him. He'd never seen her like this. Hair loose all around her. Lips puffy and bruised from kissing. From him. From *his* mouth.

Her wide, dark eyes looked a little glazed as they stared up at him. As though she didn't know how to work through what had just happened.

He had a fairly good idea on how to work through it and it involved finding the nearest bed. A task that wouldn't be too difficult in this house.

Frustration stabbed at him because he knew that couldn't happen. One look at her, already peering around him as though searching for the nearest escape, and he knew that wasn't a possibility. For a few fleeting moments she might have responded to his kiss, but she wasn't up for a continuation.

He clamped his hand around her wrist and pulled her along. "Come."

She hurried to keep up with him.

He tried to quell his frustration and remember

who she was. She was a lady he'd always given proper deference, as one might any other friend's mother.

Now when he looked at her, she would always be someone other than that. Someone he'd kissed. Someone whom he knew to frequent Sodom—and that was a jarring thought.

How many times had she visited here? How many men had she taken to her bed? And why did he want to kill every single one of them?

HE SEEMED ANGRY. His feet moved so quickly she had difficulty keeping up with his swift stride. Her skirts slapped at her ankles and her fingers dug into his hand that gripped her own.

"Where are you taking me?" she finally asked, breathless.

"I'm not *taking* you anywhere. I'm getting you out of here," he said tersely.

"Oh." She winced inwardly, despising the tenor of that single meaningless word. She sounded disappointed.

"That is what you wanted. What you asked of me," he reminded, flexing his fingers around her hand and casting a quick look over her shoulder in the direction of the room where he had just shattered her so thoroughly. "Isn't it?"

She nodded doggedly. "Yes." That is what she had asked him, after all, when she spotted Marcus in the hall. Before Strickland had hauled her into that room. Before he'd kissed her.

The kiss. Mad as it seemed, it felt as though her life could now be separated into two parts. Before she kissed Lord Strickland. And after. Because the kiss had changed things. She felt different. Altered.

Her lips still tingled and her body burned in places that she wasn't entirely certain had ever felt sensation before. And considering she was a widow and knew a man's touch, that was saying a great deal indeed.

She took a shuddery breath. She needed to be free of him and alone to think about what this change meant for her.

He led her down a back stairwell, different from the one she and Mary Rebecca had taken to reach the second floor.

"You actually came here alone?" he asked with a hint of wonder in his voice as he descended in front of her, his hand still holding hers, pulling her along after him.

"No. My friend—"

"Lady Talbot?" he guessed, and there was something else in his voice at that inquiry.

"Why, yes. How did you know?"

"I've seen her here before and I know you and she are friends." His lips curled in a half smile. "She's a frequent visitor."

"Is that so?" she muttered, despising that smile and all that it implied. Mary Rebecca was a welcome and regular visitor to Sodom. Graciela experienced an unwanted pang of jealousy.

Immediately she wondered if he had kissed Mary Rebecca and liked kissing her. Perhaps they had done *more* than kiss. Mary Rebecca couldn't be expected to tell her about her every encounter at Sodom. Mary Rebecca was a lovely woman, and Colin, without a doubt, had his charms. Of course her friend would find him attractive.

Graciela scanned his strong profile as they touched down on the first floor. Who would not? Presented with an opportunity to be with him, how could her man-loving friend not desire him?

And yet the thought of him with Mary Rebecca unsettled her. She resisted the urge to touch her lips where she still felt the burning imprint of his mouth. She was singed for life. He'd done that to her.

As he settled his gaze on her, she made certain her hand stayed firmly at her side. She had no wish for him to see her touching her mouth as though reveling in the memory of his kiss. Definitely not. He needn't know the impact he had on her. He would likely have to stave off laughter. He probably went about kissing women all the time and it meant nothing to him. It shouldn't mean anything to her either.

She would reserve the touching of her mouth and the recounting of that shattering kiss for when she was alone.

They stood in a narrow foyer. A weathered wooden door loomed at the far end that had to be a servant's entrance—or an entrance for guests who wanted more discretion.

He sighed. "I never thought to see *you* here." Disapproval was writ all over his face.

Apparently he smiled only at the mention of Mary Rebecca frequenting Sodom. Not Graciela. Such activities were not for her, it seemed

She inhaled through her nose, undeniably offended. Who was he to judge her? Her dearest friend could be a regular here and not Graciela?

He released her hand and turned toward the door, clearly expecting her to follow.

This would be the moment to explain that this was the first time she stepped foot inside Sodom and that the experience had been too much for her and she would never dare repeat it. Except pride kept those words bottled up inside her.

She squared her shoulders. "Just because we've known each other for years, does not mean we really know each other, Lord Strickland."

He stopped and turned to fully face her again. He stared at her for a long moment and she felt the weight of that silvery blue gaze as though he were a magistrate rendering harsh judgment on her.

"Lord Strickland now, is it? You've been known to call me Colin in the past."

True, she did at times use his Christian name. Only now that felt much too intimate given the circumstances.

"We kiss and suddenly I'm Lord Strickland." Mockery hugged his tones. She chose to ignore it.

He'd done it. He'd mentioned the kiss. Named and identified that great giant beast in the room so it could not be avoided. She sighed. Perhaps this was for the best. They needed to discuss it and put it to rest.

She swallowed and glanced around. The space in which they stood suddenly felt suffocatingly small.

"About that kiss," she began. "I appreciate what you were doing . . . helping me, but we need to forget that it ever happened."

She expected a look of relief from him. She was giving them both a way out of this uncomfortable scenario. They would simply go back to before. Pretend it never happened.

He stepped closer, which was disconcerting. Especially as she was confronted with those eyes and the way they were looking at her now. Usually they stared at her kindly, full of mild-mannered courtesy. The perfect gentleman.

But right now the blue of his eyes fairly glowed at her. He didn't look like a gentleman. He more resembled a devilish pirate from a novel. The air charged and sparked in the tight space around them. She felt trapped, like she were caged with an unpredictable beast that might decide to bite.

"You didn't like it, Ela?" His voice rumbled between them, deep as distant thunder. "Could have fooled me."

The skin near her eye twitched. She inhaled through her nose and tried to ignore his nearness—and how very alone they were now. There was no Marcus to interrupt them. No roomful of strangers to offer distractions—not that they hadn't engaged in a thoroughly devastating kiss with all those distractions anyway. But who knew what could transpire between them when they were well and truly alone? It was not a good situation for a woman who had decided only this night to seize her life and experience adventure for herself. Anything could happen now between them. Her belly clenched. All the decadent images she had witnessed tonight flashed through her mind. Purge. Purge them from her memory.

"I'm Marcus's stepmother." The weak reminder came out the smallest whisper.

He shrugged. "So? Marcus doesn't have to know."

She stared, struggling to grasp what he was suggesting. "You mean . . ."

He waved a finger between them. "He doesn't need to know about anything that passes between us."

It took her a moment to fully absorb what he was saying. "Are you suggesting . . ."

"Us," he smoothly inserted. "You. Me."

A sharp laugh escaped her. She couldn't help it. Her nerves were overwrought and what he was proposing was ludicrous.

He scowled. "I'm not jesting. It is what you came here for tonight, is it not? To find a man to warm your bed?"

How could he so accurately guess at her motives? "I—I . . ."

"It takes more than curiosity for someone to come to Sodom." He spoke in so even and moderate a voice—as though he were explaining a simple concept. "People come here when they're looking for something . . . wanting something. Someone." He stared at her, waiting.

She swallowed, wishing she could deny the charge, but then Evangeline's face rushed across her memory. Once full of life, now she was lost, buried deep underground.

Graciela knew that such a fate would be hers eventually. Death came to all. She simply wanted to live more before that happened, to experience all the colors life had to offer before that inevitable day arrived.

So far the rainbow of her existence consisted of only a handful of colors, and most of them were because of her daughter. Clara provided all her joy and had given her life purpose during the bleak years of her marriage and even after she buried her husband.

Colin was right.

She had come here because she wanted something. *Someone*. Perhaps *want* wasn't even the right word. She *needed* to find other colors to fill her life.

Gazing at Colin's handsome face, she was tempted to believe that he was that someone for her, that he was the lover she was seeking here at Sodom.

Except it was preposterous for her to consider that a young, virile man like him, at the pinnacle of life, so beautiful to behold, not even married or yet a father, could be the lover she sought. He could have his pick of young women. He had so many other options. It was arrogant of her to think he would want her.

She shook her head slightly. "Lord Strickland, I'm much too old for you."

He stared at her for a long moment. "Is that your excuse? You're not that much older than me, Ela."

"Six years."

"A pittance."

She shook her head. "You should be paying court to all the young debutantes coming out. Choose one of them. Marry one of—"

"I'm not suggesting marriage to you, Ela," he cut her off. Laughter tinged his words. As if the very idea of marrying her, a woman his senior and well beyond childbearing years, was a jest. Heat slapped her face—and shame.

Of course it was a jest.

All laughter faded from his voice as he answered, "I'm suggesting an affair, of course."

"Of course," she echoed, feeling instantly hollow inside. She knew that's all that could ever be between them, but it did not lessen the sting. She was good enough for a quick tumble but nothing else. Nothing honorable. An empty, meaningless affair was all she was worth. With one hand skimming the wall, she skirted past him and headed for the door.

His feet sounded behind her, following. She hurriedly opened the latch of the back door and stepped out into the night, plunging into the frigid air. It was a welcome shock to her overheated body. She lifted her face to the air and took a bracing breath.

A street ran in front of her, parallel to Sodom, and she glanced up and down its length. Even at this late hour, carriages passed along the lane. This was a busy part of town with several gaming hells and clubs.

She signaled for a hack, not bothering to wait for him to do it for her. Right now she wanted only to go home to her bed. Alone.

He arrived at her side. "Ela, I meant no insult. We have known each other for years and I would hate for—"

She whirled to face him, dropping her arm. The momentary relief she'd felt stepping outside quickly faded. She shivered in the cold, wet air. "Years of acquaintance notwithstanding, we don't really know each other, my lord. I see no reason why we should change that fact now."

A nearby streetlamp cast his features in light. She did not miss the tensing of his jaw. "I think I know you fairly well, Ela."

"Only in the most superficial way," she countered.

He was fuming. It was strange. She had only ever seen him as an affable young man, but tonight she had observed him in several states of emotion—none she would characterize as affable. All that made him quite the dangerous man—the darkly handsome character from a Gothic novel whom the heroine did not know to be hero or villain.

"So I'm nothing but a stranger to you?" he challenged, stepping ever nearer, a great encroaching wall of pulsing energy she felt certain would singe her if she were so foolish to touch it.

She masked her unease with a shrug.

"Is that not what you were looking for, then?" he pressed in a hard voice, reaching out a finger to trace the stiff edge of her domino. "An anonymous shag? Someone to rub that itch between your legs and afterward you can return to your polite life as the Duchess of Autenberry as though it never happened?"

She gasped.

His words were brutal and blunt . . . and not untrue. Even worse, they sent a spike of heat straight to her core. Her gaze feverishly scanned his handsome face, a single, horrible chorus chanting through her mind: *Yesyesyyesyesyesyesyes.*

"I can be that man for you," he added, his lip curling, revealing a flash of straight white teeth. "I felt the way you rode me as I kissed you. You wanted me deep inside you." Her stomach flipped and churned and twisted as his gaze crawled hotly over her. "I still can be."

She sucked in a breath, aware that she should soundly slap him for speaking to her in such a way.

A horse neighed as a coach clattered by, serving to remind her that civilization existed and she would not resort to histrionics and slap him like some overwrought damsel.

She lifted a hand and this time a nearby hack responded, slowing to a stop beside them. The driver hopped down to open the door for her.

She stepped close to Strickland, brushing a hand against his chest, a gossamer touch, barely making contact. Leaning forward, she breathed her response near his ear, ignoring the way his proximity made her heart race. "Rest assured, if I've an *itch* that needs rubbing, I'll find someone other than *you* to rub it."

Turning, she fled inside the hack, a deep sense of gratification sweeping through her. He had offended her. Not so much with his offer to be her lover, but with the laughter in his voice when he assured her that he would never consider marrying her. Let him think she would seek another man. Perhaps she would.

She heard the earl give her address to the driver outside. She leaned back on the squabs, holding her breath until the conveyance rocked forward, signaling she was moving away from Sodom and across town.

She sat rigid and anxious until she reached her town house and she was safe inside. Her maid, Minnie, helped her undress and climb up into bed.

Once there, tucked beneath the covers upon the colossal mattress, she gazed into the dark blindly.

The winter wind tapped at the panes of her mullioned window. It was a lonely sound but it gave her comfort. This was familiar. Alone in her bed was familiar.

Tonight marked her first kiss in over ten years.

She replayed it in her mind. Everything right

down to those outrageous parting remarks with Strickland. *Colin.*

She dragged her knees up to her chest and curled into a tight ball. In this moment, lying aching in her bed, she imagined that she had taken him up on his offer. Right now he could be filling the awful clenching throb between her thighs.

Her hand slipped between her knees to cup her throbbing mound. She felt hot in her hand, the ache there deep and almost painful. She moaned in frustration. Wicked as it was, she fondled herself, pushing the base of her palm against her womanhood, rubbing at that little pleasure point until she was shaking and panting. She worked for her climax, but it was elusive. She finally gave up, so unfulfilled she could weep.

She brought her hand out from between her legs and rolled onto her back. Her ragged breaths filled the air between her and the canopy.

It felt like she hovered on a great precipice. Change was inevitable after this night. She was on the verge of something significant and she needed to decide what that could be.

When she was a little girl, Papa's groundskeeper, Francisco, would take her fishing. Whenever she caught a fish, she would study it carefully, memorizing its shape and the shimmer of its iridescent underbelly, carefully disengaging the hook from its gaping mouth and then setting it free back into the dark waters of the bay. Francisco's voice surfaced now and echoed through her mind: *Every creature has its limitations. A fish cannot live out of water. Learn what it is you cannot live without,* mi niña, *and never let that thing go.*

Unfortunately, Graciela still wasn't certain what that was. She'd married and buried a husband and suffered numerous miscarriages. She knew loss and she knew joy. Her daughter was certainly the light of her life.

And yet as much as she loved her daughter, Clara was growing up and starting to pull away. It was only fair and right that her daughter find her own path. Even though it made her heart hurt, Graciela knew this was inevitable. She would have to let her daughter go soon. Clara could not be that one thing she couldn't live without. She would soon have to learn to live without her.

And that left Graciela standing on that dock again, overlooking the water as she tossed her fish back in the bay, wondering what it was she couldn't live without.

It was time to find out.

She would begin by taking a lover.

Chapter 6

The following day, Graciela returned to the town house and expelled a heavy sigh, wearied from the ordeal of saying her final farewell to Evangeline. She glanced down at the heavy black bombazine she wore, so eager to rid herself of the dress that the notion of burning the garment did not even strike her as dramatic.

The funeral had been as grim as the vigil, replete with old dames gabbing on about women they'd known over the course of their lives who'd also expired young. One such tale featured a young baroness who walked off a cliff in a fog whilst looking for her pet pig.

At least the somber event saved Graciela

from being interrogated by Mary Rebecca over last night's deeds. She saw the question in her friend's eyes. She knew she wanted an explanation as to why she vanished last night, and Graciela wasn't quite prepared to give it. She could lie or prevaricate, of course, but she wouldn't. She made certain to take her own conveyance to and from the funeral, avoiding time alone with Mary Rebecca. She was her closest friend and the one person she could confide in about anything. In good time, she would tell her, but not today.

"Good afternoon, Your Grace." Mrs. Wakefield greeted her in the foyer, a ready smile creasing her face. Graciela looked up at the imposing woman several inches taller than herself.

The housekeeper shooed away the footman and collected Graciela's cloak and gloves and bonnet herself. "You must be chilled to the bones. It's a dreadful cold day to be outdoors, Your Grace."

"Indeed. It was a dreadful day altogether," she said, moving toward the stairs, eager to be rid of her gown and relax within the comfort of her chamber.

Evangeline was gone and in the ground. The realization left her as cold as the winter outside.

Last night Graciela had felt warm and alive.

When Colin hauled her onto his lap, she'd felt an undeniable sizzle of excitement. As though she might burst out of her skin. Somehow she would get that feeling back. Only not with Colin. She would find someone else. Someone more suitable.

"His Grace is in the library. He arrived over an hour ago."

"Marcus?" She froze, one hand on the balustrade, her heart starting a fierce rhythm. Could he be here for any particular reason or was this simply a social call?

For a moment, she feared that Lord Strickland had told Marcus everything, but then she knew that he wouldn't do that. He had gone to a great deal of trouble to get her out of that club without her stepson learning her identity. He wouldn't have surrendered the truth after all that effort.

"Yes." Mrs. Wakefield nodded. "Are you up to seeing him or would you like to retire?"

There was a lengthy pause before she replied, "I'll see him, of course." Lifting her skirts, she made her way to the library, feeling like a black crow sweeping along the corridor in her swishing ebony skirts.

The library had always been Marcus's favorite room in the house. Even though he kept a house across town, new books appeared every season, ordered at his specification. It was an impressive collection.

The door was cracked. She entered, spotting her stepson reclining on the sofa before the fireplace, jacket removed and cravat loose—the height of casual comfort.

"Hello, Marcus. This is a pleasant . . ." Her voice faded as she stepped through the door and saw that he wasn't alone.

Colin sat in an armchair, his legs stretched out before him, fingers loosely holding a glass of whiskey. Unlike her stepson's, his glass appeared hardly depleted.

Both men stood at her arrival.

It shouldn't have surprised her that *he* was here, too.

Colin could often be found in Marcus's company. Years ago when they still attended Eton, Colin tagged along when Marcus came home on holidays. Her heart had always ached for him, orphaned at an early age with only an uninterested grandmother who spent all of her time in Bath with all the other grand dames of the ton rather than attending to her grandson.

"Lord Strickland, how good to see you." Her voice emerged small and tinny.

"Your Grace." He inclined his head very properly. She quickly looked away lest she stare too long and with too much yearning at that mouth of his that she now knew intimately.

Marcus stepped forward to press a kiss to her cheek. "You're looking well, Ela. I was sorry to hear about your friend."

She dipped her gaze to study her hands as though they were of vast interest. "Yes. It's a terrible tragedy."

Marcus motioned for her to join him on the sofa. She claimed a seat for herself, arranging her skirts carefully and pasting a smile on her face. She felt Colin's stare but didn't glance his way again. She nodded with seeming interest, attempting to carry on a conversation with her stepson. She must have conversed passably. Marcus didn't remark to the contrary. Not that she did a very good job focusing on his words.

He caught her attention only when he addressed Colin. "Lud, I can't believe you're really about this, Strickland." Marcus's expression was disgusted.

She glanced between the two men, her gaze resting on Colin a fraction too long. He must have felt the weight of it. He turned to stare back at her, his face unreadable.

"You're much too young to get leg-shackled," Marcus added.

"I seem to recall you were considering leg-shackling yourself to Poppy Fairchurch not too long ago," Colin responded evenly, his gaze still fixed on her as he spoke.

Leg-shackled? Her mind raced. Colin was getting married? To whom? When?

It shouldn't have mattered, but she couldn't deny the swift stab of discomfort in the center of her chest. He'd kissed her only last night and offered to scratch the itch between her legs. Her face burned at the memory.

And he was on the verge of marriage?

She knew that fidelity wasn't a high priority among noblemen, but somehow she'd thought Colin was better. At least before last night. Now she knew he was as lust driven as the rest of them.

"A mistake. A remnant of my coma." Marcus fluttered his fingers in the air. "Side effect, no doubt, of trauma to the head."

Graciela stifled a snort. It was her assumption that her stepson had proposed marriage to Poppy Fairchurch to thwart his bastard half brother. At least in part. Poppy Fairchurch was sweet and appealing and she didn't doubt that had some influence over him as he pursued her. But she was penniless and titleless and without connections. These things mattered to a duke like her stepson. She should have known something else was afoot when he proposed. Something like stealing the girl away from the half brother he loathed.

Fortunately, Poppy loved Struan Mackenzie every bit as much as he loved her and they were happily married now.

Marcus noticed her again and asked suddenly, "Would you like me to ring for your favorite Madeira, Ela?"

"No, thank you. I'm fine," she said, deciding she couldn't feel comfortable in Colin's company. Perhaps never again, sadly. It wasn't to be borne . . . feeling the heat of his stare, knowing he was thinking about last night.

She rose to her feet in a swish of skirts. The men stood, as well. She motioned for them to resume sitting. "Please. Stay as long as you wish. It's been a long day."

"Of course." Marcus gave her a quick embrace. "You must be very heart heavy for your friend. Take some time for yourself and have a long nap."

She winced. It was the manner of advice one would give to an elderly parent. Next he would be offering to mash up her food for her.

It stung a little that Colin bore witness to such treatment. He was probably kicking himself for his fleeting lapse with her and thanking the heavens that she had refused him.

"Yes." She nodded in agreement. "A nap sounds like a fine idea." Let them think her old and infirm.

She left the room, still not sparing a glance for Colin, no matter how much the urge beckoned. She had to be strong and put things back in their proper perspective. She would pretend last night never happened. After all, Graciela knew how to play the game of pretend. She was well versed in it. She had pretended for years to be happily married, and even now when her husband had passed away, she still pretended he was the good man he wasn't—all for the sake of Clara and her stepchildren.

She was almost to the door of her bedchamber when she heard steps behind her. A glance over her shoulder revealed Colin following on her heels.

She stopped and whirled around, her heart immediately jumping to her throat. "Colin . . . what are you doing?" Mistrust laced her voice, which was absurd. She had nothing to fear from him. She knew that. It was more an issue of her not trusting herself . . . and reverting to that lonely, needy creature from the night before that melted the moment his lips touched hers.

"I just wanted to make certain you're well."

"I'm well," she quickly assured him, hoping he would turn and leave her.

"You don't look well." He stopped in front of her, thankfully a respectable space between them.

She forced a light laugh. "That's a fine thing to say."

His gaze narrowed and flicked over her features. "You know what I mean." His tone was no-nonsense. Clearly her attempt at levity had not fooled him.

She hadn't been well since she learned of her friend's demise . . . and she hadn't been fine since stepping into Sodom. Since coming face-to-face with Colin. Since that kiss and those blunt words exchanged outside the club.

"Today was a trying day." Blast if her voice didn't give a telltale shake.

He nodded. "Of course. That's understandable. But I was referring to last night."

No. Please. She didn't want to relive that with him. "What about last night?" she asked quickly. Too quickly.

He cocked his head. "Have you forgotten so soon?"

Forgotten? As if that were possible.

She glanced past him, fearful Marcus would come up behind him in that moment and catch on to their discussion.

"No, my lord. I haven't forgotten but I will set it aside from my mind. Just as you should." She took a step closer and lowered her voice to a conspiratorial pitch. "What happened between us . . . you have to forget all about it." She made a swiping motion with her hand.

"Do you think it that simple?" His gaze moved over her face, as though he were seeing her features for the first time. Or at least seeing her in a new light. She was certain that much was true. She was definitely seeing him in a new way. "As eventful as the night was?"

She shook her head. *Eventful?* She could think of a dozen more-apt words.

His gaze grew more intense on her face, his brows drawing closer. "I doubt I shall ever be able to put it from my mind."

"My good sense has returned in full. I've learned my lesson." The lesson that she would look somewhere other than Sodom for a lover—and she would obliterate the memory of his kiss by replacing it with another's. Posthaste.

"No more jaunts to places like Sodom, then?"

Heat fired in her cheeks. "Rest assured, no." She would simply be smarter as she went about the acquisition of a lover.

He continued to stare at her in that oddly intent way, almost as though he could read her thoughts. His pale blue eyes gleamed like silver in the shadows of the corridor. Exactly as she remembered from last night. She resisted squirming beneath his regard. How could things have ever been easy and natural between them? The air between them was spiked and charged. Not easy. Not natural.

Time, she told herself. In time, things would go back to the way they were before. Last night was an anomaly and would simply become a dim memory. Besides, if he was to marry soon, he wouldn't be hanging around her so much. He'd have a wife to fill his time with . . . and soon they would have children.

This thought didn't supply nearly as much comfort as it should have.

She moistened her lips. "Did I hear Marcus correctly? You're to be married?"

The silence crackled before he replied. "I'm not engaged. Not yet. My grandmother has merely brought it to my attention that it is time to start filling the family nursery."

"How splendid for you. And your family." The words felt like rocks spitting out from her mouth.

"Yes. The next in line after me, according to my grandmother, is a wastrel second cousin in America. She would like at least two great-grandchildren, in fast succession."

"An heir and a spare," she remarked a touch bitterly, well familiar with the English adage. "You best accommodate. This season boasts a lovely crop of debutantes."

He sighed, not appearing thrilled at the idea but dutiful. Always dutiful. "I do have a few prospects in mind, supplied to me by my ever-helpful grandmother, of course."

She nodded. "Of course. I'm certain your grandmama is full of recommendations, but I'd be happy to steer you, as well. I know of several accomplished ladies that would be proud to call you husband."

Did she just offer to help him pick out a bride? She needed a gag to stuff in her mouth at once.

One corner of his mouth kicked up. "Are you offering me your assistance in selecting a bride?" The mocking tone of his voice brought the heat creeping back into her face. Considering their activities the night before, it was a ludicrous suggestion.

She stammered, "I-If you should require my opinion, it is yours. Friends help one another and we are that, are we not, my lord?" What rot was she spewing now?

"Yes," he said slowly, his voice solemn. "Always that, Your Grace."

They held each other's gazes for an interminable moment.

She felt as though she were facing a stranger, contrary to the nonsense she was spouting. A man who was stripping her of her clothes with his eyes to see all that lay beneath.

Chapter 7

"I'm not sure about this, Mary Rebecca," Graciela whispered, careful that no one overheard her. Two of Mary Rebecca's daughters sat on the seat across from them, identical smiles of excitement etched onto their glowing faces.

Graciela was most definitely the only one in the carriage not looking forward to the evening ahead. And yet somehow she was here, coaxed into attending Lord Needling's musicale by her friend.

"Ela, please," Mary Rebecca whispered back, tugging and plucking at the neckline of her gown with a militant eye, making sure the satin rose-buds edging the brocade had the proper fluff and framed her cleavage to maximum effect. "Lord Needling has long been an admirer of yours. And considering he has never been interested in me, despite all my most ardent efforts"—she arched a reproachful eyebrow at Graciela—"you should have him."

"Thank you?" she murmured as their carriage rolled to a stop before the viscount's town house, a questioning lilt to her voice. She didn't bother pointing out that Lord Needling was a grown man and not an *item* to be given.

"Ah! We're here. Come." Mary Rebecca shooed her girls toward the door.

"He did not invite *me* directly, Mary Rebecca," she muttered as they lifted their skirts and followed young Marianne and Aurora down from the carriage.

Mary Rebecca landed on her feet with a huff. She whirled on Graciela and seized her by the shoulders, giving her a little shake. "You know he was hoping I would bring you. He is always asking about you. Truly. If you weren't my friend, I would hate you." Her gaze flitted over Graciela's shoulder. "Marianne! Don't run. Have some decorum, please."

Mary Rebecca hurried after her daughters up

the steps toward the front doors of Lord Needling's Mayfair home.

Graciela slowly fell in behind them, moving at a more sedate pace, doubts plaguing her. Coming here tonight, uninvited, was waving a flag of surrender in Needling's direction. She chewed her bottom lip in agitation. It was one thing to decide to take a suitable lover and another thing to go about the motions of making that happen. She wasn't certain she was ready for this.

You were ready a couple days ago when you straddled Colin's lap and rubbed yourself all over him like a cat in heat.

She shushed her inner voice, just as she had done countless times since that night. That episode had been an anomaly brought about by the suggestive atmosphere of Sodom. It wasn't real. It was as artificial as something dreamed up . . . at least this was what she had convinced herself.

She had not been blind to Lord Needling's interested gaze over the years. As much as he had made his admiration for her known, he had only ever been gentlemanly toward her. An ideal choice for dalliance. He was a widower purported to have loved his late wife—that alone esteemed him in Graciela's eyes.

He would be discreet. He was handsome. He was of appropriate age, perhaps five or six years older than herself. He was everything she should want in a paramour. She wrapped herself in these emboldening words and stepped inside the house.

They were escorted to the drawing room, where chairs had been arranged for Lord Needling's musicale. A father of three daughters, all of marriageable age, he often hosted such events to showcase their talents. His middle daughter was quite good friends with Marianne. Mary Rebecca's daughters almost immediately abandoned them to join Dorothea, who was tuning her violin at the front of the room.

"Ladies, welcome, welcome." Lord Needling greeted them warmly, his gaze resting on her overly long. "Your loveliness brings light to the room." The viscount bowed over their hands. Mary Rebecca cut Graciela a smug look over his bowed head.

"Thank you for allowing me to invade your evening's musicale, my lord," she murmured, still feeling a bit of an interloper.

"Nonsense!" His soft brown eyes twinkled merrily. Not a tall man, he was trim and self-possessed with a full head of black hair streaked with gray. "If I had realized you were in Town, I would have happily extended an invitation."

She was not so certain of that. She had long ago dismissed the invitation in his eyes, and he had respectfully kept his distance.

But that would change now. He would soon realize that she was receptive to him. That was the point of her attendance this evening, after all. Before the night's end, he would grasp that she had changed her mind and his pursuit would be welcome. A wave of nausea overcame her and her gaze darted about the room, assessing for where she might be sick in the event of an emergency.

Mary Rebecca conveniently drifted away to speak with Mrs. Pottingham, Lord Needling's sister, leaving her alone with the viscount.

Graciela did not miss, however, the condemning stare of Mrs. Pottingham. The lady's hawk-like gaze traveled over Graciela as she examined her from head to toe with slightly flaring nostrils . . . as though she caught the scent of something sour.

Graciela's hand drifted to her bodice. Her neckline was modest, but she still felt vulnerable, her golden skin laid bare before one of the ton dames who found her so clearly defective. It was not the first time she was treated to such a stare. She knew what it meant . . . knew that her presence, her appearance, her very voice heavy with accent, was offensive to many.

She cleared her throat and removed her gaze from Mrs. Pottingham. If she allowed Society's opinion of her to dictate her actions, then she would never step foot in public. Graciela had always endured it. Now was no different. Fortunately, Clara, as the late duke's daughter, was more accepted.

"I'm looking forward to the evening's entertainment, my lord," she said. "I understand your daughters are quite the accomplished musicians."

He chuckled lightly. Taking her elbow, he guided her to a seat at the front of the room, even farther away from the other guests, who milled about the opposite side of the room near the refreshment table. "Lies, all. Fortunately, they have their mother's beauty, so their musical talents shan't be their only lure in attracting a husband."

Graciela smiled, not bothering to voice her opinion that he would do well to cultivate other things in his daughters and not rely on their beauty to snare husbands. If her late husband had admired more than her face, he might not have been so disappointed in her as a wife. But it wasn't her place. She was trying to let this man woo her, not run him off. "Your girls are lovely."

"So is your daughter. Much like her mother. I'm sorry she can't be here tonight."

"She is enjoying the country right now with her sister. She is quite the horsewoman. She enjoys the open space to ride. She will be here for the season."

"Perhaps we can bring the girls together then. She's close in age to my Dorothea, is she not?"

Graciela nodded, her gaze drifting to the youngest of his three daughters, sitting at the pianoforte. "I believe so."

"Splendid. We've much in common, Your Grace." He sank into a chair beside her.

She nodded, although other than raising a daughter, in his case multiple daughters, she wasn't sure what those commonalities might be. She didn't really know much about him. Instead of disagreeing, she said, "Indeed, we do." She held his kind gaze a trifle long. It was as forward as she could manage. She'd once known how to flirt, but that skill had grown cold some time ago. It was no longer within her repertoire to be coquettish.

"It's regrettable that we did not reach this realization sooner, Your Grace." His eyes grew heavy lidded as he uttered this. "We've wasted precious time. Time we might have spent about more pleasurable tasks."

The husky pitch of his voice shouldn't make her skin crawl. She knew this, and yet she longed for a bath where she might wash her skin clean of his gaze.

She forced a smile, telling herself this was simply new to her. She wasn't accustomed to exchanging seductive repartee.

He cast a quick look about and then leaned slightly closer. "It is right for us to come together, Graciela."

She started at his use of her name. She had not invited him to do so, and yet coming here, she supposed, indirectly, she had.

He watched her, assessing, gauging her reaction. This would be the moment when she could put an end to this familiarity once and for all, thereby quashing any intimacy between them before it officially began.

She held silent.

His hand inched toward hers atop her lap and lightly grazed the pinkie finger of her hand. It was the subtlest of actions, but that was Lord Needling. Subtle. Not at all confident or aggressive. Not at all the type of man to haul a woman onto his lap and kiss her like she were the last bit of food on earth and he a man starved.

Lord Needling was ever polite. He would probably make polite love to her. *Begging your pardon, may I do this? And may I put this here, Your Grace?*

She lifted her fingers to her mouth to smother a giggle. Heavens, she was one breath away from hysteria.

A polite gentleman to make polite love to her was the safest choice—and that thought jarred her. She had decided to add excitement to her life. A safe, dull lover was in direct opposition of that. The notion of taking Lord Needling to her bed shouldn't fill her with apathy. Her purpose had been to put an end to the blur of days leading to her demise. She would not end up like Evangeline, dead too soon with only regrets to carry into the hereafter.

She brought her focus back to Lord Needling, searching, hoping for some evidence, some sign, that he was the right choice and she would not live to regret him.

Just then Forsythia, Lord Needling's eldest daughter, called out in excitable tones from the other side of the room, "Lord Strickland! You came! You came! How delightful!" She hopped in place, clapping her hands like a girl much younger than her eighteen years.

Graciela's heart galloped loose in her chest as she followed the girl's gaze to Lord Strickland.

He stepped into the room, smiling as the girl barreled toward him with all the eagerness of a charging elephant.

Her mind raced, trying to grapple with what the sight of him here signified. Then the truth came to her. His presence could mean only one thing. He was here to pay court. Lord Needling's daughters must be on Colin's grandmother's list of bridal candidates.

She closed her eyes in a long agonizing blink. He was here to court Forsythia and Graciela was considering Lord Needling for a lover.

Could this situation be any more excruciating?

"Forsythia." Lord Needling sighed. "Eighteen but she is still very much a child. An exuberant child."

"She's beautiful," Graciela said softly, admiring the girl.

"Indeed, she is. And an heiress, so she needn't be overly eager." Judgment laced his voice as he frowned at his still-bouncing daughter. "She'll have her pick of suitors this season."

And yet the best candidate stood before her now.

Lord Strickland had yet to see her and she was free to study his handsome profile. He bowed over Forsythia's hand. They made an attractive couple. She with her fair hair and he with his dark head of hair and silvery blue eyes. They would make exceptionally beautiful babies. A pang pierced her heart.

"She'll be a lucky girl if the suitor she snares is Lord Strickland." Once the words were out, she regretted them. What was she doing recommending Strickland?

And why shouldn't she? She had no claim to him. She needn't be selfish and try to keep him from an ideal match.

"Is that so?" Lord Needling considered him with fresh eyes. "She pestered me to invite him this evening. It seems he is much favored with all the young ladies."

Of course he was.

"He's a gentleman," she said, the words unbearably tight in her throat. And it wasn't only young ladies who favored him.

"Hm. His line is an old one. His grandmother ruled Almack's in her day." He scratched his chin thoughtfully as though weighing Strickland's worth. "I suppose I could do worse for a son-in-law."

"Indeed." She nodded stiffly, hating that she should agree, but it was true.

"Pardon me, would you, my dear?" Lord Needling asked. "I should greet him."

"Of course."

He covered her hand with his and held it there, his eyes searching hers, as fervent as a puppy eager to please. "Don't move, Your Grace. I should like to sit with you during the musicale."

She fought to swallow against the sudden lump in her throat, her fingers shifting slightly beneath the foreign weight of his hand.

In that instant, she *felt* Colin's gaze. It landed on her, as palpable as a touch . . . a fiery brand that sent searing shivers across her skin. She held her breath and schooled her features into blankness as she allowed her gaze to find him.

As suspected, he was staring directly at her, his bright blue eyes wide with an emotion she could not quite identify

He blinked, the sight of her here clearly startling him. His gaze drifted from her to Lord Needling sitting beside her. His mouth pressed into a flat line. His gaze dropped to where their hands touched and his expression turned to hard stone.

Heat crept over her face. She slipped her hand out from under Lord Needling's, suddenly guilty and self-conscious—even though she ought not to feel that way. Being here, with Lord Needling, made much more sense than visiting Sodom. This was by far the more appropriate scenario. It was entirely within propriety for a woman her age—a widow of ten years—to be seen in public with a gentleman friend.

She watched Colin closely, waiting for him to give her a nod of greeting, for his stony expression to crack with a smile. It never happened.

With a blink, he turned his complete attention to Forsythia, dismissing her. His smile returned in full force for Forsythia. He even tossed back his head and laughed at something the girl said. Her stomach churned as she observed the handsome pair.

Lord Needling joined them and the gentlemen exchanged pleasantries. Colin didn't glance her way again.

She stuffed her hurt way deep down. She didn't have a right to such an emotion. There was nothing between them. That much had been made clear. She didn't have a right to even think of him as Colin. He was Lord Strickland, friend to her stepson, and nothing more to her. If she said it enough times, surely it would start to sink in.

He dipped his head closer to Forsythia as they conversed, his dark hair brushing the girl's golden tresses. Forsythia grazed her hand along his arm. They looked the perfect couple.

As they should.

A handsome young nobleman. A beautiful heiress of noble blood—*English* blood. They were meant for each other. He shouldn't waste a moment looking her way. Graciela was nothing. Always an outsider. Nowhere near the first blush of youth. A woman of advanced years incapable of giving him any of the things he required in life.

"Your Grace?" Needling's voice drew her attention back to him. She sat up a little straighter and looked at him. Here was a man she could be with and delight in the joining. "Shall we sit together?" he inquired.

She fixed a smile on her face . . . the same one she had learned to wear years ago when it became clear to her that the kind of marriage she had always wanted, one of love and happiness, was never to be hers. "That would be lovely," she replied.

WHAT IN BLOODY hell was she doing here?

Scratch that. One glance at Lord Needling's hungry gaze crawling all over her body and he knew precisely what she was doing here.

She was actually acting on her words.

If I've an itch that needs rubbing, I'll find someone other than you to rub it.

He had not taken her seriously when she tossed

those heated words at his head outside of Sodom. Now he knew that was because he didn't want to, but he should have realized she meant them. If she had been bold enough to step foot inside Sodom, then this would not be such a leap for her.

Staring at her, a rose in this garden of lilies, he felt his heart pound in his chest. As more people arrived, he worked carefully to mask his face so that he revealed none of the turmoil churning through him. He kept her in his line of vision as Needling's daughters warmed up on their instruments, shifting so that he could spy on her through bodies and over the heads of guests.

He had thought tonight would be uneventful. A polite gathering at the home of one of Grandmother's favored candidates. A girl he might wish to pursue, but the distraction of Ela here was too much. He couldn't even think about Forsythia. The significance of Ela's presence was a bitter draught that threatened to choke him.

She was entertaining the notion of that dull prig as a lover. He inhaled a deep breath.

This realization ran as a litany through his head.

Hell, no.

Perhaps she was not merely *entertaining* the notion. Perhaps she had already taken him to her bed. Jealously of the likes he had never felt sank deep into him, seeping past muscle and sinew and striking bone. Air hissed silently past his teeth.

His hands clenched around the edge of the small plate that had been forced into his hands by the eager Forsythia with the instructions that he must eat every bit of Cook's apple tart because it was the tastiest thing in creation.

Staring across the room at Ela, her profile lovely and gentle in repose as she listened to whatever drivel Needling was spouting to get into her knickers, he knew this to be false.

Ela was the tastiest thing in creation. Her lips chased through his dreams. Her warm skin. The fullness of her body rocking against him. He told himself it was simply because she was forbidden and yet he had been granted a brief taste. The reality of her couldn't be nearly as sweet as he imagined. All of this made sense, but it didn't matter. She was a fever in his blood and there was only one way to purge her.

He set the plate down lest he snap it in half, his hand slightly trembling. He didn't know which urge was stronger. The one to grab Ela and shake her until her good sense returned . . . or the one demanding he haul her into his arms and finish what they started at Sodom. He stifled a groan. Very well. He knew which urge was stronger.

He knew what he wanted. Knew what they had to do.

Fuck each other senseless until he had exorcised her from his thoughts.

Previous to Sodom, this would have been an unconscionable thought. Out of respect for his friend *and* respect for her, he'd never seriously considered the idea of bedding her, much less bedding her with the intention to ultimately cast her aside. He'd never thought she could be agreeable to such a thing with *him*.

But that night at Sodom had changed everything. That kiss . . . the words that passed between them. They couldn't be undone. She was in search of a lover. Why not him? He offered her discretion. More than any other gentleman. And he knew she was not immune to him.

"Can you believe she's here?" He overheard Mrs. Pottingham whisper to the lady at her side, whose name he did not know. A quick glance over his shoulder revealed the lady stuffing the famed apple tartlets into her mouth. She spoke around a mouthful, crumbs spewing in the air. "Look at the way she is throwing herself at my brother. Shameful!"

Oh, he'd been looking but he saw quite the opposite. Lord Needling wasn't paying attention to anyone other than the duchess. He listed to the side, making certain that his body was in direct contact with hers. Graciela was either unaware or amenable to the proximity. The fool woman. Did she not understand people were taking note? That *he* was watching? Clearly she didn't care.

"Duchess or not, she's a light-skirt, I say," Mrs. Pottingham remarked, her voice a fraction above a whisper now. "My brother would do well to steer clear of a woman like that."

He turned and leveled her a cold glare where she stood on the opposite side of the refreshment table.

The lady froze, another tart halfway to her lips, her gaze trained hesitantly on him. The other lady, her companion, looked wide-eyed between the two of them.

"In my experience, a light-skirt is on a higher rung than a commonplace gabster."

Mrs. Pottingham gaped, revealing a mouthful of half-chewed food. Her companion covered her own mouth with a napkin to muffle her snickers, whilst Mrs. Pottingham turned several shades of red.

"Well!" With a huff, she plopped several more

tartlets on her plate, whirled around and marched away, her friend following on her heels.

Idly, he realized it was probably unwise to set himself at odds with the relation of a girl he was considering for matrimony.

Despite the encounter, the more reasonable side of himself knew the activities of one widow did not overly matter in Society. There were much greater scandals.

Ela was no blushing debutante or married lady. She was free to dally where she chose and despite the nattering of one busybody, if she and Needling had an affair, it would hardly cause a ripple.

The butler called for everyone to take their seats. The performance was to begin. The wave of guests began moving toward the array of chairs.

There was no need for him to feel so protective of her. No need for him to move away from the table and take his seat directly behind where Ela sat beside Lord Needling, where he had a perfect view of the couple.

Chapter 8

It was torture.

The girls' musical ability was less than passable. Every time Forsythia would slip up on the keys, she would giggle and cast an adorable look Lord Strickland's way that seemed to promise she was good at *other* things. Or perhaps those were merely Graciela's unkind thoughts. She couldn't see Colin's face and she didn't dare turn to glimpse behind her. It was enough that she felt him there, his presence radiating heat she was certain only affected her.

When they stopped for an intermission, she was the first to her feet.

Lord Needling rose, looking concerned.

"If you'll excuse me."

He nodded, too gentlemanly to pry as to her destination. As she passed through the room, she was careful not to seek out Colin with her eyes. She couldn't bear the thought of seeing him looking moon-eyed at that child, Forsythia.

At the door, she asked a maid to direct her to the ladies' retiring room. Several ladies were already walking down the corridor, heading that way, including Mrs. Pottingham. Deciding she did not want to stomach that particular lady's glares or stilted conversation, she slowed her pace and ducked down an intersecting corridor, hoping to find a quiet room where she might have a moment's respite to gather her composure.

Voices traveled on the air. More people were coming. Determined that no one spot her and drag her back to the party, she opened a random door. Peering inside, she saw the room was mostly dark, the hearth cold. A feeble ribbon of moonlight spilled into the room from the French doors, allowing her to make out pieces of furniture draped in cloth. This room wasn't in active use, then. No one would find her in here. She should not be disturbed.

Satisfied, she stepped within the chilly interior and closed the door after her.

She was alone.

Graciela strolled deeper into the room, her gloved hands coming up to chafe at her arms, attempting to rub the gooseflesh away. She was wondering how much longer she could tolerate the frigid room when she heard the door open behind her.

She spun around, her heart loud in her ears as the door snicked shut. He had followed her. Colin stood here, his tall frame leaning back against its length for an extended moment.

Her chest lifted on a breath. Her slippered feet carried her back, farther into the room. She rounded a chair and placed her hands on the back of it as though needing the support.

She moistened her lips. "You shouldn't be here." Her voice rang tinny on the air. They could not be discovered together here like this, alone in a darkened room. She pointed an imperious finger. "Go."

He pushed off the door and came at her, his legs eating up the distance, stalking her in a manner that urged her to take flight, to bolt. It took all her will to hold her ground.

He stopped in front of her, the chair between them. "Why are you here?" he demanded.

There was no urgency to him, no fear that they might be discovered. No, that was only *her* fear. The hard hammer of which pulsed through her now. Her gaze darted several times toward the door and back to him. What if someone entered? He held himself boldly, as though he had every right to be here. And what would it matter to him if they were discovered? That was the dichotomy of men and women. Women had reputations to lose. Men merely had reputations.

"Why are you here?" he repeated.

"It is a party, is it not?" she snapped, her ire rising for the unfairness of it all. That he should have no worries whilst she had so many things to consider. That he should be so very appealing and so very out of her reach simultaneously. "There are a great many people here. Why shouldn't I be here?"

He ignored the reasonableness of her question and angled his dark head in a manner that could be described only as faintly menacing. "Are you and the viscount lovers now?"

She came out from behind the chair, skirting him. "That's none of your business," she retorted even as heat flooded her face.

She moved about the room evasively, making

progress toward the door. She never presented her back to him. That seemed a foolish thing to do.

She kept her gaze trained on his face, on the glitter of his gaze. She had been alone with him before and it never felt like this—all crackling space and too-hard-to-breathe air.

As she stared at him, it was hard to recall he was the same Lord Strickland she had known almost half her life.

Everything about him was different. He treated her . . . differently. Looked at her in a manner that made her skin feel too tight for her body.

Or maybe it was that *she* had changed. After all, she had become the manner of female who visited pleasure clubs and contemplated taking a lover.

He knew that about her now. So of course he would look at her differently and behave differently toward her.

Her gaze fixed on him as he closed the space between them. She held out a hand as though to ward him off. There shouldn't be this strangeness between them. He should *not* look at her the way he was. He should not make her feel the way he did.

She was still Autenberry's stepmother.

Still a duchess.

Still forbidden.

Those words never came, however. They were on the tip of her tongue, but she lost them when she bumped a table that held a lamp. Glass clinked in discord, and she turned, steadying the surface with shaking hands.

When she turned around again, it was to find him before her. She gasped at his sudden closeness and leaned back against the table, her gloved hands falling flat on the surface.

"I'm waiting for your answer."

"What was the question?" She breathed, her pulse an urgent charge that ran all the way from her throat to the core of her . . . making her press her thighs together.

"Are you and Needling lovers now?"

For him to wonder such a thing was not outrageous, she supposed. Not given her activity of late. It was only outrageous in that he would think he had any right to ask.

Her fingers curled and dug into the cloth-covered surface of the table. The heat in her face did not abate. Any other man who dared to utter such words would be treated to the flat of her palm. It was only their long-standing connection that stopped her from slapping him.

"I do not see how that is any of your concern."

He smiled slowly. Actually, it was more a grimace than a smile. His lips peeled back from his straight white teeth. "True, it's not any of my business, but did you not only recently pry into my affairs regarding my intentions to marry? I think you even offered to help in my quest. I assumed that meant we were sharing confidences."

She squared her shoulders and tried to pretend not to notice his gaze dip to her décolletage. A difficult task when her skin seemed to warm from the inside out at the stroke of his gaze. "It is not the same."

His hands came to rest beside hers on top of the table. She felt all of him then aligned with her body. It was shocking. Even dancing, she had never felt a man's body so close. Not since her husband.

"How so?" he pressed.

She struggled to focus, struggled to ignore the distraction of his proximity. Her eyes ached from lack of blinking. She really needed to blink. "It's improper to ask me such a thing, whereas my inquiries are polite . . . an extension of my maternal interest—"

"Bollocks," he growled, his hand coming to fist the side of her gown.

She swallowed against the impossibly thick lump in her throat at his hand there, gathering the fabric slowly up, radiating heat into her hip. "What?"

"Don't." The word puffed out in a breath.

"What?" she managed.

"Lie."

He brought his other hand to her skirts. His body crouched slightly as his fists tightened, bunching the fabric, lifting her gown to her waist until cool air kissed her stocking-clad legs.

She opened her lips to speak but only a squeak escaped as he jerked her closer, mashing her breasts into his chest. Holding on to her waist, he lifted her and plopped her down on the table, wedging himself between her splayed thighs.

"Shall I show you just how much you lie?"

Without waiting for her reply, one of his hands dove between her parted legs.

He moved with such skill and swiftness to the slit in her drawers that she knew he was quite familiar with lady's undergarments. He knew what he was about. Her head was spinning and she had yet to gain her voice before his fingers were gliding through her womanhood.

"Let's just crush the idea that what you feel toward me is maternal once and for all," he growled, his fingers growing more confident, stroking and circling around that tiny button of pleasure at the top of her sex.

Her head fell back with a strangled cry. "What are . . . you . . ." Her voice surfaced in a rasp. As far as protests went it was pathetic, but then, her body was one clamoring ball of need at the moment.

All she could do was gaze in astonishment at the stark handsomeness of his face. The burn of his stare matched the heavy throb low in her belly.

It had been too long since her body received any kind of attention. Even longer since her body knew true satisfaction—perhaps it never had. There was something about his hooded gaze that promised satisfaction—to say nothing of his hand working between her thighs, stroking that most intimate part of her.

Her body shook in her eagerness, her muscles tightening like a coil. She leaned back, giving him greater access.

She still recalled that trip to Sodom. The smell of sex and desire ripe all around her. It was as though the single experience had infected her, leaving her feverish and aching, afflicted with a deep craving for this, for *him*, even if she happened to be in the middle of a party at Lord Needling's house. It mattered naught. She realized that now. When you had gone without for all your life, nothing else mattered when the opportunity finally presented itself.

She whimpered, her arms starting to tremble on the table from holding her weight. There was no denying herself this.

He explored her, circling her opening and then moving back up, so close to that aching nub, and then darting away again. Close but never quite touching it. She could weep for the torment of it. Her hips started to move, pelvis lifting, seeking his touch.

"So wet, Ela," he groaned and dropped his head in the crook between her neck and shoulder. "You feel like honey and silk."

His teasing became too much, unbearable. Soon she felt herself wet and slippery against his fingers. Embarrassment stabbed at her, but she pushed it aside as his hand continued to work its magic between her thighs.

She bit her lips to stop herself from begging. Autenberry had never touched her like this. Until Sodom she had not known that men petted women in such a place on their bodies . . . nor had she had any notion that it could feel so good.

"Do you like this, Ela?" His deep voice scratched her skin, traveling over her and abrading her in her most tender places—places she hadn't known could feel sensations like this.

And that's when she realized he wanted that. He wanted her senseless with need. He wanted her to beg for it. Damn him.

She gnashed her teeth to stop her pleas from escaping.

"Say it. Tell me." Colin's finger brushed the tiny bud nestled at the top of her folds and she jerked as though burned, sucking in a hissing breath.

In the gloom of the room, his eyes glowed like moonlight. He continued to toy with her, circling around that button faster, tantalizingly close without actually making contact, bringing her to the brink of something.

She could hardly hold herself up. Her entire body quaked. She fell back on her elbows, making the dangling beads of the lamp jingle.

He squatted, shoving her legs wider apart. He looked up from between her thighs at her. "I'm going to taste you as you come apart, Ela." She gaped down at him, bewildered, her body a throbbing inferno at his outrageous words. But he didn't stop there. He continued to talk, to say the most scandalous things that made her already pulsating body vibrate with want and need. "And then after you come apart, you're going to beg me for more. For me. Inside you. Not bloody Needling. Not any other man."

Then his hands gripped the slit of her drawers and tore the fabric wider, giving him greater access. Her chest froze, the air trapped in her lungs as she watched his head dip. His mouth was *there*. On her. He took the oversensitized nub he had just been teasing moments before and sucked it deep in his mouth, his tongue flaying it as his teeth scored the tender flesh.

She gasped, her hands diving into his hair. It was too much. She tugged on the strands but his face just burrowed deeper between her legs. But then she felt it. The coming apart he had promised. A tidal wave of sensation washed over her. Moisture rushed between her legs.

She choked, overcome, lurching off the table as she shattered and came apart. A shriek tore from her lips, but his hand shot up, covering her mouth and muffling the cry as his own mouth continued to devour her below, riding out her pleasure.

She drifted back to earth gradually. Small sobs spilled from her throat. She couldn't help herself. The aftershocks continued to come. Tears pricked at the corners of her eyes and she couldn't stop shaking.

She was dimly aware of his hands tugging her skirts back down as he rose. She should be grateful for that, she supposed. And yet she couldn't motivate herself to move. Her muscles had the consistency of jam. Her legs hung limply off the sides of the table.

He grasped her arms and pulled her off the table to her feet. She wobbled on her legs and he reached out to steady her. She stared at him, still feeling dazed and fuzzy headed.

He smiled down at her, looking so smug and satisfied. Embarrassment brought a fresh wave of heat to her face. She'd come apart for him just as he predicted. This was also the moment, after she came apart, that he predicted she would beg him for more.

He hadn't forgotten his promise either, for his next words were just as smug as his expression: "When I claim you, it won't be on a table."

A shiver of anticipation shot through her, followed fast with regret because she had no business feeling anticipation.

She really was shameful. She'd allowed him—*Lord Strickland! Que el cielo me ayude*—to do the most wicked things to her whilst the girl he was courting played the pianoforte a few rooms over. And despite all that, Graciela still wanted him. She wanted him to do *more* wicked things to her. *Every* wicked thing.

She had clearly lost herself. Anger welled up inside her. Anger at herself . . . anger at him.

His eyes stared down at her so knowingly. He thought he had her. He thought he'd won.

Her hand twitched at her side and before she realized her intent, she slapped him.

For a moment neither one of them moved. Their breaths crashed between them, the only sound in the silent room. He touched his cheek where her hand had left a stark white handprint on his face. He looked utterly calm as he gazed back at her.

Her chest heaved. She felt anything but calm. She wanted to hit him again, irrational or not, and that shamed her, too.

"Feel better?" he asked.

No. She felt worse. The strange urge to cry overwhelmed her. She didn't know what this was. She didn't know *who* she was.

She shook her head. "No more." It was all she could think. All she could manage to get out.

It was enough to garner a reaction from him. His eyes narrowed. "I'm assuming you're referring to us."

She nodded.

He chuckled and the rough laughter startled her. She eyed him warily.

"You really are naïve if you think we will never do this again, Ela. We started something here. It's too late to go back."

His words sent a sharp sting of panic through her. Was he right? She was suddenly desperate to prove him wrong. He had to be wrong. They had to go back to the way things were before. She winced. Very well . . . maybe that wasn't possible, but she definitely knew they couldn't move forward. If someone ever found out about them—and people always found out—it would be disastrous.

He dropped his hand away from his face. The white handprint had faded to leave a reddened cheek behind. "If you were honest with yourself, you would admit we both want this and then we could quit wasting time and find the nearest bed."

She should hate his words. Hate him for all the grief he was putting her through. Instead she felt a treacherous little thrill. She was still wet between the thighs from him and terribly sensitive. Her body hummed, ready for the *more* that he had promised.

She took a bracing breath, suppressing her body's traitorous longings and reached for logic—for sanity. "You need to be an adult, Colin."

His nostrils flared and she knew she'd insulted him with the insinuation that he was a child. "I am an adult," he growled.

"Then you should know that you can't always have what you want."

"I'm adult enough to know that this thing between us isn't simply going to go away. We might as well indulge in it, purge it from ourselves."

She bit her lip, silently arguing that he was wrong. Giving in to this thing between them would make everything worse.

In the distance, music started, signaling Lord Needling's daughters had resumed playing. It was like a douse of cold water, effectively killing all the yearning she felt. A necessary reminder. He belonged out there, wooing his future bride. Not in here committing all manner of licentiousness with her.

She turned in the direction of the door, motioning at it with her hand. "I'm sure Forsythia is looking for you. Save your kisses for her. She will gladly take them." The image that produced cut her like a blade. Forsythia with Colin—his head ducking between her thighs to do all the wicked things he had just done to Graciela. The idea actually hurt; it was a physical ache in her chest.

Just then a sound reached her ears. Footsteps. A door opening and closing, the noise echoing down the stretch of corridor.

Someone was coming.

Her panicked gaze flew to Colin's face, but he was already moving, diving behind a large piece of furniture draped in cloth just as the door cracked open.

Lord Needling peered into the shadows. His gaze scanned the room, stopping with a jerk on her. His expression lightened. "Your Grace! I've been searching for you. I worried when you had not returned. The recital has continued."

She stepped forward, pasting a smile on her face and pretending not to feel the evidence of what she had just done beneath her skirts. The rent fabric of her drawers flapped against her upper thighs.

"I just needed a moment. The retiring room was quite crowded," she lied, assuming he would not contradict her. How would he know what it was like inside the ladies' retiring room?

He nodded agreeably, offering his arm. She stepped forward to accept it, eager to leave the room where Colin hid. After they departed, he would slip out and presumably return to the musicale, no one the wiser.

Her heart hammered in her chest, the fear of discovery enough to choke her. She wouldn't breathe easy until she was in her seat. Perhaps not even then.

Her fingers settled in the nook of the viscount's arm. She resisted the urge to look behind her into the shadows to assure herself that no part of Colin was in sight. She needn't draw Lord Needling's attention anywhere except to her.

Needling covered her hand on his arm with his own and gave it a squeeze. "I'm so glad you came tonight, Your Grace."

She nodded, shaking inside, her nerves stretched thin. She tried to step forward so that they might continue out from the room but his hand tightened around hers, holding her in place.

His eyes roamed her face. "Are you well, Graciela?"

She nodded, an uncomfortable knot forming in her chest at the avid way he was looking at her combined with the knowledge that Colin was in the room listening to their exchange. She prayed he would make no sound even as she wondered, what must he think? Then she told herself it didn't matter what he thought. Despite what just occurred between them, he had no claim on her.

"Yes, of course," she said, willing to say just about anything to get him to lead them out of this room.

He released a nervous sounding breath. "Brilliant. Then while I have you alone here, I must do what I have longed to do since I first clapped eyes on you all those years ago. I confess, even when my late wife was alive, I felt a strong pull toward you."

She shook her head, horror filling her as he drew closer, his head inching her way. No. No. No. This wasn't happening. He wasn't saying these things. He wasn't moving toward her with puckering lips and passion-glazed eyes.

She pressed the flat of her hand against his chest and strained away, hoping to stop him from encroaching further. "My lord . . ." she began, glad that he wasn't a very big man. He was scarcely taller than she. Not that she imagined she would have to wrestle free of him, but if necessary she likely could.

"Graciela, my dark siren," he crooned. She turned her head from his descending mouth. His lips landed on her cheek, but his voice filled her ears, desperate and frenzied with need. "I've dreamed of you in my arms for too long. There have been others since my wife, but none have been you despite how I liked to pretend—"

"My lord!" The idea that he *pretended* he was with her when he was with other women revolted her.

"Your sunlit skin," he panted.

"No!" She pushed harder at his chest.

"Your glorious breasts." His hand closed around one, mauling it roughly, with all the finesse of a drunken ox, through the bodice of her gown. "I've ached for these in my hands for so long."

A strangled shriek escaped her and she pulled back her arm to slap him but never got the chance. Colin was there, yanking the viscount away from her. She staggered free, watching in horror as he pulled back his arm and delivered a hard blow to Needling's face. It sounded awful. Like bone striking bone.

She felt the color bleed from her face. There was no saving her now.

The smaller man fell to the carpet with a mewling cry. Colin didn't even appear finished. Bloodlust gleamed in his eyes.

She attached herself to Colin's side, seizing his arm just as he stretched it for Needling again. "Colin, no, no!"

He attempted to shake off her hand, his stare fixed hard on the older man. "He touched you," he growled.

Needling rolled on the floor, holding his nose and moaning. Blood seeped out between his fingers.

"You stopped him," she argued, trying to find the words to calm him. His face was fearsome in its intensity, skin flushed red with temper, his eyes vowing murder. He was normally so affable. If anything, Marcus was given to fisticuffs. He had brawled on the streets of London with his half brother, after all. Colin, however, was always the calm and steady one. She'd never seen him like this and it alarmed her. She didn't know what to do to bring him back to himself.

"I'll kill you. She said no," he snarled at Needling, leaning over the man and kicking his listless boot. "Get to your feet."

"Colin!" She took his face in both hands and forced him around to meet her gaze.

His brilliant eyes raged with the storm of his fury. Still holding him, she did the one thing she could think to do to distract him from thrashing Needling to within an inch of his life.

She kissed him.

Chapter 9

It took all of one moment for Ela to blind him to everything. To Needling, to his surroundings. The entire world faded away.

Her mouth fell hungrily on his, demanding. She kissed him as though this were the last kiss in the history of all kisses.

She clung to his face, her short little nails digging deep into his cheeks as her soft, pliant mouth slanted wide for him. She bit his bottom lip before thrusting her tongue against his. His cock grew hard against her belly, but she didn't appear to care. Didn't care that she was kissing him. Didn't care that they had an audience. She pressed herself into him with wild abandon. Her hands dropped to his shoulders and he grabbed her by the small of the back, holding her lush body against him as he kissed her back with equal intensity.

"I see the way of it," Needling rasped. "Of course, it would have been nice to know I was wasting my time."

Colin growled and started breaking away from Ela, but her hands tightened on his shoulders. She increased the pressure of her mouth. He knew what she was doing. He knew she was attempting to distract him from thrashing Needling—and for the most part succeeding.

"If you were otherwise involved, Your Grace, you should have said as much before you traipsed inside my house and made a fool of me."

At this, Colin finally tore himself away from Ela and squared off in front of the viscount. "You need very little help from us to do that."

She made a plaintive sound in her throat, her wide eyes flying to the viscount. She attempted to step forward as though to place herself between them. Colin snatched her hand and hauled her behind him. No woman of his needed to protect him.

The possessive thought jarred him the moment it crossed his mind, but he didn't waste another moment on it as Needling advanced on him, mopping at his bloodied face with a handkerchief. He fluttered the bloody rag in the air between them. "Had I known that the two of you—"

"You know now. She's mine," Colin snapped.

Ela sucked in a breath behind him as though preparing to speak, doubtlessly to protest that statement. He gave her hand a squeeze and sent her a quelling look over his shoulder indicating she could argue that point later. After she'd just kissed him bold as you please, Needling wouldn't believe her anyway.

"I should call you out," Needling sputtered. "You're a blackguard, Strickland."

"Am I? I caught you manhandling the Duchess of Autenberry. What does that make you?"

"I thought she favored my attentions!"

"She said no. Quite forcibly as I heard it."

"She made a fool of me. And you, Strickland. I welcomed you into my house to court my daughter. What were you two up to before I happened upon you?" His eyes narrowed. "I've been made a fool by the both of you!"

"Indeed." Colin nodded, feeling a deep sense of satisfaction.

Ela hissed behind him. "How are you helping?"

He continued, "I doubt you should like the world to know that fact, my lord. You can well imagine the great amusement everyone will take at your expense. I can just hear the men at White's laughing now."

He knew the precise moment this clicked in Needling's mind. All the men at his club . . . laughing because the Duchess of Autenberry made merry with his daughter's suitor beneath his roof whilst he thought she wanted him. It was a tangled shrub and Needling the unfortunate dunce at the center of it.

The viscount flushed red, shaking his head vigorously. "This episode need go no further than us."

"Quite so," Colin said crisply.

Squaring his shoulders, Needling managed to demand, "I take it you will quit your suit of my daughter."

Colin nodded tersely. "Of course."

Relinquishing his suit of Forsythia was no hardship. He'd already crossed her off his list—not that he was thinking much about his list right now. Needling as a father-in-law would be a definite toll to endure. Forget the fact that Colin had quite possibly broken the man's nose—he'd never be able to forget the way Needling had groped Ela. No, there were countless debutantes from whom to choose. Colin need only look to his grandmother's list.

Needling bobbed his head as though satisfied and then looked over Colin's shoulder where Ela stood.

He felt a snarl well up inside his throat. He didn't even want the man looking at her. He could still hear the bastard calling her his "dark siren" and wanted to smash his face in all over again. He wasn't usually given to violence. She did that to him. Made him react and feel things he hadn't felt before. He told himself it was because he had known her for so long, but that explanation felt a little weak even to him.

The fact that Ela had even been considering taking the viscount—or someone else—into her bed struck him hard. If he had not seen her the other night at Sodom, she might very well be with someone else now. Colin might not have kissed her or tasted her or even right now be planning how he could be alone with her again.

Needling must have seen some of his urge to commit violence again in his face. Sniffing loudly, he edged toward the door, saying, "You both can see yourselves out. If anyone asks, I'll make your excuses."

"Good of you," Colin replied in a voice that was anything but appreciative.

The viscount departed the room. Colin listened for a moment to the sounds of his footsteps scurrying away.

"We best leave before the performance ends. No one will notice if we slip out now."

She nodded in agreement, still staring at him warily. "I came here with Lady Talbot."

"I'll see you home."

If possible, she looked even more wary. Gone was the woman who had just kissed him with fire and zeal.

She stepped past him and out into the corridor. He followed her, reaching for her elbow.

She glanced down at his touch on her arm as though she would reject it but then trained her gaze forward again, her lips flattening into a thin line. As though she would endure his touch. Still, he did not release her until they'd departed the house and settled in the confines of his coach.

He took the seat across from her, deciding not to push his luck by sitting next to her.

The carriage began rolling, the wheels clattering on the road outside.

"Will he keep his word?"

"Or risk becoming a laughingstock?" he asked, understanding her meaning at once. "He will keep his word. His pride will guarantee his silence."

She exhaled and he noticed her shoulders eased a little, some of their rigidity slipping away. He was glad for that. He didn't wish to see her worried or afraid and the encounter with Needling had left her feeling both those things. She lifted her gaze to the curtains. They were closed, but she stared at them as though she were seeing outside. Evidently she would rather look anywhere than at him.

"How long will you remain in Town?" he asked. He knew with Clara and Enid in the country she would not be here too long.

She lifted her dark eyes to him. "I don't know. I suppose I should return soon." She paused, frowning. "Perhaps the sooner the better. This visit to Town hasn't been free of its problems—"

"You mean you and me."

She held his gaze and merely arched a dark eyebrow. "We've both been behaving recklessly of late."

"I'll allow that."

She sniffed. "It has to stop. If Marcus or the girls ever knew . . ."

"So let's stop behaving recklessly."

"What do you mean?"

"Let's have a proper affair, conducted with total discretion. I can arrange it so no one ever knows. A time and place so that no one will ever know."

She stared at him a long moment, swaying slightly with the carriage's movement. He took heart in the fact that she did not deny him right away. She did not laugh at the suggestion. She was considering it and he had to contain his excitement. Somehow, in a short time she had become his sole desire. He wanted her with an intensity that would not go away until it found its release.

"Simply promise to consider it."

The carriage slowed as it approached her town house. It rocked to a stop and she still hadn't answered him. He didn't know if this was a good sign or not. The groom was at the door, opening it. She sat forward, ready to descend, her eyes averted. His heart sank a little. She couldn't even look at him.

She gripped the handle above the door, on the verge of stepping down. "I will consider it," she murmured, her softly accented voice nearly inaudible. But he heard it.

He released a breath, ridiculously elated.

And then she was gone.

THE DAY DAWNED bright and cold and with it came the flood of everything that happened the night before. As she opened her eyes to peer out at the frost-crusted mullioned windowpanes of her bedchamber, she remembered everything in painful detail. She had told Colin she would consider an affair with him.

She pulled her pillow over her head and groaned. How could she have done such a thing?

"Morning, Your Grace," Minnie called, poking the logs in the hearth at the other side of the chamber before then adding more logs. That explained the chill. The fire had died down in the night. "Shall I fetch your breakfast or would you like to eat downstairs?"

"A tray please, Minnie." She pulled the pillow off her face and released a great breath.

She had clearly lost her mind if she was thinking that she would do such a foolhardy thing. Today she would not step outside her bedchamber. Nothing could go wrong if she stayed locked up in her room.

A knock sounded at her door. She bade entrance. Mrs. Wakefield entered. "Good morning, Your Grace. Lady Talbot has sent her card twice this morning. She said she would call in a quarter of an hour. She is quite insistent on seeing you today."

She sighed. Of course she was. Two nights in close succession she had disappeared on her. Vanished with no explanation. Mary Rebecca likely wanted to know what was going on. Graciela owed her an explanation, she supposed. She flung back the coverlet. "Very well. Ring for Minnie, please."

She'd best make herself presentable.

Chapter 10

"What's his name?" Mary Rebecca demanded.

"Begging your pardon?" Graciela attempted to school her features into cool neutrality.

"It's a man. I can tell. What is his name?"

"H-how can you tell?" She winced at that telltale quaver to her voice.

"You look as though you haven't slept in a week. A man will do that, too." She nodded sagely. "He'll either keep you awake at night, occupying you with more carnal pleasures . . . or drive you to such distraction that you cannot sleep."

She could only stare at her friend for one long

beat. As ridiculous as her logic seemed, it was sound. Perhaps the time had come for confessions. It would feel good to talk to someone.

She cleared her throat. "Remember the night at Sodom? When I disappeared—"

"I knew it! I knew it!" Mary Rebecca bounced on her seat, the curls gathered at the sides of her head bobbing. "Who is he?"

"Nothing happened," she stressed. "Well, merely a kiss and that was only for convenience's sake."

"Convenience? What on earth are you talking about? A man does not kiss a woman out of convenience." Mary Rebecca released a *pfft*.

"Well, perhaps it's more fair to say he was rescuing me." She plucked at the velvet trim of her gown. "You see, my stepson was there that night."

"Autenberry." Mary Rebecca's eyes grew enormous in her face. "No! How incredibly awkward. I have seen him there a time or two." She cringed and looked remorseful. "I should have warned you."

Yes, that would have been nice to know before she agreed to join her, but that was neither here nor there now. "Well, he almost saw me." She inhaled. "But Lord Strickland intervened."

"How did he accomplish that?"

"Not with ease. He had to kiss me . . . and behave

as though we were embroiled to remove me from the room before Marcus realized it was me."

Mary Rebecca whistled between her teeth. "How very magnanimous of him. I mean, that must have been awful." Her voice turned teasing. "Kissing you must have been revolting for him."

She swatted at her friend's arm.

Sudden understanding lit Mary Rebecca's eyes. "You disappeared last night with *him*! That's why you both vanished during that dreadful musicale. You're having an affair with that delicious Lord Strickland!" She slapped Graciela's arm. "You wicked creature. Bedding a younger man! I'm so envious. I want to hear all about it! Leave nothing out. I must find all my vicarious thrills from you."

She shook her head, a hot blush stealing over her face. "I'm not bedding him."

Mary Rebecca looked her over carefully. "Not yet, then."

She continued shaking her head. "No. It won't happen. Ever. It cannot."

Mary Rebecca looked merely amused.

A brief knock preceded Mrs. Wakefield's entrance into the drawing room.

"Begging your pardon, Your Grace. You have some deliveries." With great flourish, she pulled the door wide, admitting several footmen bearing vases of hothouse roses. Her eyes widened as they simply kept coming. Several footmen. Several vases. Too many to count. "These just arrived for you." A smile played about the housekeeper's lips as she stepped forward and extended a small card to Graciela.

"Roses!" Mary Rebecca exclaimed, gawking at the parade of them. "This time of year? They must have cost a fortune."

Graciela accepted the card with trembling fingers. "Thank you, Mrs. Wakefield."

Still wearing that knowing smile, the housekeeper left the room on the heels of the army of footmen.

Mary Rebecca looked ready to burst as she waited, lips pressed into a tight line, for the door to shut. As soon as it did, Mary Rebecca erupted, "Open it! Open the card."

Dread pooled in her stomach, mingling with something that felt suspiciously like excitement, and she had no right to feel that way. If Colin was the sender as she suspected, this was the opposite of discretion as he had promised.

Her wide gaze scanned her drawing room. Every surface was covered in flowers. This was flagrant and brazen.

"He promised discretion," she muttered.

"Open the blasted card!" Mary Rebecca writhed where she sat. "The anticipation is strangling me."

With a sigh, Graciela broke open the envelope and read it.

"Read it aloud!" Mary Rebecca demanded.

After reading the scant line several times to herself, she obliged. Clearing her throat, she recited: "Ever hopeful we can come to a mutually propitious agreement."

Propitious. As though this were a business arrangement and not a personal matter. She looked up to meet her friend's gaze. "He signed it *C*."

Mary Rebecca held still for a full thirty seconds before clapping and bouncing again where she sat. "Oooh, you've a loooover, Ela. How exciting."

"Mary Rebecca," she hissed, shooting a glare to the door. "I have no such thing and would you be so good as to behave with the maturity of a toddler? At the very least?"

Mary Rebecca stuck out her tongue and then supplied, "*Yet.* You're not lovers yet, but it is a mere eventuality."

"No, it is not," Graciela stated evenly. "He promised discretion if we were to do this . . ." She waved a hand around them. "And this is hardly discreet."

"Oh! Poo! You're being too difficult. He didn't sign his name. Nor did he say anything inflammatory in that note."

"This is not a good idea," she grumbled, rising to smell one of the plump blooms on a nearby bouquet. It was fragrant and heady . . . quite like this entire relationship with Colin.

She brushed the petal almost resentfully. No one had ever sent her flowers. Not even her late husband. Their courtship had happened extraordinarily fast. Papa was simply so proud that she had won an offer from so eligible and prestigious a man. After she and the duke took marriage vows, there had been no such courtesy, of course. At that point, she was Autenberry's property—bought and paid for. No wooing. No flowers. The only jewelry he gave her was everything that had belonged to the long line of Duchesses of Autenberry before her.

"You deserve some happiness, Ela. And diversion," Mary Rebecca said gently.

She twisted one shoulder in a semblance of a shrug. "If he were anyone else. Not a family friend. An older, more mature gentleman—"

"Nonsense. I'm tired of you talking as though you have one foot in the grave. You're still young and attractive."

"I'm aware that I'm not in my dotage. I could perhaps overlook his youth if he were not—" her voice dipped to a whisper as though she was still worried servants lurked near "—Marcus's closest friend."

Mary Rebecca nodded thoughtfully. "I admit, that gives one pause, but there is no reason your stepson should ever learn of what is a private relationship." She arched her neck and sighed heavenward. "For goodness' sake! Do it just once! Find out what it is you've been missing all these years, Ela. I mean, look at whom we are talking about. My toes curl just thinking about him . . ."

More than her toes curled. Something twisted and pulsed within her. A deep, longing ache. She was beginning to understand—and fear—that it went beyond desire, and that was a terrifying concept.

He'd already given her a sample of what she had been missing when they were at Lord Needling's. The memory of that night would have to be enough. She would hug that memory close and wait until she could find some semblance of it again with a more suitable candidate.

She blinked eyes that felt dangerously close to tearing. This wasn't about denying herself pleasure and adventure. It was about denying herself *him,* which was the safest action to take—at least in terms of self-preservation.

"This is already much too demonstrative." She scanned the room and gestured to the flowers. "What if Marcus stops by and sees all of this? How shall I explain it?"

"With the truth. You have an admirer. He need not know whom."

An admirer? That was by far too quiet of a word. She couldn't look at the flowers without her face catching fire.

Suddenly she felt him between her thighs again. His mouth on the very core of her. Her hands buried in his thick hair, urging him on.

She sucked in a shaky breath and shook her head, hardening her heart against that part of herself that turned all hot and quivery inside at thoughts of Colin.

"No," she said, her voice resolved. "I must get rid of these flowers. All of them." She must leave no evidence that there was a man in her life. Marcus would investigate. He would deem it his duty. "And I'll send him a missive, as well, leaving him with no confusion that we will not be entering into a relationship."

Mary Rebecca sighed, her expression disappointed. "I hope you don't look back and come to regret this decision."

"I'm certain I won't," she lied, an awful feeling stirring in the pit of her stomach.

Because she wasn't certain of anything. Only days ago she had vowed to start living, and this felt an awful lot like running.

Mary Rebecca rose and moved to the nearest vase of roses. "Well, I might as well take one of these home with me if you're just going to throw them out. They are lovely."

"Take as many as you like as long as they go."

At that moment the drawing room doors opened and Marcus strode inside wearing a loose smile on his lips. Her hand drifted to her suddenly contracting throat. The act of drawing air was a struggle.

She shouldn't have been surprised at his sudden and uninvited presence. For years, before he acquired his own residence, this had been his home when in Town. He still treated it that way, coming and going as he pleased.

He opened his mouth, but the greeting never made it out. He froze and turned in a small circle, surveying the room. "Wow," he murmured. "What happened here? Did someone die?"

Graciela's stomach sank as waves of dread washed over her.

Mary Rebecca leaned in close beside her and whispered, "Looks like it's too late. I think he's seen the flowers."

Chapter 11

Colin stared, unmoving for several moments as his eyes traveled over the meager words etched on the missive in his hands.

I've thought over your proposition and my answer is no.

G.

She'd given him her answer. Perhaps the flowers had been too much and scared her off. He reread the note and smiled to himself. Not for one moment did he believe she meant those words. Scared or not, it didn't change anything. It wouldn't do any good.

He was still coming for her.

The doors to his drawing room flung open. Marcus strode in the room with Colin's harried butler scurrying behind him, belatedly clearing his throat in an attempt to announce the duke. It was the same scene every time and yet Lemword did not give up trying.

Autenberry collapsed inelegantly on the sofa before the fire. "When is this hellish winter going to end?" he grumbled as he stared into the fire. "Town is a right bore with everyone rusticating in the country."

With an apologetic glance to Colin, the butler closed the doors on them, leaving them alone.

Colin folded Ela's note and stuck it in his top drawer. He knew he would likely reread it several more times as though something could yet be gleaned from those so few words.

Just then Autenberry looked away from the fire. "Should we go to Sodom tonight? That might be diverting."

"I wasn't planning on it." No, he *had* been plotting on seeing Ela again—even if that meant scaling the balcony of her room. Her note had definitely put a halt to that thinking. Now he needed to carefully rethink his next step.

Perhaps he should do just as she demanded and forget about her—about *them*. He wasn't one of those pushy gentlemen to force his unwanted attentions on a female.

However, this was different. Ela wanted him as much as he wanted her.

"Come, now. Perhaps you can meet up with that tasty little bit of muslin you disappeared with last time."

He would have to bring up Ela—even if he didn't realize it. Colin shrugged as though the possibility made little difference to him.

"No? Well, then, perhaps I'll have a go at her."

Colin tried to mask his grimace by turning his gaze to the fire as though the writhing flames fascinated him. A hot streak of possessiveness battled with a flare of guilt. He had no right to feel possessive or jealous. His friend would be horrified to know he was talking about his stepmother in such a manner.

Marcus had built this fiction in his head of how noble and loving his father had been. In truth, Colin remembered him as uninterested and distant. Everyone knew old Autenberry bedded anything in skirts. He imagined Graciela didn't know the extent of her late husband's philandering ways. Any time she mentioned him it was in glowing terms. To hear her describe him, the old man was a saint.

Ela had been the one to hold the family together. Enid, Marcus and Clara. They had regular dinners and picnics and went to Sunday church. They sang carols at Christmas and went hunting for holly. They did all manner of things that good, wholesome families did. He knew Marcus loved her for that.

Hell, she'd even made Colin feel welcome.

"I'm not in the mood for Sodom tonight," he said, adopting a casual air. "Perhaps another time. You're welcome to stay for dinner here. I'm sure Cook is making something tasty. We can play a few hands of cards."

Marcus patted his flat stomach. "I had luncheon with Ela today. She always feeds me as though it is my last meal. Quite a repast. I don't think I can eat for days. I still regret not taking Cook with me when I set up my own house."

Everything in him tensed and yet he fought for calm as he asked, "You saw Ela today?"

"Yes." He sat up a little straighter. "Which reminds me. I believe my stepmother has a suitor." He waved with his hand. "The entire drawing room was a putrid explosion of flowers. It looked like a florist's shop. Disgusting, really. Some fool thinks he can get into Ela's bed by sending her flowers."

Colin paused slightly, trying not to let Marcus's words sting. That wasn't what he was doing, after all. Not precisely. "Do you, now?" Thankfully, his voice sounded mild and revealed none of his inner turmoil.

Marcus tapped his fingers on the cushions on either side of him. "Indeed."

"Did she tell you who?"

"She brushed it off and tried to imply she didn't know." He made a snort of disbelief. "Of course, she was lying. She could hardly look me in the eyes."

"Of course," he echoed.

"Don't worry. I'll find out who."

"Not to be a voice of dissent, but why is it so very important that you find out? Your stepmother is no green girl. Your father has been dead for many years—"

"Because this is Ela. I'll not leave her prey to the wolves of the ton. Trust me. I know their sort."

Naturally. *They* were *him*.

Marcus continued, "I've seen the way the ton looks at her. I'll not have her abused or made a point of gossip after some man has his sport with her and casts her aside."

Colin nodded once, feeling oddly detached, as though he were observing this scene from a great distance, watching two other men rather than the ridiculous pair they made. "And when you find this fellow?" Yes, Colin was referring to himself. Again. Ridiculousness. "What then?"

"I shall make him understand that he chose the wrong lady for dalliance and that he needs to steer clear of her."

And because he was the Duke of Autenberry and an imposing man in his own right, he would be obeyed. That was his assumption. Except for one thing. He did not know they were speaking about Colin. He thought they were talking about some dandy who would quake before Autenberry's foreboding visage.

"And if this man doesn't steer clear of her?" Because at this point that was not even possible for him. It was as though an invisible string connected them. A string with the strength of Prometheus's chains.

"Then I will make it abundantly clear to him." His hand opened and closed into a tight fist on the arm of the sofa. Colin did not mistake his meaning.

"I see."

It was his turn to gaze into the fire. Perhaps he should attempt to drop this infatuation with Ela. He did not imagine that Autenberry would approve.

Except there was that string between them. Impossible to break.

Marcus sighed deeply. "I suppose it's all moot now at any rate."

"What do you mean?"

"She's leaving."

Colin stilled, his fingers staying on his knee, gripping tightly, exerting so much pressure his fingertips whitened. "Leaving?" he asked, his voice deceptively quiet.

"Yes. She's returning to the country tomorrow. I doubt this admirer of hers will follow her to the country."

AFTER BRIEF CONTEMPLATION, he decided to scale the wall outside her bedchamber after all.

It was a drastic measure, but after Autenberry's announcement he felt desperate measures were called for. Dramatic of him perhaps. It wasn't as though he would never see her again. And yet if she left for the country now, it was because she was fleeing him. The next time they came face-to-face would be God knew when. Months perhaps.

By then she would be as resolute and grim as a bloody statue around him. She would be a perfectly composed Duchess of Autenberry, impregnable to his charm or influence. Forever out of reach. He knew it just as surely as he knew the sun would rise in the morning. He couldn't stand the thought of it.

He couldn't let that happen.

Naturally, he'd never entered the duchess's private rooms before. But he knew the house well enough to know the location.

He slapped hand over hand, fingers burrowing between chilled bricks covered in thick ivy as he pulled himself up, only the moon's glow showing him the way.

By the time he reached the balcony, his heart was hammering . . . and not because he'd exerted himself. It was the prospect of seeing her again. Of being alone with her. In a bedchamber, no less. He couldn't pretend that didn't weigh heavily on his mind.

He swung his leg over the balcony and dropped down silently on booted feet. His chest lifted on a deep breath as he contemplated the closed French doors. A faint reflection of himself stared back at him from the shining black windowpanes. It was disconcerting. He felt as though he was doing something illicit.

That would be because you are. Shoving the voice aside, he closed a hand around the latch and turned it, easing the door open.

The room was cloaked in darkness except for the faint glow of a fire dying in the hearth. He left the balcony door open behind him, letting the moonlit air bleed into the room and light his path to the colossal bed at the center.

He'd always thought his own bedchamber was ridiculous in size. He'd gone directly from living in the nursery to residing at Eton, where he'd shared a room with other lads. After finishing at Eton, he'd slept in the master bedchamber that had once belonged to his father, but even that was not as grand as this. Even in the near dark, he felt as though the vaulted ceiling stretched on forever.

He advanced on the bed, making out the outline of a body beneath the counterpane. Not any body. Ela's body.

He stopped at the edge of the bed and looked down. Her back was to him and he couldn't see her face. Just the shape of her on her side and the dark spill of hair, like ink across the white bedding.

His palms itched to gather that mass up, but he wouldn't touch her. He wasn't here to paw and grope her in her sleep like some predator of the night given to assaulting women while they were at their most vulnerable.

He cleared his throat. "Ela?"

Nothing. She didn't so much as stir. Granted, he had not spoken very loudly. Her name merely felt like a clamoring shout inside of him.

She shivered and rolled onto her back, pulling the coverlet fully to her chin. That's when he became conscious of the bite of cold at his back from the open door.

He strode from the bed and shut it, then moved to the giant fireplace and stoked the dying embers. He added a few more logs to the waning fire, satisfied that should bring it back to life and warm her well enough.

Standing back, he watched for a few moments as the logs started to smoke and then catch flame.

A slight noise behind him had him turning the precise moment an object came barreling at his head.

Chapter 12

Colin jerked to the side, narrowly dodging the object as it whistled past his ear. He turned, following it with his gaze, identifying it as a candlestick as it clattered to the floor.

Whipping around, he held out a hand to ward off Ela, armed with a second candlestick, charging him. "Ela! Stop! It's me!"

Either his words did not penetrate or she didn't care. The candlestick was coming straight at him. He reached out and caught it, his hand wrapping around her clenched fist.

"Let go!" she cried, trying to tear the heavy crystal free of his grip.

"Ela!" He said her name again, giving the candlestick a yank and wresting it out of her hand for good. He tossed it down to the thick carpet at their feet and then wrapped an arm around her waist, hauling her against him.

She at once felt familiar against him, her body pliant and lush. Familiar yet agonizingly unknown. He wanted to know her. He longed to sink himself inside her and know her as well as he knew himself.

"Colin!" Her dark eyes gleamed like gemstones in the dancing firelight as she stared at him, absorbing him for a long moment before adding, "What are you doing here? In my chamber?" She pressed her small hands against his chest, simultaneously arching her body away and shoving at him.

His gaze dipped and stared at the way the soft fabric draped over her lush breasts. The darkness of her nipples was quite clearly outlined against the material. It wasn't a sexy nightgown. It didn't even show any hint of cleavage or skin below her throat. It wasn't meant to entice but it was the single most provocative article of clothing he had ever seen on a woman.

"It was brought to my attention that you were leaving on the morrow."

She stilled at that, her hands no longer pushing

against him. "And that made you break into my room in the middle of the night? How did you get in here? The hinges on my door always squeak. It would have woken me." Her gaze darted about as though searching for some hidden door.

"I came through the window."

Her gaze shot to the now closed balcony doors. "I'm on the second floor!"

He shrugged. "I scaled the wall."

"You could have broken your neck."

"I assure you as a lad I scaled far greater heights."

"You're no lad anymore."

He smiled widely. "How nice of you to finally admit that," he growled.

Her eyes widened and then narrowed. "This is not a time for jesting. You need to leave this room, this house, at once!"

"Oh, I'm not jesting. This is quite serious for me. Finishing what has started between us, taking it to its most natural progression is a very serious matter. I only wish *you* would take it nearly as seriously. Instead of running away."

"I'm not running away!" Even in the dimness, he detected the ruddy cast to her features.

"No?" He snorted. "Your departure on the heels of what occurred at Needling's seems rather coincidental."

Despite that he stood several inches over her, she somehow managed to look down her nose at him. "I should not be surprised that a carefree bachelor such as yourself would have difficulty imagining motives that are not selfish." She was good at prevaricating and distracting from what was really afoot. He would give her that. If he didn't have direct evidence to the contrary . . . if he had not felt just how much he affected her, he would have felt about two inches tall right now.

"Pray enlighten me."

"Not that my travel plans, whatever they may be, are your business, but I've left Clara and Enid to their devices for long enough. I realize you have no concept of duty, but those girls are my responsibility."

She was trying to shame him. He wouldn't let her.

"We are something to each other, Ela." He held her gaze, his arm tightening around her. He wouldn't say what that something was—perhaps he couldn't even put a name to it—but it was more than they were a week ago. However distantly she attempted to treat him now, he would not let her pretend he were a stranger overstepping his bounds with her.

She shook her head, looking sad and a little frustrated. "Did you not receive my note?"

"I did. It is what brought me here."

"And what did you fail to understand?"

Her tone in that moment reminded him of a schoolmaster taking a disobedient child to task. He did not enjoy how it made him feel. He was a man, not a child, and well she knew it.

"My difficulty," he began, "rests in the fact that you are lying. A reoccurring condition of late."

"Lying?"

"There is no way you properly considered my proposition. A full day has not even passed."

She released a single bark of laughter. "I fear your wounded ego is the problem here."

"*My* ego?"

"Yes. You're unaccustomed to hearing 'no' from the female gender. I'm sorry to be the first one to say it, but I'm certain I shan't be the last."

She was maddening! His temper quickened. "My ego is well in balance. In fact, I am quite self-aware."

She snorted.

He continued, "You, on the other hand, could use a little self-examination. Why not take a hard look at yourself and admit that you fear your reaction to me? Admit that you fear you might enjoy being with me too much. Admit you're worried that I might discover that I mean more to you than your late husband ever did."

She sputtered. "That—that—"

"That," he heard himself saying, "might shatter the fairy tale you've spun for the world? Myself included. Yes." He nodded. "I've observed your pretenses all these years. Never believed them but didn't believe it gentlemanly to call you out."

She continued to sputter. "Fairy tale? What are you talking about?" She shook her head, all that dark hair flowing like a banner of rich silk around her.

"I'm speaking of the fairy tale you've pranced about in front of your family and for anyone who will listen. The fairy tale that you and the late duke were a love match . . . that you cared for him and he cared for you and you mourn for him every day. It's an entertaining bit of fiction but why don't you confess it's a lie?"

His demand rang out between them, the hard echo felt long after the last word was uttered.

"How could you say such a thing to me?" she whispered, her voice an angry scratch on the air. Indignation hummed along her frame, but he suspected that was because he had called her out on her years-long charade and not because his words were untrue.

"Oh, make no mistake. You play the bereaved widow admirably. Everyone believes it. Hell, Marcus believes it so much he's blinded himself to just how big of a bastard his father really was. Easy enough to do when his stepmother goes along with the lie. Trust me, you do him no favors. The moment he can acknowledge who and what his father was, then he'll see everything more clearly . . . Maybe he can even have a relationship with his half brother and generally stop being such an ass."

"Marcus being an ass is my fault?"

He shrugged. "You've created the beast."

"Let us be clear. You don't know anything about my relationship with my stepchildren and you certainly don't know anything about my marriage."

He took a step closer, but she held her ground. Her eyes burned fire, but call him a masochist because he wanted only to get closer to that fire—to feel it scald him everywhere. This—a furious Ela—was far better than an Ela en route to her country manor and away from him.

"I know your marriage left you cold and that you've been hungering for more . . . for warmth and heat and passion. You wanted that even before the old man died."

She averted her gaze.

He flexed his fingers against her, compelling her to look back at him. Swallowing, he then confessed a memory he'd never forgotten. "I saw you. The moment that you broke. The moment *he* broke you and you realized you would never have the life you wanted with him."

Her mouth parted on a little gasp and he knew she understood what he was talking about.

One never forgot the moment of one's ruin. It stayed with a person. A forever stain that sank past the surface and burrowed deep into bone.

He shouldn't have been a witness to it all those years ago, but he had been there. At the time he'd vowed to himself that he would never be such a husband to any woman, that he would never dishonor any female in such a manner. That he would never be like the Duke of Autenberry.

"What did you see?" Her soft voice rose up between them, a warble of fear in its depths.

"I saw you. It was a long time ago. After Clara was born. At her christening."

She went still in his arms, and he knew she remembered. "Go on," she whispered. "What did you see?"

"I'd just arrived. I saw you heading toward the late duke's drawing room and followed you so that I could pay my respects. I wasn't very far behind. I watched as you knocked once and then pushed the door open."

Her eyes suddenly looked haunted . . . like she wasn't quite in his presence anymore but somewhere else, lost in that day of her disillusionment. "You shouldn't have been following me," she murmured, her gaze somewhere over his shoulder, and he knew that she was no longer with him but back there again, standing in the threshold of the late duke's study.

"I know that," he returned. "But I did. I was there, standing just beyond you."

Her gaze snapped to his face. "You saw him then? My husband."

He nodded.

"Say it, then," she commanded, her voice like flint. "You've had all the words up until this moment. Don't let speech desert you now, my lord."

He nodded once. "I saw your husband shagging a servant girl upon his desk."

The scene was still vivid in his mind. At the time, Colin had been a young man, with limited experience, scarcely more than a boy. The very carnal image of Marcus's father bending a maid over his desk and taking her so savagely had shocked him.

"Come, come. It wasn't simply a servant. Let's be accurate if we are going to reflect," she said bitterly, her features screwing tight with contempt. "That particular female was Clara's new nanny. She was the first in a long line of nannies to warm Autenberry's bed."

"Your face when you turned around—"

"I didn't see you." Accusation sharpened her voice.

"I ducked behind a large vase of flowers."

She nodded jerkily, her gaze darting away before coming back to him.

"Seeing him like that wrecked you. Whatever tender emotions you felt for him died then. I saw it in your face, just as surely as a flame snuffed out—"

"Don't be so dramatic." Her mocking tones shook between them.

"He bade you to close the door on them." He well remembered the duke's autocratic voice calling out the command. *Damn it all, Graciela. Did no one ever tell you to knock? Shut the bloody door! I'll be out when I've finished.*

She flinched and he knew she was hearing it

again, too. "I was very young then. I had yet to understand the reality of ton marriages."

"You were very beautiful with a heart full of hope and love."

"Yes." She lifted eyes that shimmered with emotion. "As I said, *very* young. I now know better than to let such things as hope and love rule me."

"That tender heart is still in you. It longs for more." His hands tightened on her waist. "That is what brought you to Sodom. Ill advised, perhaps, but with a friend like Lady Talbot it is a wonder you resisted for this long. I suppose I should be grateful that I was there when you went."

Her body felt suddenly warmer against him, the proximity too much. Or perhaps he was simply burning for her.

"You've known of that day all this time." She shook her head. "Every time I said something about my late husband, about how wonderful he was or how much I adored him . . . you were laughing at me."

"No. I'd never laugh at you."

"Then you pitied me. Even better." She dropped her head and laughed humorlessly, her expression pained.

"Ela—"

"No," she cut him off. "Stop speaking to me in

that soft voice. Like you know me and care about me. It's pity you feel for me along with some twisted determination to win."

"To win?"

"Yes. Ever since Sodom you've been badgering me." She stopped and released a gust of breath. "I wish you hadn't been there that night."

Her words did the trick and stung him for the split second he allowed them to. Then he dismissed them, not accepting them as truth for one moment. "Indeed? You wish some other man had kissed you? Perhaps you would have made use of one of Sodom's private rooms had you met someone else there."

"Perhaps I would have," she returned hotly, eyes sparking.

"You really are very adept at lying," he growled.

He wrapped his arm around her waist and hauled her in closer. He feathered his lips over hers, speaking his words directly against her mouth. "The other night at Lord Needling's? Do you regret that, as well? You didn't taste like regret to me." He kissed her then, slow and deep. She melted against him, her mouth softening under his, sighing open as their tongues met and tangled. "You don't taste like regret now."

He backed her toward the bed. Their feet

moved until they were falling, sinking together on the luxurious softness.

She gasped, tearing her mouth from his. Desire thickened her voice. "I *do* regret what happened at Lord Needling's." Her hands dove between them, feverishly tearing at his clothing, in direct opposition to her panted speech. "And I shall regret this, too. Make no mistake of that."

And yet it was finally happening.

He leaned back and shrugged out of his jacket and vest. His fingers worked quickly, tearing loose his cravat. She found the bottom of his shirt and tugged the voluminous garment over his head, then flung it to the floor.

Her palms landed on his chest and skimmed the flat plane of his stomach. "Your skin," she breathed heavily. "It's like silk on steel. I didn't—" She stopped, killing whatever she would have said with a hard blink. She gave her head a slight shake. He knew the almost words likely compared him to her dead husband. He saw that in her eyes. She lowered her gaze as though she had committed some offense.

He tipped her chin back up, forcing her to look at him. "You don't have to hide from me. Hide from the rest of the world if you must, but not me. Never me."

She nodded slowly.

He continued, "I'll never tell you what to say, think or feel."

In that way he was not like old Autenberry. Indeed not. It wasn't merely the way his skin felt. It was *who* he was. He'd never treat her like a possession. Never shame her or dishonor her.

And there was the not so minor fact that he intended to make love to her like her bastard of a husband never had.

He brought his hand up under her nightgown, skating it along her bare thigh. Just the sensation of her. The warm, full flesh giving beneath his hand, the swift intake of her breath, all conspired to unman him.

He nestled his weight deeper into her. "*Your* skin is like silk."

He brought both hands under the skirts of her nightgown, sliding them along her thighs, her hips. His hands curved under her lush backside, palming each cheek and lifting her up, grinding her into him. He burrowed his mouth against her neck, hating the fact that he was still dressed at all.

The only problem with getting undressed was that he would have to take his hands off her, even for just a moment, and he couldn't bear the notion of that.

Her sharp gasp sounded in his ear as he squeezed and fondled the delicious rounds of her ass. This woman was made for him. Never had a female felt so right.

A rhythm built between them, driven by need and instinct. He squeezed her bottom as she simultaneously pushed her quim up against his cock.

They were both groaning and panting.

"Colin," she pleaded, dropping her hands to tug at his trousers. No words were needed. He felt the same desperation, but he didn't want this over too quickly. He might not have allowed himself the fantasy of this ever happening between them, but it felt as though he had been waiting his entire life for this moment. He wanted to savor it. He wanted this to be good for both of them.

And part of that was touching her everywhere. Learning her body as surely as he knew his own. He slid his hands around to her belly, delighting in discovering all her secrets.

He dragged his fingertips down her navel. The tender skin of her belly quivered. He longed to press his mouth there and follow the slope down to where he had already tasted her. Where he longed to taste her again.

She tensed, her hand coming to lock around his wrist.

"I—I'm not young," she murmured, a shake to her voice. "And . . . I—I bore a child. I'm not like the girls you are accustomed to. I—"

He silenced her with a full-mouthed kiss.

Almost at once she melted into the mattress again, kissing him back and looping her arms around his neck. He sank deeper into her, loving how she molded to him.

"The idea of any other female pales beside you. Don't ever doubt that." His hands gathered two fistfuls of her nightgown and swept it over her head in one motion, laying her completely bare beneath him.

His gaze devoured her. She was better than anything he had imagined. Wide hipped and narrow waisted. Breasts that would overflow in his hands. Honey skin with dark, penny-sized nipples that made his mouth water.

His cock was painfully hard.

He felt like a green lad, close to spilling himself before they even commenced with the act.

She bit her lip, fidgeting under him, and he

knew doubts plagued her despite his earlier assurance.

He reached up and brushed a lock of dark hair off the swell of her shoulder. "I have a confession to make."

"A confession?" she asked uncertainly, her voice as tremulous as a feather. She looked like she wanted to snatch her nightgown back and cover herself up.

He touched her cheek, his fingertips grazing the soft skin. She was so lovely it offended him that she thought of herself as anything less than that.

His thumb traced her mouth. "I've dreamed of you this way before. Naked. Under me. Although the fantasy doesn't even compare to the reality."

She stilled for a moment and he wondered if he had offended her . . . if he had gone too far, but then those long lashes dipped, fanning dark shadows on her cheeks. The look was pure seduction. "Tell me, my lord." Her accented tones turned low and throaty. "When did you have this fantasy? And how exactly did you imagine me?"

"I always thought you beautiful, but I kept a tight leash on my imagination as it concerned you. My first fantasy about you happened one Easter. Marcus brought me home with him from

Eton. I was seventeen. Do you remember that time?"

She paused. "Yes. I think so."

"I remember thinking Autenberry was one lucky bastard during that visit . . . and that he didn't deserve you." But he hadn't allowed himself to ponder much more than that. No lustful wonderings. He'd been careful to keep his thoughts in check. But his dreams had been another matter. Beyond his control. He'd woken gasping her name.

"It was a definite weakness to dream of you, but how can one control one's dreams?" His eyes roamed over her as he spoke. "I was back at Eton when it happened. In the dormitory. I woke up cock hard and in a sweat. It was wrong . . . the wicked things I had been doing to you in that dream."

"What things?" she asked breathlessly.

"I was doing this to you." Bending his head, he closed his mouth around her nipple, pulling it deep and wrapping it with his tongue until she was arching under him and releasing a keening cry.

After some moments, he turned his attention to her other breast, but he didn't forget the first one, palming it almost roughly. The action only drove her wild beneath him.

"What else?" she demanded, her hands diving through his hair, all her reticence forgotten as heat exploded between them.

His hands dropped to his trousers, unfastening them hastily. "I was doing this, too."

He shoved down his breeches, gripped his manhood and rubbed it along her folds, wetting himself in the evidence of her desire.

It took everything in him not to slip between her folds and sink inside her.

He rubbed the head of his cock higher, directly against her clit.

A sob broke from her, racking her entire body. Her hands clutched his arms, her nails scoring deep. "What else?"

He moved down and fit the head of his cock at her entrance. "And I was doing this to you," he gritted out, finally sinking into her wondrous, sucking heat.

It was better than any dream. Better than *anything.*

He buried himself deep and held still inside her, fighting to not lose control of himself prematurely as her inner muscles acclimated around the throbbing length of him. She might not be a maid, but she felt surprisingly untried.

As though she read his mind, she gasped, "It's been a long time."

"Feels like it," he ground out. It felt bloody perfect.

She wrapped her thighs around his hips and tilted her pelvis, urging him on. "Show me more," she encouraged.

He grasped one of her thighs and hiked it higher, angling her for deeper penetration. He set a faster pace, thrusting harder. And it was eerily like that dream all those years ago except better because this was real. He was no boy with his secret lusts and longings.

He was a man now and he knew precisely how to make her unravel. She was already starting to shake beneath him when his hand slipped between their bodies, finding them where they were joined. He found that little bud and bore down, rolling it as he continued to work in and out of her.

"Colin!" she shrieked, coming up off the bed, clinging to his arms, her eyes wide with wonder as she came apart, shuddering and jerking against him.

He let himself go then, hammering toward his own climax, surrendering with a low groan.

He bowed his head, gasping for breath over her as he released himself inside her, unfamiliar sounds swelling up from his chest.

She undid him.

He lifted his head and stared down at her. Her dark eyes glowed up at him in the gloom of the room, still looking every bit as astounded as she had when she had reached her climax.

Pleasure unfurled in his chest. It was almost as though she had never experienced this before. Which was absurd. She was a passionate woman and no maid. And yet if he was the first one to bring her to physical release, he felt a profound sense of satisfaction.

Her hands fluttered to his chest, her fingers feathering lightly against his skin as though she still needed permission to put her hands to him.

"That was . . ." Her sultry voice faded away. She blinked as if not certain of anything. She looked out of sorts and that only increased his pleasure. He had done that to her.

He smiled down at her. "Yes," he said. "It was."

She glanced left and right, clearly unsure what to do next. He imagined her late husband wasn't much for intimate conversation.

"I—" she started and stopped again. She had never been one short for words and he enjoyed this new side to her. Knowing that he could so fluster her. He watched her, waiting. She looked back at him. "I never knew it could be like this."

He stared at her for a long moment before answering. "It's only going to get better."

He shifted slightly, still lodged inside her, letting her feel that he was hard again and ready for another go.

Her eyes widened as she felt him immediately. "W-what? You cannot mean—"

He slid almost completely out from her and then drove deeply back inside, pushing her up on the bed from the force of his thrust.

"Oh!" she cried, her hands flinging above her head, grasping fistfuls of the counterpane. "I didn't know . . . I did not think one ever could—"

"You're going to discover many things you didn't know before." Bending his head, he took her mouth in a deep kiss, silencing her from any further shocked utterances as they simply fell into each other. Again.

After that there was little talking. Only cries and gasps and moans of pleasure as he showed her what he meant.

Chapter 13

Ela opened her eyes to a chamber tinged in murky air. Dawn had arrived and the world felt different, changed somehow.

She felt different.

She was exhausted, but pleasantly so. Euphoria tingled along the edges of her nerves, leaving her, oddly enough, energized. She shifted and stretched and places that she had never given much notice to before twinged with soreness.

She never knew the things they'd done could happen more than once in a night. She never knew it could be so shattering, so good. She never knew she had it in her to *not* be dull. Autenberry had made her feel so uninspiring as a lover. He never hid his disappointment and she had only ever assumed he was correct. He'd had a score of lovers. How was she to know any differently?

An arm snaked around her waist and dragged her back, settling her against a hard male body. She gave a small squeak and looked over her shoulder.

"You're still here?" she whispered, knowing she should be concerned, cross even. It was morning. Her maid could walk in at any moment to stoke the fire. He shouldn't be here.

And yet waking up in his arms . . . a part of her thrilled at it. It was a novel experience. Autenberry had never stayed the night. After he finished with her, he always took his leave.

After the third time she and Colin came together, she had drifted off to sleep almost immediately.

Three times. Heat crept over her face. Thinking, remembering . . . it sounded positively debauched.

"You think I would leave without saying goodbye?" he growled.

"It's almost morning. The staff will be up soon."

He nuzzled her ear and bit down on the lobe, sending a swift spike of heat straight to her core. "My staff is already up."

She gasped at the naughty words, his implication clear. "Again?" She choked back a laugh.

"It's been a few hours. I'm ready again. Aren't you?"

"You're insatiable," she moaned as he nudged her thighs apart. She felt his *staff* then, hard and seeking, gliding through her sex.

"I'll never *not* want this." He drove inside her, stretching and filling her.

Even tender from the activity of the night before, she was already wet for him as he fit himself in her overly sensitized channel. She turned her face into the bedding to keep herself from crying out. Sore or not, her sex wrapped around his thick member, her body as hungry for him as ever.

All at once he grasped her waist and turned her, guiding her to her knees. It was new, the angle different, the sensation different, too. She flattened her palms on the bed and arched her spine, holding herself up as he pumped in and out of her, his big hands spanning her waist as he took her from behind.

It was astonishing. From this position, she felt his penetration deeper than ever before. With every stroke he pushed at that hard-to-reach spot inside her. Her legs shook and he wrapped one arm fully around her waist, hugging her close as he increased the speed of his thrusts.

It was wondrous. After three bouts of love-making in close succession, she didn't imagine it could still be so thrilling. She didn't imagine she could want more. She didn't imagine he could bring her to climax again, but he did. He wrung it from her until she was blubbering in her native tongue.

He pumped a few more times and stilled, pouring his seed deep inside her with a low groan that sent shivers down her spine. He ran his broad palm along her spine as though he could see the ripples of sensation there and meant to soothe.

She collapsed flat on the bed. He followed, propping himself up with his arms to keep from crushing her. It was a pleasant sensation, being caged in by his warm male body. She could get accustomed to such a thing.

And that was very dangerous thinking. This wasn't forever. It was a one-time occurrence. She couldn't permit her thoughts to drift into the arena of forever. That would be the foolish whimsy of a lovesick girl, and she was most absolutely not *that*.

She sighed, sated and content. If she was a little sad to know that this was over, she didn't let the emotion surface as she said, "You best leave."

"Must I?" he asked idly. "I can think of nothing more I'd rather do than spend the day in bed with you."

She turned onto her side. That did sound heavenly, but it wasn't possible. He must know that. He fell on his back. She propped up on her elbow to loom over him. "You jest. We can't do that. I've a houseful of servants. Any single one of them could talk."

He pushed a strand of hair behind her ear. "Very well. Then when can I see you again?"

She hesitated.

"Ela?" he pressed, his expression darkening as her silence stretched.

"It's best if we end this now. We spent a lovely night together—"

"And you think you've had your fill of me now, is that it?"

She stared down at him. All of him. His handsome face and virile, young body was more of a temptation than he could ever know. It simply wasn't to be. He wasn't to be hers. He belonged to someone like Forsythia.

"Colin. You'll see. I must return to—"

Just then the doors to her chamber burst open.

She flipped over to gawk at her unannounced visitor, her back to Colin.

Heart pounding in alarm, indignation bristled through her. She pulled the covers over her bare breasts. It was still quite early and any member of her staff should know better than to burst in upon her so unceremoniously.

"Mama!"

Clara.

She sent a quick glance over her shoulder, satisfied that Colin was tucked under the counterpane. He was a misshapen lump that could simply be mistaken for rumpled bedding.

Clara froze halfway to the bed, her lovely brown eyes widening. "Mama, you haven't any clothes on."

Ela clutched the sheet to her throat. "Yes, my dear. I grew overly warm in the night and shed my nightgown."

Her daughter's eyes widened even further. "You slept *nude*?"

"I did not account for a visitor." She forced an airy laugh, eyeing her daughter and assessing that she, too, still wore a nightgown. "How is it you came to be here? And in your nightgown?"

"We arrived last night. Enid and I decided to join you. I asked Mrs. Wakefield not to say anything to you when we arrived. I wanted to surprise you myself."

"Oh," she said faintly. "I'm surprised." The great length of Colin radiated heat beneath the covers. He was holding himself admirably still, but what if Clara decided to join her on the bed. It wouldn't be the first time. She had done it countless mornings.

Thankfully, her state of undress seemed to have given her daughter pause. She hovered, shifting on her bare feet as though uncertain how to proceed.

"Why don't you ring for your maid and dress for breakfast, my love? I'll join you and we shall decide how to spend the day."

Clara nodded happily. "Are you very surprised to see me, Mama?"

"Astonished." She nodded, her belly a sick, twisting mass. Her daughter stood mere feet before her while she had a naked man in her bed. A naked Colin.

Just then she felt his hand sliding along her thigh. She jerked and then forced herself into stillness. He really was wicked. How could she never have guessed this about him?

"Go on with you, my dear." A tick spasmed near her eye. "I'll be down once I've dressed."

Clara smiled brightly and then rushed across the remaining space to press a kiss to Ela's cheek. She stopped breathing at the sensation of her daughter's kiss—so sweet and innocent so close to the site of her wantonness.

She really was a shameful creature. She had never questioned her worth as a mother. Until now.

As soon as the door closed, she bounced out of the bed and snatched up her nightgown, pulling the billowy garment over her head, not even caring that it was inside out. The fabric settled over her, chafing against all her newly sensitive skin.

Colin's head appeared from beneath the covers, an unabashed grin on his face. He sighed and tucked his arms behind his head, clearly in no rush to go. He watched her in a way that reminded her of all the intimacy they'd shared. Familiar heat crept up her neck into her face. How would she ever look at him without her face going hot? And the way he was looking at her now? Well. That had to change. He couldn't look at her like that in public. It was positively . . . *carnal.*

Spying his trousers, she bent and tossed them at him. "Out! Out with you at once."

He caught the garment and shook his head at her. "No need to be frantic."

"*Frantic* is a pale, inadequate description for what I'm feeling. My daughter is here. She just walked in on—"

"She didn't see anything. She didn't see me."

And for that she was exceedingly fortunate. She took a bracing breath. It had been much too close, though. He couldn't possibly understand that such a risk was unconscionable to her. And that just seemed to underscore the difference between them.

She was a mature woman, entering the latter half of her life, a mother who must and always would put her daughter first. Perhaps Graciela needn't worry about ruining her own reputation, but something like this could adversely impact Clara. Even Enid would suffer.

He would never understand that. Never understand *her* and just how worlds apart they were.

"You need to go." She nodded with surety.

"Very well." He flung back the covers and stood, bold in his nakedness.

She stared for a moment at his tall, lean frame until wrenching her gaze away.

"You blush and avert your eyes now? After the night we shared?" Laughter hugged his voice over the whisper of fabric.

She forced her stare forward. He was correct.

She need not be a shrinking violet now. Save that for the Forsythias of the world.

Thankfully, he wore his breeches once again. He was in the process of buttoning them up, which only made his chest and arms flex deliciously. He really was temptation incarnate with that strong body and his rich brown hair falling over his brow. When she was a girl, she had dreamed of a man such as he. He would stride onto Papa's estate and sweep her off her feet. Instead Autenberry had come. At the time she'd told herself she was fortunate. She would come to love him. Even if not with grand passion. Love was love.

"When shall I see you again?"

She shook her head. This was not love. It was something else. Something she must crush at the root.

It was a little late for that.

He stepped forward, his voice dipping to a smoky pitch that was at once familiar because she had heard it in her ear all night. "I can always find my way back to your room tonight."

"No," she blurted. "You cannot do that."

He inclined his head slightly. "Very well. You can come visit me or I can arrange a meeting at a location—"

"No, no, I can't. We can never do this again."

He stilled.

She continued, "This was just this one time. We explored our desires for each other and now we are done."

He shook his head slowly. "You think we are done? That this is finished? That we have explored all that we will ever wish to?"

"With each other? Yes."

A dangerous light entered his eyes and she had the eeriest sensation of having tossed down a gauntlet. "Have you a wish now to explore with someone else—"

"What? No. No, I don't." She glanced at her door, fearful they would be interrupted again. "I merely mean to imply that you can be free to explore your desires elsewhere. With a female more your match. With Forsythia, for instance." The notion may have turned her stomach but she did nothing to reveal it. In fact, she stepped forward and proceeded to push him toward her balcony doors. If this was the way he had entered, then it must be the way he departed.

Hopefully, he would not be spotted in the light of dawn, as there really was no other choice. He couldn't stay in her chamber and he certainly couldn't waltz out the front door.

"I'll go," he agreed evenly.

She breathed a little easier.

At her balcony doors, he stopped and looked back at her. "But know I'll not be *exploring* with any other ladies when it's only you I can think about. You, Ela."

Her heart squeezed foolishly. "You needn't make such promises. Truly, I don't want them."

Half his mouth kicked up in a smile. "And yet you have them. They're yours." That said, he turned on his heels and left her.

She stared after him, not moving for several moments before jarred to action. Her daughter and stepdaughter were here. It was time to return to reality.

Chapter 14

Four days passed and she immersed herself with Clara and Enid's visit, working diligently to distract herself with their happiness and be the mother she was before everything happened with Colin. The mother she was meant to be . . . not a wanton and reckless creature of passion.

They visited the museum, took tea with Lady Mary Rebecca and her daughters, and dined with Marcus most evenings. They even braved the cold one afternoon for a ride in the park, only to quickly return home and warm themselves by the fire with cups of chocolate. She'd missed her girls. Even Enid, reserved as she was, succumbed to gaiety as they played whist.

Colin, however, never appeared. She suspected that he might accompany Marcus on one of his visits. He often had in the past. It would not have been unusual.

His absence both disappointed and satisfied her. She really was a contrary woman

"Mama!"

She jerked in her seat, where she sat penning a letter to Poppy Mackenzie. Her friend had gone north for the winter. Poor dear. She must be freezing. At the sound of her daughter's screech, she lurched back from her writing desk and was halfway across the salon when the doors burst open.

Clara erupted into the room, holding a tiny little ball of fur close to her chest.

Ela's heart steadied at the sight of her daughter, hale and unmaimed, before her. It was always the same. Parenthood was a state of constant anxiety over your child's welfare. She didn't know if it was that way for every parent or for only her. Clara was her sole child and, according to Ela's physician, her birth had been a miracle. Old Dr. Wilcox had told her she should count her blessings, for she would never conceive again. He had been wrong, however. She had conceived again. Twice. She had had two more miscarriages.

"Clara, you gave me a fright," she reprimanded, flattening a hand against her racing heart.

Enid followed, entering the room at a more sedate pace, her hands clasped demurely in front of her. Her stepdaughter was not an excitable creature. Unlike Clara, Enid was quiet, most of her thoughts and emotions held tucked away inside her. She was clever and well-read. Even at the age of ten, when Graciela first met her, she had seemed wise beyond her years. Certainly, Graciela's English had not been very strong then and she'd felt rather foolish around the ten-year-old whose vocabulary far outshone her own.

Graciela was waiting for the day when Enid might break free from her shell. She was still young. Enid might not show any interest in marriage or starting her own family, but that did not mean Graciela had given up on the prospect for her.

"Mama!" Clara stopped before her and now she could see that the furry little ball in her arms was a puppy. A small brown face with a pointy little nose lunged for Ela, its tongue slapping the air. Clara let the canine go and Ela caught the madly wiggling body.

She cried out as the dog started drowning her with wet kisses. "Clara, whose dog is this?"

"Ours!" Clara reclaimed the puppy.

"What?" she demanded in her sternest voice. "This puppy is not ours—"

"Yes, it is. The lad who delivered the puppy to Mrs. Wakefield said it's ours. Go ahead. There's a card. Read it."

"What card?" she asked even as her stomach sank.

"This." Enid stepped forward, holding out a small envelope.

Ela took it, noticing that Enid was looking at her with a speculative gleam in her eyes. The seal did not appear to be broken on the little envelope. She turned it over, dread filling her.

"Open it!" Clara insisted.

Nodding, she opened it, and that sinking sensation in her stomach plunged as she read the card:

Ela,
Something to keep you warm this winter when I cannot.

She gasped. Her gaze flew to Enid. Her stepdaughter studied her with those much-too-clever gray eyes of hers.

"What does it say?" Clara buried her nose in the little terrier's neck. "She's ours, isn't she?" She hopped once, still very much like a little girl even though she tottered on the edge of womanhood. "I knew it!"

Frustration bubbled up inside her. She couldn't very well say no and crush her daughter.

Forcing a smile, she nodded. "Yes, she's ours."

Clara squealed and whirled in a circle with the small dog.

He'd done this. He hadn't signed the card, but he'd most definitely sent the puppy. She hastily tucked the card back inside the envelope. He knew precisely what to do to make it impossible to forget him—not that she had been in danger of doing that. But for heaven's sake! Puppies! *Dios no!*

"Who is it from?" Enid asked as they watched Clara plop down on the rug to play with the adorable little beast.

Ela struggled to arrive at an answer to the very valid question. Her mind raced. Colin had boxed her into a corner with his actions and she couldn't think how to reply.

To complicate matters further, Marcus chose that moment to join them, strolling into the room with his elegant, long-legged gait.

"Marcus! Look!" Clara held the dog aloft. "We have a puppy!"

"A puppy?" he echoed, smiling easily as he joined them. He pressed a kiss on each of their cheeks in greeting.

Enid eyed the clock above the mantel. "Marcus, you're here in time for dinner. What a coincidence."

He winked at her. "No coincidence, I assure you."

Clara giggled and fell back on the floor as the puppy found her ear and proceeded to devour it.

Marcus squatted over them, observing the spectacle with fondness in his eyes. He reached down and petted the animal between the ears. At the attention, the puppy yipped and lunged at Marcus, clearly overjoyed to find a newcomer in her sphere. Laughing, he caught the wiggling little body against him. "What have we here? Where did you come from, little one?"

"Ela was just about to tell us that," Enid said, her pointed gaze falling on Graciela.

"Oh, you know . . ." Graciela waved the envelope helplessly, tempted to march toward the fire and cast it into the nest of flames.

Marcus looked up while still rubbing the belly of the puppy, who looked ready to pass out in ecstasy. If only her life could be that simple. A simple belly rub and all was right and well.

"You don't know where he came from?" Marcus arched an eyebrow.

"Why, yes, I do, o-of course," she stammered.

Marcus's grin slipped. His eyes turned flinty. "Ah. It is like the flowers, then. This little pet would be from your admirer."

"Mama!" Clara stared at her in astonishment. "You have an admirer?" It seemed all these years of living like a nun made such a notion ludicrous in her child's mind.

"It's nothing," she insisted.

"A man gave you a puppy," Enid stated. "It must be . . . something."

"I have to agree with Enid," Marcus said. "It must be *something*." Scowling, he glanced at all three of them as if their presence was suddenly problematic. He then looked back to Ela. "Weren't you leaving for the country?" Evidently, from his manner, that was where he preferred them to be.

"But we only just arrived," Clara cried. "I don't want to go back. It's dreadfully dull and much too cold. I can only stay outside for a little while."

"Dull sounds right." Marcus nodded once. "I think you need dull." He might have been addressing Clara but he was looking directly at Ela as he spoke. Ironic, of course, because only recently he had suggested she find herself an adventure. She resisted pointing that out, however. She did not wish for him to think that adventure was her goal. He might wonder what she'd been up to, in truth.

She fought to hold his gaze. Looking away implied guilt and that she had something to hide. "We have a shopping trip planned for tomorrow. I can't disappoint the girls."

He grunted and then turned to Enid as she engaged him in conversation, but Ela still felt his stare, speculative and unsure, drifting toward her.

She blinked burning eyes and settled her gaze on the puppy. The little beast was panting, its tongue lolling happily from its mouth as it suffered a brisk rubdown from Clara.

Colin had bought her a puppy. She would kill him.

ELA RETIRED EARLY after dinner, leaving her family in the drawing room. Enid played at the pianoforte (some tremendously complicated piece that she'd taught herself) whilst Marcus and Clara played cards.

She'd complained of an aching head and excused herself. Once in her chamber, she changed into a simple gown of dark blue wool . . . something she would use to pot flowers in the greenhouse behind the town house during the spring months. She didn't need to wear anything extravagant to go about her task tonight.

In front of her dressing table mirror, she loosened her hair and then tied it into a simple plait that she wrapped around the crown of her head. Then she simply stared at herself, imagining that she saw a different person gazing back. A woman awakened to desire and all that she had missed in life. Disappointment lanced her heart that she couldn't continue to experience such things with Colin. Matters had become much too complicated. It wasn't as though she could simply openly profess a relationship with Colin. No one would approve.

But perhaps it wasn't too late. Perhaps she could still have this.

Vowing to consider that later, she swung her fur-trimmed cloak around her shoulders and rang for Minnie. Clandestine activities were not her forte but she knew that she would need assistance to accomplish her task.

Minnie entered the room and paused, obviously assuming she was there to help ready Ela for bed. She looked Ela up and down, and the sight of her mistress dressed to go out, even humbly so, clearly put that notion to rest.

"Your Grace?" she queried, angling her head curiously.

"I'm going out," she announced, holding her chin aloft. She didn't require Minnie's approval, but that wasn't to say she didn't care for her good opinion. The woman had served her ever since she moved to England and she was fond of her. "I require your assistance . . . and it goes without saying that I would like my outing to remain . . . um, undisclosed."

"Of course." Minnie nodded and stepped forward. If she had an opinion on Ela's covert plans, she kept her expression neutral. "You should depart through the servants' entrance at the back of the house. I will make certain to leave the door unlocked tonight so that you can return without anyone detecting you."

"Thank you."

Apparently Minnie was well versed in clandestine matters. It almost made Ela feel guilty to realize she had been underutilizing her all these years. She had untapped talents, to be sure.

"You will require a hack." Minnie tapped her lip and nodded decisively.

Ela considered that for a moment. It had not even occurred to her that she might not want to take one of their very recognizable carriages with the Autenberry coat of arms on the door out about London. Especially this late and while out on an assignation.

"Yes, that would be wise. Thank you."

Minnie nodded. "Give me a few moments. I will come back to fetch you, Your Grace."

Nodding, she watched as her maid slipped from the room. Squaring her shoulders with as much dignity as she could muster, she waited for Minnie to return, telling herself not to change her mind and surrender to the cowardly voice inside her that told she shouldn't leave tonight. That this would all just go away if she ignored it.

In the distance, the puppy barked—*yipped* would be a more accurate word—and she was reminded that he had given her a puppy. A *puppy*! It was the height of manipulation and it had to stop. *No más.*

Not that she could entirely blame him. It was her fault. She had not been firm. She had allowed him into her bed. She had been weak in her dealings with him because deep down she wanted him. She liked how he made her feel. She reveled in it and he knew it.

She would revel no more.

Chapter 15

When the cloaked lady was shown into his private sitting room, he could not feign surprise. Upon sending the puppy today, he knew he would hear from Ela soon. He hoped it would prompt her to break from hiding behind the skirts of Clara and Enid.

The puppy had been a calculated move. Admittedly a bit of a bastard move. With Clara on the premises, he knew the puppy would be welcomed with open and exuberant arms. There was no way Ela would be able to deny the dog a home. Unlike the flowers he sent before, she couldn't just throw the puppy away, and that fact would only anger her. Every time she looked at the adorable little canine, she would think of him.

Her black cloak with its trim of violet ermine blanketed her. If he didn't recognize that cloak, he might have had some doubts as to her identity. She was so deeply burrowed in the garment's voluminous folds she could have been anyone.

And yet she wasn't anyone.

"Your Grace." He rose to his feet and executed a sharp bow. "To what do I owe the pleasure?"

She flung back her hood and stabbed him with accusing eyes. "You sent me a puppy!"

"Did you like her?" he asked mildly.

She scowled, which wasn't a normal expression for her. It shouldn't have made her even more tempting to him. "No!"

"No?" He motioned to take her cloak. She hesitated before unhooking the clasp at her throat and letting him assist her out of it. "Who doesn't like puppies? That's simply unfeeling and not at all in keeping with your character," he teased.

She growled. There was no other word for it.

He dropped her cloak over the back of the sofa as she blew out a breath and propped a hand on her shapely hip. She was wearing a plain blue gown with nothing in the way of embellishments, but it did more for her beauty than any of her finest gowns. The same could be said of the simple style in which she wore her hair. It was pulled into a plait that wrapped loosely around the top of her head, several dark wisps escaping to frame her face becomingly. "Oh, you know nothing is wrong with the puppy. She's fine—"

"Fine?" He'd handpicked that puppy himself. She was the chubbiest and cutest of the litter by far.

"Very well. Adorable," she snapped. "Clara adores her as you knew she would."

He shrugged, neither admitting nor denying.

"But you cannot send me any more gifts. Marcus knows I have an admirer—"

"An admirer?" He crossed his arms over his chest and laughed lightly. "Is that what I am?"

"His words, not mine."

"Because *lover* would be more accurate, don't you think? Or even *paramour*."

"Stop. You're none of those things. *We* are none of those things to each other."

"Oh, indeed? Shall I recite you the definitions of these words, then?"

"Please do not." She held up a hand. "My English is good enough. I know what they mean. I know what we did and what we were, but that is in the past. I don't want to be with you."

He stared at her for a moment, processing the militant light in her eyes. This time she held his gaze. She did not look away.

I don't want to be with you. She couldn't be any clearer than that. He'd said the words before himself, when ending a relationship. Cruel perhaps, but honest in a way he'd always felt an individual deserved to hear.

Still, with the memory of their time together, he felt jolted. He had not thought his feelings so very one-sided, but he wasn't infallible. She could very well have had her fill of him and was done.

He knew his insecurities. Living as an orphan, even with wealth and privilege, left one with them. He hadn't been enough even for his own father. That was always there, niggling in the back of his mind. A valiant little seed of discontent.

What made him think he was good enough for someone he might really want?

He released a breath. "Indeed." He felt like an ass, seeing himself as he imagined she viewed him. Immature and overly eager. "Very well. I will stop pursuing you. My mistake. I thought you might have longed for me as I longed for you." He inched toward her with measured steps and stopped before her, careful not to touch. There would be no touching. No more seducing or cajoling. He had his pride. He'd never begged for a woman before.

You'd never been with the likes of Ela.

She lifted wide eyes to him. "Don't." The single word sounded very much like a plea.

"I'm not touching you. I'm giving you what you want. Promising to stop. No more gifts. No more anything from me."

She nodded, distrust or some other such emotion still brimming in her brown eyes. For some reason he wasn't certain if the distrust was directed at him or herself.

"Because that's what you want," he reminded her. "You've made that clear enough now."

"Thank you. Yes," she murmured, moving hesitantly toward the door. Obviously, she didn't expect such easy relent from him.

When she reached the door to his sitting room, she looked back at him questioningly. Did she expect a fight from him? After her words?

He nodded at her. "Go on," he encouraged. "You said what you came here to say."

Still, she did not move, even with one hand closed around the door's latch.

"Unless there was something else you wanted," he added. Was he really still hoping that she would stop and change her mind?

Say yes. Say me. Say you want me.

He'd told her to never lie to him. To be herself. He willed her to be that right now with him. No more pretenses. If this wasn't what she wanted, then God willing she would snap to her senses and admit it and put both of them out of their suffering.

She gave her head a small shake as if coming back to reality. Evidently satisfied, she turned and exited his sitting room. The door snicked shut after her.

So much for that.

He sank down on his chair and sat there for some time, the book he had been reading forgotten by his side, the crack and pop of the fire the only sounds in the room other than his own breathing. It was much the same as during all his life. He was alone. Only now he felt the aloneness more acutely than ever.

Suddenly he heard the rushing of footsteps. The door burst open again. Ela shut it, leaning her body against it for a moment, her chest rising and falling with deep breaths within her modest neckline. His excitement at her return abated at the sight of her stricken expression.

"Ela? What is it?"

"It's Marcus. He's coming up the stairs."

"Quick!" Colin seized her arm and shoved her into his bedchamber. "Stay in there," he commanded over her stammers. "He'll not enter this room. He has no cause."

He shut the door just as the door to his sitting room flew open, once again the harried butler fast on Marcus's heels, sputtering his introduction.

"Ah, there you are," Marcus declared as though he were not certain that he would find Colin here in his own rooms.

"Here I am. In my house. Where I live." Colin gestured widely. "It's a strange set of circumstances, is it not?"

Marcus ignored his sarcasm and helped himself to his Scotch.

"It's rather late."

"Is it?" Marcus settled himself before the fire. "I've just left my stepmother's. Fine dinner. The pheasant was excellent. You should have joined me."

"Perhaps next time. And how is your family?" he inquired. Because it was the thing to do. The thing he had done countless times over the years.

Marcus stopped and looked heavenward. "My stepmother had this puppy. Damnedest thing. It's a gift from that secret admirer of hers. We really need to find this fellow and set him straight."

"Do we?" Colin's gaze shot to his bedchamber door and then skittered away.

"Indeed, we do. He bought her a puppy. I fear things are escalating with this Lothario, and now that the girls are here, Ela is in no hurry to return to the country, so there is no telling how much further this *business* shall go. Damn nuisance, I tell you. This is the last thing I wish to contend with. I always thought it would be Enid or Clara that I would need to safeguard. Clara, I'm certain I still will, once she's come out. She is pretty and of cheerful disposition. Enid, however, did a fine enough job all on her own frightening men away. Not even her dowry can entice them." He dropped a fist into his hand with an aggrieved air. "A man should not have to play the role of protective father when the female in question is his stepmother!"

"Hmm," he murmured noncommittally, forcing his gaze not to stray to his bedchamber door again. Marcus continued to drone on, but he couldn't focus on a word he was uttering. Colin could think only of Ela in his chamber, on his bed. He'd envisioned her there several times but not under this circumstance—hiding from her stepson. Bloody hell. He was no lad anymore who had to skulk about in the shadows with girls from the village so that none of his teachers caught him. He was much too old for this.

Suddenly, he realized Marcus wasn't talking anymore.

He fixed his gaze on his friend, who had gone unnaturally still. "Marcus?" he prompted. "You were saying?"

He was saying nothing at all. He simply stared at something just over Colin's shoulder. Colin turned his head and followed Marcus's gaze, attempting to see what had snared his attention.

And he saw it. Ela's cloak draped over the back of the sofa just to the right of his shoulder. Bloody, *bloody* hell.

Marcus stabbed a single finger in its direction and asked in an eerily calm voice, "What is my stepmother's cloak doing here?"

He opened his mouth, prepared to deny that it belonged to Ela. Any number of excuses—both plausible and implausible—flitted across his mind. Very well, the majority of them were implausible. Nevertheless, they were something. Anything other than the truth.

Instead the words that fell from his mouth were the last thing he expected. "I set it there when I assisted her from it."

Marcus's blue gaze snapped back to him. "And what was she doing in your private rooms?"

Still more honesty spewed forth. "She came to see me." He paused and prodded within himself to see if he was really about to admit this to his lifelong friend. "She was here because she was angry with me. For buying her a puppy."

Marcus's hand tightened dangerously around his glass, the knuckles whitening. "And why did you do that?"

"Because she and I are . . ." Here he paused, searching for the most sensitive word. He arrived at ". . . involved."

Tactful or not, Marcus understood his meaning. He understood it all too well. As only a man who had been *involved* with many women in the course of his philandering life would understand.

THEIR VOICES WERE muffled even with her ear pressed to the wall, but there was no mistaking the loud crash followed by several thuds. She jerked and stared at the door.

Que en los cielos?

A bellow of rage left no doubt as to what was happening in the other room. Without wasting another moment, she wrenched the door open and stepped into the fray.

Marcus and Colin were locked in struggle, twisting and knocking into furniture. Glass littered the rug, the remnants of a decanter. The ripe smell of Scotch reached her nose. A side table had been overturned, glasses scattered on the rug beside it.

"Marcus!" she shouted as she spied him standing over Colin. His arm was cocked back, ready to deliver another blow to Colin's face.

Colin stared up at him, passive and accepting of the abuse.

At her shout, Marcus's head whipped in her direction. His eyes flared and then narrowed at the evidence of her here, standing before them. Clearly it was all the proof he needed.

Marcus moved in a blur then, bringing his fist down.

Colin took the punch, willingly, his head snapping back from the blow, and she feared he was going to let her stepson beat him senseless if she didn't do something to stop him.

She lurched across the distance, wedging between them, using her hands and elbows to separate them. "Marcus, no, no, stop!"

He sneered down at her. "What's wrong? Afraid I'll mar his pretty face?"

"What? No—Yes!" She shook her head. "Marcus, you're overreacting. This is Colin! He's your friend!"

He stood back, breathing heavily, looking back and forth between the two of them. "He *was* my friend! Before he shagged my stepmother."

She shook her head at him. "No," she whispered, swallowing miserably. This was everything she feared coming true.

"Just tell me this. How long has this been going on?" His stare flipped from Graciela to Colin in hot accusation. "Was this happening when my father was still alive?"

Horror punched her in the chest. "What? No!" Did he really think such a thing of her? Of Colin? Her husband may have never been faithful to her, but she had never strayed from her vows.

"No," Colin seconded, his voice a low growl. He gingerly tapped at his swollen lip as he spoke. It was cut down the middle, an angry tear of red. She had to fight the urge to go to him and press a handkerchief to the wound. "And you damn well know it."

"Do I?" Marcus glared at them both with such contempt that she felt it, as palpable as a cold vapor. "I'm not certain I know anything about either one of you anymore, because I never would have thought my *best friend* and *stepmother* capable of this."

"And what is it that we've done that is so abhorrent?" Colin challenged. "We're both adults entitled to our happiness, are we not? Before this moment you would have claimed to want that for the both of us. We aren't harming anyone."

She nodded, feeling all at once emboldened. Her mind deliberately shied away from the fact that he was equating his happiness to being with her. She was sure he did not mean it in any permanent fashion. Still, that would be for later consideration. Something she could turn over in her mind and examine another time. "You told me to have an adventure," she reminded.

Marcus stared at her, his eyes wide with incredulity. "Indeed! I thought you would learn to play the viola. Or take the girls on a trip to the Lake District."

"She's more than that," Colin retorted. "You've spent your entire life seeing her as one thing that fits into a certain box. There is more to her." He heaved a breath. Several heartbeats passed before he added, "*I* see that."

"I don't need you to lecture me on how I should view my stepmother." Marcus returned his stare to her. "As I said, I meant find a hobby," he clarified, his tone no less scathing. "Not fuck my best friend."

Colin snarled and moved as though to lunge for Marcus, but she stayed him with a look.

"Tread carefully," Colin warned. "Any other man I'd strike down for—"

"I'm not any other man, though, am I? I was your friend? And that makes you one bloody bastard."

"It only just happened the one time," she defended.

Marcus scoffed. "I'm expected to believe you."

She squared her shoulders, understanding the ugliness of his implication—even if he was the last person she expected to hurl such an insult at her. He'd always been her stalwart supporter. From the day she stepped onto this oversized island, she knew its inhabitants didn't embrace her. It was years before her own stepdaughter looked at her without a sour expression. Marcus had always been the bright light, accepting and friendly, amid a sea of smirks and leers.

"It's the truth," she insisted.

Silence stretched as he stared at her. "Maybe everyone was right about you."

Colin moved so quickly then that she practically missed it. Suddenly he was on Marcus and they were on the floor. Gone was the reticent, apologetic Colin willing to take whatever punishment Marcus heaped upon him.

Colin straddled her stepson and pounded his face again and again.

She grabbed his arm, catching it midblow. "Colin, don't, please!"

He looked over at her, his eyes fierce with a savage spark. For *her.* The sight rattled her.

Then she glimpsed her stepson beneath Colin and she felt awful. This shouldn't have happened but it had. Because of her. Because she had been so weak as to give in to temptation.

"Stop it!" Somehow her final shout penetrated.

Colin pulled back. Marcus scrambled out from under his best friend and yanked his rumpled jacket into some semblance of order. "I'll see myself out."

"Marcus, please." She reached for his arm. "Let's talk about this."

"There's nothing to discuss. You two enjoy yourselves. Don't let me stop you. In fact, forget about me."

He turned on his heels and slammed out of the room.

"Marcus!" she called.

He didn't reappear.

She spun around and her gaze shot to Colin. Blood still trickled slowly from his lip and his cheek bore an angry red stain. "Ela . . ." he started to say, but she shook her head. His words died off.

"There's nothing more to say. Exactly what I feared would happen has happened. Marcus hates us both now. And my family—" She stopped abruptly, her voice choking. She didn't know yet what this had done to her family. That was still to be seen. Hopefully, her reckless actions had not damaged things irreparably.

Eyes burning, she snatched her cloak from the floor where it had fallen—even though she would rather cast it into the fire than look at it right now.

"Ela," he said evenly, "there is nothing to hide anymore. No reason we should even attempt to. No reason why we should not continue—"

"There is *every* reason. It's not right. Marcus doesn't approve. How can I face him or my family?" She pressed her fingers to the center of her forehead and rubbed. "What will the girls think?"

"Are you so very ashamed, then?"

"It is so very easy for you, a man, to ask that. You needn't feel guilt or shame. What have you to lose? A reputation? Your fortune? A *family*?" She snorted. "I think not."

Too late she realized her words had stung him. He was not lacking family by design and she had just callously flung at him that he was alone, the only relation left to him an indifferent grandmother who never deigned to see him.

She blinked slowly, painfully. This day had seen its fair share of hurt. She'd best leave before she carved the blade any deeper.

"I do have something to lose."

She moved toward the door, ready to quit this evening and hopefully put it all behind her, when his voice stopped her. "I have you to lose."

Her back still to him, she flinched. Damn him for saying the one thing he could say to make her feel necessary. It had been a long time, if ever, since she felt that with a man.

"Ela?" There was heavy request in the sound of her name.

She couldn't do this. Not now.

Right now Marcus was somewhere thinking the worst of her. Perhaps he was even telling Enid. And all because she'd been selfish enough to surrender to her desire for a man she had no right to.

"Good night, Colin."

Chapter 16

Four days later Graciela sat ensconced in a well-padded chair in the conservatory, Mary Rebecca beside her, sipping tea. She balanced a small plate of mostly uneaten sandwiches on her lap and smiled at their girls playing croquet on the expanse of indoor lawn. A somewhat tricky task with potted trees and other plants and shrubbery to maneuver around. As cold as it was outdoors, the day was bright and the sunlight that beamed through the glass warmed the large room considerably.

"Come, eat, and tell me what you have been doing with yourself. Your cook makes the most delicious fare." Mary Rebecca motioned to her neglected plate. "I really must steal her away from you."

It was easy in moments like this, with Mary Rebecca teasing and their girls laughing and the sun shining through the glass, to forget that so many things were amiss in her life. Things like the fact that Marcus had disappeared. Well, perhaps *disappeared* was too dramatic a word.

He'd closed up his town house and left the morning after discovering her with Colin. When she inquired to his man of affairs as to his location, she was informed simply that he went to visit one of his properties in the north. He owned countless properties, the farthest being in the Black Isle. Her late husband's mother had a fondness for dolphins and her husband had purchased her an old remote castle along the shoreline where she could observe them from her solarium.

She couldn't imagine Marcus retreating there this time of year. The weather would be treacherously cold, but given his current mood, she couldn't hazard to guess where he was or what he was thinking. She hoped only that he would surface eventually. He did have sisters whom he loved and who loved him in turn. He wouldn't neglect them forever. She prayed that when he was ready to see them again, he would have forgiveness in his heart for her. She sighed. For Colin, too.

She refused to accept that she had come between the two men's lifelong friendship. They would patch things up. That's what friends did. And when they did, she would be only a proper duchess, keeping *proper* distance from Colin. He would become Lord Strickland to her once again.

As though the thought of Colin invoked him, Mary Rebecca asked, "Have you seen any more of that delicious Lord Strickland? Received any more gifts? I feel as though I haven't seen you in an age. You much catch me up."

Heat crawled like ants over Graciela's cheeks. She stammered for a reply, regretting taking Mary Rebecca into her confidences now that everything had fallen apart so miserably.

She'd been overwhelmed and bewildered and fit to burst with all that had transpired. Mary Rebecca had seemed a likely candidate for such confidences—the *only* candidate. Who else could she talk to about her peccadillos, after all, than the very person to drag her to a pleasure club? Except this recent matter with Marcus discovering them, she preferred not to discuss.

And yet now here she sat with a burning face

and twisting stomach. Mary Rebecca giggled and swatted at Graciela's hand. "You needn't look so embarrassed, you wicked creature. To think I begged you to join me at Sodom for *years*. One visit there and now you're a veritable seductress."

A seductress? Hardly. Their tryst had been wild but unintentional. There was nothing of her behavior that had been calculated enough to be termed seductive.

"No, I have not seen him. In fact, I'm thinking this little holiday is over." She injected a cheerful note to her voice, hoping to project that she wasn't troubled over anything. "I'm returning to the country with the girls."

Not a complete falsehood. She had stayed longer than she'd intended, and she wanted to put London, the site of all her transgressions, behind her. She needed to remove herself from Colin's sphere. He would soon forget about those mad moments of passion they shared. He'd pick out his debutante, marry her and start filling his nursery with progeny enough to delight his grandmother and satisfy the ghosts of his line.

"So soon? You haven't been here very long and the girls only just arrived." Mary Rebecca tsked. "I'm certain they don't want to leave."

Graciela shrugged lightly. She couldn't think

about that. There were bigger things at stake than the girls' disappointment.

Mary Rebecca arched one well-shaped eyebrow. "I suspect you leaving has nothing to do with missing the country air. You're running away."

"Running away?" She snorted and shifted uncomfortably in her seat. "From what?"

"From *who* would be a more accurate question and we both know the answer to that." She sighed and leaned forward to cover Graciela's hand with her own. "You're a woman with needs, Ela. Your husband passed away a decade ago. It's acceptable, you know. You can claim pleasure for yourself. Just because he died does not mean that you did, too."

Was it acceptable if the man she chose was so *unacceptable*?

"I'm not running away," she denied hotly, not bothering to admit that her rash behavior had given her more pleasure than she had experienced in all the years she'd been married to Autenberry. Mary Rebecca would only insist she repeat such behavior and seize more pleasure, and that simply couldn't happen.

Mary Rebecca inclined her head as she took a bite from her iced biscuit. She chewed for a moment, her head cocked thoughtfully as she studied Graciela. "I can understand why you might be a little unsettled at all of this. This is all new for you. Change is frightening for the best of us. Taking a lover, conducting an illicit affair. And I am certain Strickland is an excellent lover—I have heard things. Talk, you know."

An unaccountable stab of jealousy pierced her in the chest. Of course he had lovers in the past. And he likely would in the future. In addition to whomever he married. Forsythia's sweet young face appeared in her mind. That knife of jealousy twisted deeper.

She had no cause to feel possessive. He was entitled to such things in life and she had no claim on him. She told herself this repeatedly as she sat there. Unfortunately, it did little to alleviate her ugly feelings.

Mary Rebecca continued. "This was quite possibly beyond your scope of experience." Mary Rebecca's gaze turned knowing. "There's no cause to run away. You will soon grow accustomed to it. He was simply your first. If you're that perturbed by Strickland's close relationship with Autenberry, then move on to someone else. You have several admirers that I can think of as I sit here. What of Lord Higgins?"

At the swift shake of Graciela's head, she shrugged. "Higgins is rather long in the tooth. Very well, then someone else. A younger man since you seemed so fond of those." She winked impishly and Graciela rolled her eyes. She hadn't chosen this affair with Colin. It had simply . . . happened.

"The point, my dear," Mary Rebecca added, "is that a few more lovers and you will be quite versed in the language of these things."

A few more lovers?

Her stomach took another dive and this time bile rose up in her throat. She didn't judge Mary Rebecca for her active love life, but it simply wasn't for Graciela. She couldn't contemplate jumping into bed with another man. Especially after Colin and what they shared.

Hands that weren't Colin's touching her . . . another body driving into hers the way his had done. Their single night had shattered her. Reduced her to this—a woman who hid in her town house, both terrified and hopeful that she might see him again.

Mary Rebecca selected another biscuit, unaware of her tumultuous thoughts, and plopped it on Graciela's plate. "Here. Have one. I know how much you love them."

She shook her head, her stomach too knotted to eat. She pressed a hand to her belly as though she could quell the churning. "Perhaps later. My stomach is a little off at the moment."

"Since when do you turn down lemon biscuits? I've been sitting here eating half a dozen and you've yet to consume one. They are your favorite."

She lifted one shoulder in a half shrug. Suddenly speech seemed much too taxing.

Mary Rebecca leaned forward to look her over more closely. "Now that you mention it, your color is a little off, too."

Graciela sighed. "My appetite has been off lately."

"Hmm." She scrutinized Graciela. "You look a bit weary. Have you been sleeping well?"

"No," she confessed. Even without thoughts of Colin and Marcus plaguing her, it had been impossible to get comfortable in the giant four-poster bed. Granted, it was the bed she always slept in when she came to Town, but she almost believed someone had gone and changed the mattress on her. Try as she might, she could not find a comfortable position where her back and muscles did not ache. She wondered if she had some manner of ague.

"It shows."

She let out a single rough laugh. "Well, thank you," she grumbled. "I might be coming down with an ague. You should probably keep your distance. Perhaps you should take your girls home . . ." If a little hope laced her voice, Mary Rebecca didn't detect it.

In fact, she didn't seem to hear the suggestion at all. She continued, "Then you should wait before traveling. You would not want to fall ill along the way and be stuck at some roadside inn with your girls."

She gave a slight nod, acknowledging the wisdom of that. "Perhaps. A few more days wouldn't hurt . . . until I'm feeling hale again."

"I wonder if Lord Strickland is ill, as well." Mary Rebecca's lips twitched as though amused. "You were in close proximity, after all. I hope he's not unwell."

Graciela shook her head in forbearance of her friend's wicked sense of humor. "Unlikely. It's been a little over a week since we were together . . ." Her voice faded.

Clara squealed and danced in delight as she knocked Enid out of the game. Enid shook her head, smiling indulgently over her half sister's unfettered glee.

Graciela lost herself for a moment, gazing at the girls swinging their mallets and contemplating her night with Colin. It had been more than a week since they'd come together. *Multiple* times in one night. She'd never known such a thing was done. She hadn't known that such stamina was possible, that any man could possess such virility.

The silence stretched as her mind raced, retracing, *counting* . . .

The silence came to an end when Mary Rebecca sucked in a sudden breath, practically making Graciela jump. "Perhaps he in fact did . . . *infect* you with something?" She waved her hand in a small circle, nudging toward a point that Graciela was grappling with herself. She didn't want to acknowledge it. She didn't want to say the words aloud . . . as if that would somehow make them real.

"Infected?" Graciela echoed. It was a distasteful way to word it.

"Yes." Mary Rebecca nodded doggedly.

She stared at her friend warily. "What are you saying?"

"You know what I'm saying. I can see the dread in your face." Mary Rebecca set her plate carefully on the service table and leaned forward. Casting a glance about as if she, too, was aware of the enormity of her forthcoming words and that an abundance of servants lurked in the vicinity—any of whom could overhear—she whispered, "Perhaps he planted a babe in your belly?"

She flinched. There it was. Uttered aloud, however quietly. She was certain that so crass a topic as a Dowager Duchess of Autenberry with child and out of wedlock had never been discussed in the vaunted Autenberry town house.

"I can see you are thinking the same thing, Ela. Is it possible? Did you take any precautions?"

Trust Mary Rebecca, much more experienced and blunt than she, to ask the direct and important questions.

Graciela stared in long silence at her friend, her mind awhirl.

A babe! In her belly.

She let that thought roll around and sink its teeth deep.

Finally, at last, she reacted. Something loosened inside her chest and she laughed.

Mary Rebecca leaned back, bristling. "I'm glad to know that you find such an utterly serious topic amusing." She crossed her arms over her chest in uncharacteristic huffiness.

"Why, Mary Rebecca." She shook her head. "It was just the once." One night, anyway.

Mary Rebecca smirked. "My dear friend, once is all that is required. As a matter of fact, that is usually how it works." She held one finger in the air.

Graciela's face heated a little at that bit of truth. She sounded foolish, she knew, but there were other glaring facts. "I'm not a young girl, Mary Rebecca."

"So?"

"I'm too old to conceive a child," she stated baldly as if Mary Rebecca failed to understand her words. She was no female in the first blush of youth.

"Women your age *and* older have been conceiving children since time immemorial!"

Graciela shook her head, struggling to believe that this possibility could apply to her. She wasn't normal in that sense. She hadn't been even when she was young.

She could not be with child. She had to deny this as a possibility lest she lose her mind and fall victim to hope. Hope had crushed her before. She couldn't let it creep back in. Because even in this less than ideal situation, she felt the old stirrings of longing for another child.

It was like a vague, nearly forgotten dream. Something that teased at the edges of her memory. As ephemeral as smoke, but not forgotten. In moments like this the yearning returned in a swift rush.

"It's not simply my age. I've shared with you how difficult it was for me to conceive. I was a great disappointment for Autenberry in that regard." One of many disappointments for him pertaining to her. "I endured one miscarriage before delivering Clara and two after her birth. The physician pronounced my womb . . . defective."

Mary Rebecca reeled back where she sat. "Defective?"

Graciela remembered the word clearly because with her limited English at the time she had not understood its meaning. It had to be explained to her, which her late husband had done in excruciating and scathing detail.

You're useless. A limp rag doll in bed and you cannot even carry out the one thing for which you were put on this earth to do.

Defective. She was well versed in that word's meaning now. She had failed to give Autenberry the son he required . . . the spare he had wanted like so many men of his rank.

"Men," Mary Rebecca scoffed, patting her

hand. "What do they know about such matters? Perhaps the fault rested with Autenberry? Have you considered that?"

Graciela shook her head slowly. "No, he had Marcus and Enid. And he did give me Clara."

Mary Rebecca tossed her hands. "There are things that cannot be explained in this life. Perhaps you and he were merely . . . ill matched."

"Ill matched? I am not certain I understand your meaning."

"I mean, my dear, that your body and his were not ideally suited for purposes of procreation."

She winced a little. *Ill matched* would be an apt description of her relationship with her late husband even beyond the scope of their physical bodies.

Mary Rebecca shook her head and sighed gently. "You cannot be so very naïve to think you're incapable of begetting another child."

Hushed or not, the utterance did not stop Graciela from swinging her gaze to where the girls frolicked, panicked they had overheard the words.

Heat rushed to her face as she thought of their joining. It hadn't been civilized. She certainly hadn't thought about taking precautions.

"By the expression on your face, I gather you did not take precautions."

She snapped her gaze back to Mary Rebecca and shook her head. "I am due any day now to . . ." Her voice faded as her mind settled on one realization. She was wrong. Her cycle was *past* due. She frowned. Granted, she wasn't the best at keeping track of such things. There had been no need. She had not been intimate with a man in well over ten years. She had no reason to pay close attention to her menses.

"Ela, dearest." Mary Rebecca squeezed her hand, her voice softening. "When did your courses last come?"

Her mind raced feverishly, counting how many days she had been in Town and then the days before that in the country. She reflected on the last time she had required napkins.

"By my accounting," she whispered, a prickly cold sensation washing over her, "I should have started . . . six days ago."

Chapter 17

She did not leave Town after all.

Traveling in her possible condition didn't seem the wisest course. Yes, she was still convinced that it wasn't true, but she was unwilling to take the risk even so. After so many miscarriages, it was an instinctive reaction, even all these years later.

She might have decided not to leave Town, but she didn't leave the house either. She complained of not feeling well and excused herself from, well . . . the world.

She spent her time pacing her bedchamber, working on embroidery—never a particularly favored task—and letter writing. She wrote to her sisters in Spain and to Poppy. Anything and everything to fill the hours as she waited for her courses to begin. For reality to return. She told herself there could be another reason for being late, far-fetched and desperate as it seemed. Perhaps it was simply stress.

The second afternoon of her self-imposed quarantine, Mrs. Wakefield knocked on her door. Graciela bade enter.

"Your Grace," she greeted. "Lord Strickland awaits in the drawing room." Her gaze flickered over Graciela still garbed in a dressing gown. "Shall I convey your regrets?"

She froze, unable to disguise her reaction for anything but what it was. Panic. She couldn't see Colin. Not after that terrible scene at his house. Not after her good-bye. Not with the possibility that they had created a child.

She sank down on the edge of her bed, clutching the lapels of her robe close.

"Are you well, Your Grace?" Mrs. Wakefield inched forward, concern writ all over her face.

She shook her head. "I fear I've still a headache. Please convey my regrets. I think I should like to rest."

"Of course. I'll send Minnie to attend you. And perhaps I should send one of the grooms to fetch the apothecary?"

"Thank you, no. I don't think that necessary. A nice nap should do me wonders."

Mrs. Wakefield sent her one last lingering look of uncertainty. "As you wish."

As she slipped from the room to send Colin away, Graciela fell back down on the bed, where she did in fact drift into a restless sleep.

In it, however, she dreamed that she was lost in a dark wood, running and carrying a great basket of heavy rocks. She didn't know why she carted the rocks about, only that she did, only that they strained her arms and back but she could not let the basket drop even when hungry hounds appeared to nip and snarl at her heels.

She called for help amid sobs, at first shouting for her father, but when he never came, she cried out for Colin. She begged him to come.

He never came either. And then she remembered.

She'd sent him away.

THREE MORE DAYS passed. Then three more.

Mrs. Wakefield and the girls grew concerned even though Graciela assured them she was well and surfaced from her bedchamber to prove it. It was either that or Enid vowed to send for the physician. She was a stubborn chit and Graciela had no doubt she would do just that. Given that she was not yet ready to meet with a physician and have her condition confirmed (much less known), she relented and joined the girls for a stroll through the courtyard and gardens.

Her menses had not come.

Her breasts had grown sensitive and there was a decided darkening of her nipples. She knew this because she stared hard at herself each morning in the cheval mirror in her bedchamber without a stitch of clothing on, noting all the small signs. And they were in evidence. Or perhaps she was going mad. She certainly felt out of sorts.

She contemplated secretly seeing a physician, but fear held her in check. How could she trust him to be discreet? She was an unwed lady and could not risk word of her condition, real or imagined, leaking out.

She continued to try to convince herself it wasn't possible, that her body was *defective* as she had once been told. And then she thought of Colin, of his young, virile body, the strength and power of his physique as he buried himself deep inside of her. Such thoughts always produced a flicker of doubt. When she closed her eyes, she could still recall the throb of his manhood, the pulse of him as he released his seed into her. *Sev-*

eral times. If ever a man exuded potency and vigor, it was he. He certainly was the very picture of virility. He could probably impregnate a woman if they waltzed too close together. Was his potency perhaps enough to plant a child in her womb?

Could Mary Rebecca be right?

Perhaps Graciela hadn't been the barren one. Perhaps Autenberry had been the problem. While not infirm, he had not been a young man when they married. A fact that time, naturally, did not improve as the years of their marriage progressed. She knew he'd cavorted and taken lovers. He never hid the fact. And yet she'd heard no rumors of any by-blows he'd fathered—aside from Struan Mackenzie, whom he had fathered when he was a young man.

Or perhaps the problem had been Graciela and Autenberry . . . *together.* As Mary Rebecca suggested.

Standing before the mirror on the eighth evening of her self-imposed confinement, she splayed a hand over her belly and frowned. Her stomach appeared the same as it always did, perhaps only a little less pliant.

She'd retired after dinner, leaving Enid to her books and Clara to her drawing. She'd spent most of the day with them and even adopted a cheerful air so they didn't look at her with such concern anymore. It had taken a toll. She couldn't go on hiding from her predicament forever. A decision would have to be reached, and soon.

She'd taken a long bath, letting the warm water ease her muscles if not her mind.

She moved away from the mirror and slipped on her dressing robe, covering her nakedness. She passed by her writing desk, where she had abandoned the missive Mary Rebecca had sent earlier today demanding that they meet tomorrow. Additionally, she demanded Graciela stop hiding in her house. She sighed. Her friend knew her too well. Mary Rebecca doubtlessly wanted to be apprised of her condition.

She seated herself at her dressing table and began to brush out her hair in long strokes. Minnie knocked once before entering. "Your Grace, can I get you anything? Your Madeira perhaps?"

She smiled and shook her head. The idea of her favorite Madeira didn't appeal to her uneasy stomach right now. "I'm fine. That will be all for the night, Minnie. Thank you."

Minnie smiled, nodded and ducked back out into the hall, closing the door softly behind her.

The house settled into the quiet sounds of the night. The wind howled outside and a log popped and crackled in the fireplace. Even the constantly barking puppy couldn't be heard, likely snuggled in bed with Clara, who had confiscated her. She stared at her bed for a long moment. Sleep did not call to her.

Belting the robe snugly at her waist, she slipped from her bedchamber and made her way downstairs. The town house hummed in the late night silence and she reveled in the solitude.

She made her way to the library, enjoying the sensation of carpet under her bare feet. Enid made certain the library was well stocked with popular titles. Perhaps a book would take her mind off her worries for a bit, and in the morning a solution would present itself and she would know what to do.

She browsed the spines, tucking her hair behind her ears as she decided against the romantic novels of Mrs. Radcliffe. Moody Gothic romances were likely not a good notion.

Instead she selected a heavy book entitled *Treatise on the Catacombs of Ancient Rome*. Such material did not lend itself to emotion. She had enough of that churning through her presently. She could do without it this night.

High emotions were what brought her to this

state. Longing. Fear. Fear of loneliness. Fear of regret. That's what drove her to Sodom. From there, other emotions drove her into Colin's arms, most notably blood-pumping desire. She turned the leather-bound tome over in her hands. Perhaps this dry material would help her forget.

"So now you've become a hermit."

She whirled around with a yelp and dropped the weighty book she held. It hit the carpet with a thud. It was as though her thoughts had materialized in front of her. Colin stood in the threshold, one shoulder leaning against the doorjamb, his arms crossed casually over his chest.

"What are you doing here?" He was making a habit of breaking into her home uninvited and unannounced.

She clutched the lapels of her dressing robe together, achingly conscious of the fact that she was naked beneath it. What had she been thinking? She really should have donned her nightgown. She just hadn't thought she would run across anyone at this late hour in her home . . . especially not him.

"I know how we left things," he said, his voice gravelly thick. "But I wanted to see that you are well."

She knew how they'd left things, too. *She'd* left

things with a good-bye that felt an awful lot like the end.

And yet here he was sending butterflies spinning through her.

Perhaps she had been deluding herself. She was starting to wonder if there could ever be an end between them. If what they'd started wouldn't echo through her for all the rest of her days.

Her fingers flexed around the edges of her robe. "As you can see, I am well. You can rest easy and leave."

He leaned just inside the wall of the library, looking nonchalant and decidedly unperturbed. "I've called upon you twice. Why have you not given me audience?"

"It's my prerogative who I grant admittance into my home."

He stared at her for a long moment, revealing no expression, his eyes smoky in the shadows. "True. However, given our last encounter, I felt it necessary to speak with you again."

"Necessary?" She frowned. "Given our last encounter, I thought it clear that we should not see each other again. At least not like this."

"Like this?" He made a slight circle with his fingers and angled his head. "How do you mean?"

"Alone," she clarified.

"Ah. Imagine my growing concern when I was told you were ill."

"It was naught but an ague."

"Which kept you locked up and indisposed to visitors. Or was that only me?"

"Since when do you require to be apprised of my health?"

"Since I became your lover."

She blinked. Even after everything, he could still shock her. "You're not my lover."

"No?" His handsome lips curled. "We have evidence to the contrary of that." He pushed off the wall and walked toward her. Stalked really.

She gripped her robe more tightly. She had very nearly lost all feeling in her fingers. And yet she was afraid of letting go. Afraid of all that she would expose. All that could happen.

She moistened her lips. "One time does not make a lover."

"It was more than once."

"But one occasion."

"I see. How many occasions constitutes a lover, then?" He stopped before her.

She held her ground even though the hairsbreadth that separated them was hardly proper. They had tossed propriety aside long ago.

She winced and swallowed, fighting the enormous lump in her throat. It should not feel like this. It should not be so terribly awkward between them.

"Two occasions? Three?" he pressed, his voice a husky feather's stroke.

He inched closer, his chest pressing into hers.

She shifted uneasily where she stood, her robe chafing against her suddenly oversensitized skin.

Her already tender breasts felt full and heavy and her core throbbed and tingled with awareness. A flood of memories slammed into her. It really was mortifying how her body had a mind of its own around him.

She lifted her chin. "I don't know the criteria . . . only that one time doesn't make us lovers."

He raised a hand. She froze, watching it descend to her face. He brushed a lock of hair back from her shoulder. "Then maybe we should keep at it until there's no doubt in your mind."

Heat inflamed her face. "We can't—"

"You said that last time." He smiled, looking more roguish. And handsome. Damn him.

"This time I mean it." She hated that she sounded like a child. She squared her shoulders and tried to look more commanding. More duchess-esque.

He gave her such a look, dark and heavy with longing. "You mean you haven't thought about it?" Her lungs seized, unable to draw air. "You don't want to experience it again. With me." He touched another lock of hair, tracing it to where it draped over her shoulder, the backs of his fingers singeing her through her robe as his hand dragged lower, trailing her breast and brushing along her nipple until it pebbled against the fabric.

Her breath released and caught. His words, that barely there touch, throbbed like a pulsing beat through her body, sparking heat along every nerve. "It's all I've thought about," she admitted, her voice at a whisper pitch.

A damning confession, but she couldn't pretend otherwise.

She felt his gaze dip to the small vee of skin exposed at her throat, searing her like a brand.

"Are you wearing anything under this robe, Ela?" he asked, his voice growly and gruff. His hand slipped inside the opening of her robe, his blunt-tipped fingers rasping along her skin. A wave of gooseflesh broke out in the wake of his touch.

She sucked in a breath and stepped around him. "I cannot do this. You let yourself in. I'm sure you can show yourself out."

Proud of the coolness of her tone, she strode past him. She hadn't made it two strides before she felt his hand on her arm. With a tug he pulled her around until they were chest to chest. His nostrils flared as though he was filling himself with the scent of her. She could understand that. Right now his heady scent swirled around her, the faint smell of soap and leather and the maleness that was inherently Colin. It was hard to imagine that she might have a similar impact on him. Handsome, young and titled with a bevy of heiresses only too happy for his attentions.

And yet he was here now, making her knees go weak, appealing to all of her senses for one more liaison with him.

Just one more time. One more time wouldn't hurt.

She shook her head at the coaxing internal voice, her head falling back as she looked up at him. "Colin. There are any number of girls you can—"

"I don't want any other girl," he growled.

His hands moved then, dropped to the belt of her robe. Her voice died as he slowly untied it, his eyes never leaving her face.

She didn't speak. Didn't breathe.

He parted her robe wide, the silky fabric scraping past her straining nipples. Air wafted over her, sliding over her bare skin. She bit her lip, killing a whimper before it could escape as he surveyed her.

His chest lifted on a breath. "It seems a great injustice now that the last time—the *first* time we were together—the room was dark. I couldn't properly see you."

A rush of desire flooded her, squeezing between her legs as his gaze roamed over her breasts, her stomach, stopping on the thatch of hair between her thighs. She felt herself grow damp.

"You're the woman I want, Ela." His hand dropped and covered her sex. She gasped, singed to her core at the possessive cup of his hand over her. "I want this."

Her womanhood clenched hard in response, the sensation almost painful. Too intense to bear. A small cry escaped her trembling lips. Her hips shifted, pelvis thrusting out a little so that he had better access to her.

It was wicked. She knew it. She was shameless. Lost to him . . . to *this*.

And indeed, what difference did it make any longer? Why not listen to that little voice in her head?

They'd already been caught together—at least by Marcus. She was likely already increasing. One more time would do no harm. It couldn't possibly complicate matters more than they already were.

Chapter 18

Before she could digest how thoroughly wrong her thinking was, he wrapped an arm around her waist and lifted her off her feet, pressing her now bared body flush against him.

All thoughts fled. With her naked flesh plastered to his fully clothed body she could only feel.

A breathy squeak escaped her. She wasn't a little woman, but he made her feel petite as he held her off the floor, like one of the delicate seashells she used to collect along the shoreline back home.

He carried her several strides, his breath not even hitching. He lowered her down on the Aubusson rug before the hearth. The fire crackled, the logs popping and crumbling in the dying flames.

He kneeled beside her, his gaze traveling her length. His hand covered her breast and she arched under the pressure, hungry for more. "Your skin is so warm," he murmured. "Soft."

He ran a thumb over the rigid tip. A moan escaped her.

"I've dreamed of you like this. Of touching you again." He lowered his head, his heavy-lidded eyes fixed on her face. "Tasting." His warm breath fanned over her nipple a second before his mouth closed over it.

Her hands flew to his head, raking through the silky strands, holding him to her as she twisted and arched, offering herself more fully to him.

His mouth moved to her other breast. Pleasure spiked through her hard and fierce as his tongue and lips played with the sensitive peak. She writhed beneath him, the soft rug at her back just adding to the erotic sensations bombarding her. His hands glided over her. Her rib cage, stomach, hips. He stroked the length of her thighs as though she were an instrument created for him alone to play.

He parted her thighs and found her core, stroking her folds. "So wet." His voice was reverent and faintly worshipful.

Tears leaked out from the corners of her eyes. It was all too much. She trembled as his fingers traced the seam of her. "I've dreamed of you like this. Naked and under me."

"In your dream were you wearing clothes?"

Grinning in a way that made her stomach flip, he sat back and quickly divested himself of his jacket. His vest, cravat and shirt soon followed. He moved out of her line of vision for a moment. Even that short time was too long. She propped herself up on her elbows, watching him hungrily as he stripped off his remaining clothes.

He came over her then, naked as she was. Her mouth dried at the sight . . . at the feel of his body, his skin silk stretched over hard muscle and bone.

She could scarcely recall seeing the nude form of her late husband. He'd always come to her in the dark, but she knew he had not looked like this.

She gawked at Colin's wide shoulders and broad chest. His stomach was taut and ridged. A line of hair arrowed directly to his jutting manhood. In this better lighting, that part of him seemed so very big and yet she knew firsthand how well he fit inside her. Her stare fell on a single bead of his seed glistening at the head of him and she felt an answering throb between her legs.

Heat slapped her cheeks. The night they shared together seemed so very long ago. He hovered between her splayed thighs, on his knees. He took hold of himself, pumping once, his gaze burning.

Her sex clenched in hungry need, aching to be filled.

It all felt illicit and filthy, but she couldn't make herself stop any of it from happening. She reached for him, flattening her palm against his chest. She dragged her hand down his firm stomach, lightly scraping his skin with her nails, enjoying the way he quivered under her touch. She caught the drip of seed off the crown of him with a fingertip. Watching him, she brought it to her mouth and sucked deep.

An epithet exploded from his lips followed by her name.

His eyes glowed more silver than blue as he watched her. She brought her hand back to him and squeezed his member, sliding her moist fingertip over the straining head, playing in the weeping slit, fascinated at the way his member only deepened in color as she toyed with him.

He sucked in a breath and snatched hold of her hand, peeling her fingers off him. "Not yet. There are things I want to do first."

"Such as?" she queried.

His head disappeared between her thighs. "Such as this." She felt him breathe the words against her core a second before his tongue lapped her in one long stroke.

She jolted under him with a cry. She knew what he was doing. He had done it to her before, but it still astounded her that men did such things to women. Autenberry had certainly never bothered or even voiced an interest. If it didn't further his own pleasure, he didn't have need of it.

"Colin!" She grabbed his hair and tugged as sensations welled up in her . . . a coiling tightness that was almost uncomfortable.

"You have such a pretty, delicious quim, Ela," he growled, ignoring her pulling hands and burying his mouth deeper against her. His tongue thrust into her opening, mimicking the sexual act.

His hands dove beneath her, his fingers digging into the tender flesh of her bottom as he lifted her higher for his invading mouth—as if she were a feast he could not get enough of.

"Colin, please . . ." she choked, that great tightness forcing her to rise up again. Her hips moved, thrusting both toward him and away, too overcome, too overwhelmed. She felt bewildered and on the brink of tears.

At last she surrendered to the rising tide, her body falling back against the rug. Her head writhed, her hair tangling into snarls beneath her as he lapped at her.

Finally his tongue hit that button of pleasure nestled at the top of her sex and she came apart. She flung her arms wide above her head, hands balled into tight fists as he sucked the tiny nub, lashing it with his tongue in a way that made her lose all control and keen like she was dying. Suddenly it made sense why the French called it *la petite mort*.

She blinked several times against bright spots, gulping sobbing breaths as she floated back down. His mouth left her. She pressed a hand to the bare skin above her heart, willing the racing organ to steady and slow.

But there was no point. It was far from over.

Suddenly Colin was over her, his eyes pinning her, gazing at her intently as he pushed inside her, driving deep.

She gasped, her pulse spiking again.

He closed his eyes briefly, his expression blissful in a way she understood because she felt it, too. "Ela," he groaned. "Your quim is the sweetest thing . . ."

She whimpered in complaint as he withdrew almost fully. He waited, hovering at the entrance to her womb.

"Colin." She panted his name and sank her teeth into his shoulder.

He drove back inside her then, the force shoving her up on the rug.

Pleasure sparked out from where their bodies were joined. He dropped his head, burying his face against her neck. His lips moved against her skin as he said, "I thought maybe I imagined it was this good . . ."

"Me, too," she choked as he increased his pace, pumping into her fiercely. She wrapped her arms around his solid shoulders, hanging on and pressing her open mouth to one hard shoulder as he rode her faster, harder, the friction between their joined bodies so intense, so unbearable, that she had to wrap her legs around his hips.

One of his broad palms skimmed her thigh, fingers scoring into her skin, holding tightly, possessively, lifting that limb higher so that he could penetrate her ever deeper. The different angle struck something inside her, a sensitive never-before-touched spot that brought her to explosive release.

Her fingers flexed against the now slick skin of his shoulders, still hanging on to him as though he were the only thing grounding her and keeping her from flying away.

He let go of her leg and settled both his arms beside her head, propping himself up on his elbows so that he didn't fully crush her with his weight.

They stared into each other's eyes, panting, trying to catch their breaths. She smiled slowly, tenderly, and lifted a hand to touch his face, her fingers curling up against the bristle of his jaw. She could lose herself in his eyes.

"So does this make us lovers now?" he asked.

She stiffened. Losing herself in his eyes had its drawbacks. He made her forget everything. She couldn't afford to do that. Especially now. She needed to decide what to do, *not* block out reality.

She glanced around at the room, recalling where they were, and pushed against his chest in horror. Anyone could enter the room. They had definitely been loud. What if they roused a servant? *Por favor, Dios.* Clara or Enid?

She pushed at his chest. "You need to go."

He frowned. "We can go upstairs—"

"No. You just need to leave. We're *not* lovers, and you need to get that notion out of your head."

He sat back and reached for his clothes, his movements angry. "Keep deluding yourself, Ela. Keep running away."

"I didn't invite you here tonight," she reminded him. "You just crept in here like some thief in the night."

He laughed harshly. "Except I *stole* nothing. This wasn't even a seduction. A seduction requires coaxing. You offered not even a token of resistance."

"Oh!" She snatched up her robe, yanked it on and belted it securely. Truthfully, she was angrier with herself than him—because he was right. She'd surrendered gladly, easily. And if put to the test, she would do it again.

"You know this is wrong between us." She stabbed a finger in his direction. If he would only see that, then this wouldn't be nearly so difficult.

He stared at her and nodded. "You're right. As long as you think that, then this *is* wrong." He turned and marched out of the library, the door swinging behind him.

She stared at the space he had just occupied, wishing she could feel some finality, some closure between them . . . wishing she did not feel as though she was failing him and failing herself.

Her hand drifted to her stomach.

GRACIELA BLINKED SLOWLY awake the following morning. Sunlight poured in through her drapes, alerting her that it was well past morning. She had slept late. She lay in her colossal bed for several moments, her thoughts hazy and scattered, still lost in that in-between state of sleep and wakefulness.

Then it all flooded back to her. Colin and his late night visit. She'd succumbed to him, crumbled like bits of rocky shoreline against the waves.

Moaning, she scrubbed her hands over her face. It wasn't even the worst of it. Her hand dropped to her stomach. There was still this. A child that she had to stop thinking about in terms of *maybe* or *if.*

It was a reality. Her new reality, and she had to make some decisions.

A knock at the door had her sitting up in bed. "Come in," she called.

Minnie entered her chamber. "Begging your pardon, Your Grace, but Lady Talbot is downstairs and she insists on seeing you. She says she won't go away until she does."

There would be no putting her off. Just as there was no more putting off reality. Accepting that, she nodded once and climbed out of bed.

"DR. WILCOX SAID I could never conceive. How can this be?" Graciela asked quietly. She had just finished apprising Mary Rebecca of her situation. Or rather, the fact that her situation was unchanged and she had yet to start her menses. They sat in the drawing room, a fact that greatly relieved her. She did not think she could ever occupy the library again without recalling what she had done with Colin in there.

"Wilcox." Mary Rebecca snorted where she sat beside Graciela. "That old quacksalver. Is he even still alive?"

"I don't know that he is. It's been some years, but he told me after the second miscarriage that I was incapable—"

"You need to see my midwife. She delivered every one of my children and she understands a woman's anatomy."

"A midwife?"

"We use them in Ireland. My mother bore nine children with the aid of a midwife. Healthy babes all. You think I would let some old man with icy hands near me?" She shuddered. "What do stodgy old physicians and apothecaries know?"

She considered Mary Rebecca's words for a moment. She had not thought she could refuse Dr. Wilcox. He was simply who Autenberry sent for to attend to her. He only ever called on her to confirm if she was in fact increasing, the one time she gave birth to Clara and on the occasions she miscarried.

"Yes. I should like to see your midwife as soon as possible." She inhaled and already felt better saying the words.

She wished she could feel better about everything else. Colin. Marcus. *Colin.* The girls when they found out she was increasing, for she did not know how she would keep such a thing secret from them. And . . . *Colin.*

Her heart ached thinking about him and how she could never seem to get anything quite right with him anymore. Everything had changed between them and for all the passion and pleasure they had shared, she felt as though something had been lost, too. She missed the accord they had enjoyed. The easy smiles.

And yet she knew that had been superficial, too. It was strange to know a person for years and not really know him. Or know only one side of him at any rate. Now she knew him. Just as she knew they could never go back to before. Now she felt as though he were a part of her . . . Even if she wasn't carrying his child, she would feel that way. The thought jarred her a little.

"Ela?" Mary Rebecca said her name gently, tugging her from her thoughts, which was just as well. She didn't want to probe too much more into what it was she felt for Colin.

Chapter 19

As soon as possible ended up being the following day. The midwife, Mrs. Silver, was attending another expectant mother just outside the City, so it was late afternoon by the time she arrived.

Fortunately, Enid had wanted to visit her favorite bookseller and Clara decided to accompany her. Even as abundant as their library was, Enid was constantly acquiring new books. That's what happened when she read everything she got her hands on, devouring the pages as quickly as one did an iced pastry.

Mary Rebecca accompanied Mrs. Silver, who

was also an Irishwoman (no surprise), and the three of them shut themselves in Ela's bedchamber. Minnie asked no questions when Ela asked for their privacy and not to be disturbed.

"Don't be nervous," Mrs. Silver said kindly in her familiar accent, smiling in a way that immediately put Ela at ease. Nothing about Dr. Wilcox had ever put her at ease. This was already a marked improvement . . . even if the circumstances were far from ideal. She was no longer a married lady, hoping fervently for the news that she carried a child.

Indeed not. She was an unmarried lady . . . who still found herself a fraction hopeful that she was with child, wrong as it was.

Mary Rebecca scooted a chair up to the bed beside Ela and took her hand, clasping it between cool fingers as Mrs. Silver conducted her exam.

"When was your last menses?" the midwife asked.

She replied and moistened her lips. Her friend gave her an encouraging wink. "I've never been very . . . fruitful," Graciela added.

"Hm," Mrs. Silver replied noncommittally, pressing gently against Graciela's abdomen.

Ela continued, "I've lost three babes."

"Sometimes the reason for that has nothing to

do with your body's fertility. There can be other causes. You may cover yourself again."

Graciela pulled her dressing robe closed. Mrs. Silver helped her sit up. She slid to the edge of the bed, tightening the belt of her robe.

"Congratulations, Your Grace. You are indeed with child."

She shook her head, feeling numb inside. "Dr. Wilcox told me I was broken inside. That I could never carry a child through to term."

"That old goat?" Mrs. Silver huffed. "I've heard a great deal of him over the years. What does he know? Your body is very healthy, Your Grace. You are perfectly capable of conceiving a child . . . as you've done, and there is no reason you cannot deliver this baby. Now, take no needless risks, of course. Get plenty of rest and nutrition. Mild walks will do you and the baby good."

Graciela nodded, shoving away the painful memories of those three miscarriages. They were in the past. There was only now and this was happening. She lifted her chin and blinked back the sting in her eyes. There was only going forward.

"Should you blood-let?" she asked, recalling that Dr. Wilcox had done so. It had never been a favorite procedure.

"Heavens, no! Why would that be necessary?"

"Dr. Wilcox—"

"Of course!" Mrs. Silver muttered something unladylike beneath her breath. "It's a wonder you gave birth to even one healthy child. However did you keep up your strength with that old goat draining you?"

Graciela lowered down onto the bed, her head dropping back on the pillow. Had Dr. Wilcox given her poor care? Could that have contributed to her miscarriages? Perhaps this time would be different. Perhaps she could allow herself that hope. Heavens knew everything else up to this point had been different. Namely Colin.

As she sat there, staring unseeingly ahead, she contemplated all the strange feelings stirring within her. There was fear . . . but also elation.

She was going to have a baby.

Mrs. Silver stood back and gathered her things. "I'd be happy to assist you through your confinement and help you when your time comes, Your Grace."

She nodded. There was a great deal she had not yet decided. Her head was still spinning, but she knew she would absolutely prefer this woman to attend her rather than the likes of Wilcox.

She scarcely noticed as Mrs. Silver exchanged

words with Mary Rebecca before slipping from the room.

She turned to look at her friend, however, when she fell beside her on the bed.

"What shall I do now?" she asked with a tremulous smile.

"I shall help you. We'll arrive at a plan." Mary Rebecca patted her arm. "But first you must tell him."

She had no difficulty identifying who *him* was.

Only how would she tell him? What would she do? *Dios la ayude.* And then there was her family. Who knew where Marcus had gone, but how would she tell the girls? How would this not affect them adversely? It would not only ruin her . . . it would ruin *them*. Clara's future, all of her prospects, *poof*! Gone instantly once word of her scandalous condition made the rounds.

"Ela," Mary Rebecca pressed. "You do intend to tell him now, don't you?"

Mary Rebecca looked at her as though there were only one obvious answer to the question, but she knew it wasn't as simple as that. None of this was. Nor would it ever be. She was in dire straits here and she couldn't see an easy solution. Of course she would tell him, but she needed to think how to go about this first.

She squirmed slightly, recalling the realization she had reached earlier.

Now she felt as though he were a part of her . . . Even if she weren't carrying his child, she would have felt that way. The thought rattled her a little.

Because as entangled as they were, there had been no promises exchanged, no words of forever.

IT WAS A little after midnight when Colin was alerted to the fact that a lady had arrived at his back door. His butler had shown her to his office.

"Thank you, Lemword," he told the bleary-eyed butler as he anxiously rose from bed and slipped on some breeches. He almost didn't bother with a shirt but only at the last minute did he slip the loose garment over his head. Unnecessary, he supposed. Ela had seen him in far less. Still, she was a lady and her face would color brightly if he strolled into his office without a shirt.

That was almost incentive enough for him to strip off his shirt again. He liked it when her face colored. He liked knowing he was the one to make her react in such a manner. But there were servants about the house that he did not relish seeing him in his altogether.

His feet carried him swiftly to the office. He knew that she couldn't stay away. He'd been with enough women to know that what they had wasn't something that could be replicated or easily cast aside. Their chemistry was too strong to deny and she knew it.

The door was partially cracked. He pushed it open and shut it behind him.

He leaned back against its length and surveyed the room, finding her immediately. She stood before the fire, her back to him, cloaked head to foot as she held her palms out to the flames to be warmed. Outside his office a slow sleeting drizzle fell that almost looked like snow through the glass.

He smiled and approached slowly, his palms tingling at the prospect of touching her again. If he'd lost his best friend over this woman, it wouldn't be for nothing. He would enjoy his time with her. He'd make every moment of it count.

She must have sensed him, for she turned, pulled the hood back from her head and revealed her face.

It wasn't Ela.

His chest deflated. "Lady Talbot," he greeted, instantly on guard. What was Ela's friend doing at his house in the middle of the night?

He crossed his arms over his chest. Her gaze scanned him, not missing the fact that he was only partially attired in trousers and a shirt, his feet bare on the plush rug.

A smile played about her mouth. "Have no fear. I'm not here to molest you."

He released a short laugh, taking in her diminutive stature. "That is a comfort."

She shrugged. "I didn't want you to fear that I have designs on you."

"That is a relief. I was afraid I might have to fight you off my person."

It was her turn to laugh then. "I know better than that." The knowing light returned to her eyes.

"Let us not speak in riddles and evasions, my lady."

"Yes. Let us not," she agreed, waving a hand. "I do stand in your study in the middle of the night, after all. And you are having an affair with my best friend."

Of course she knew.

Humor gone, he asked, "Why are you here, my lady?"

"It's Ela."

He took a step forward. "What is it? Is she well?"

"Ease yourself. Although I'm relieved to see your concern for her."

"Of course I'm concerned. I . . . care for her."

"*Care* for her, do you?"

"Of course I care . . ." His voice faded and her smile deepened. She looked amused as she gazed at him.

He narrowed his eyes on her. "What are you doing here? Vetting me?"

She angled her head and looked him over. "Oh, it's not my approval you need concern yourself with."

"Then what brings you here?"

"There's something you need to know about Ela. Something she hasn't told you."

He tensed.

"I believe she will tell you. Eventually. She would never keep such a thing secret. But she's frightened, you see. Not that she would dare admit that. Such a proud soul."

"Please simply spit it out, my lady," he growled. She'd already worried him and now she was testing his patience.

"Ela is with child."

The words dropped like bricks into the space between them. She watched him with an unflinching gaze, awaiting his reaction.

He wasn't certain how long it took him to reply. Five seconds. Five hours. He could only stammer. "I . . . Sh-she . . ."

He dragged a hand through his hair and backed up until he collided with the sofa. Sinking down on it, he blew out a breath. It was the last thing he had thought to hear from Lady Talbot.

He knew of Ela's difficulties conceiving. The possibility of this had not even entered his mind. Marcus had called Clara a miracle child. Apparently there was more than one miracle to come out of Ela.

And this miracle would be theirs. A product of them. The knowledge left him reeling.

"Lord Strickland." Annoyance hugged Lady Talbot's voice. "Have you nothing to say?"

He nodded slowly. "I have a great many things to say, but they are words reserved for Ela."

She nodded in satisfaction and squared her shoulders, a faint smile on her lips. "Very well. I trust you will do the right thing. That's why I came here. You're a good man, Lord Strickland." She pulled her hood back up over her head and turned for the door. "I imagine she won't be very happy with me, but it's my hope that she will thank me later."

"I'll thank you now," he said, anger finally

starting to take root. If not for Lady Talbot, would Ela even have told him? Damn her. He'd had to hear news of his impending fatherhood from Lady Talbot and not Ela herself. It was wrong on countless levels.

First thing in the morning, she would explain herself. And then he would explain himself. He would let her know that as the mother of his child, she would become his wife.

As though she could read his mind, Lady Talbot stopped before exiting through the door of his office and looked back at him. "Oh, and you may not want to tarry too long. When I left her, she was packing for the country."

Chapter 20

Graciela couldn't sleep, so she decided to take over her own packing. Minnie had started it earlier and stopped in order to ready Graciela for bed. Only after Minnie left, she'd tossed and turned, unable to get comfortable. Finally, she'd given up.

The task of packing for the journey home occupied her time at any rate—even if it did not fully engage her mind. It was difficult not to think about Colin and the baby and her dubious future. She still found herself drifting to the mirror and smoothing a hand over her stomach as she considered herself appraisingly.

She still hadn't told the girls they were leaving

on the morrow. She winced at the oversight. There were quite a few things she hadn't told them. To be honest, it wasn't an oversight as much as it was avoidance.

She'd had an opportunity over dinner with them but decided against wrecking the evening with that announcement—or any others. It could hold until morning.

At dinner this eve, Clara had chattered on as usual, blithely unaware of the turmoil riddling Graciela. And that was as it should be. A mother's troubles should not become her child's problems. A mother's purpose was to protect her child, to shelter her from all things within her power. She would continue to do that no matter what came to pass. Clara would not suffer for her mistakes.

Clara was eager for spring and an end to the infernal cold. Over leek soup, roasted pheasant and parsnips, she waxed on about the long rides and the longer walks she was going to take and the trip to the coast that Graciela had promised before Christmas.

Graciela remembered that promise she had made even though it seemed a long time ago and she a different woman then. Untouched by desire. Oblivious to what it even was to want a man. To crave and need him as much as your next breath.

"Where has Marcus disappeared?" Clara wondered aloud. "It's not like him to not come and see us while we're in Town. He hasn't been here in days."

Graciela feigned fascination with her soup as she answered her. "I believe he decided to escape Town for a bit."

"Without telling us?" Enid frowned as she stirred her spoon into her soup. "It's not like him to leave without saying good-bye to us."

"An oversight, I'm certain." The lie felt horrible on her tongue. Enid was right, of course. Marcus had always said farewell before. Just further evidence that all was not well with him if he would punish the girls because of her.

"I wonder where he went." Clara clanked her spoon against the inside of her bowl. "Doubtlessly some place sunny and exciting."

"Hm. I believe the Black Isle was mentioned."

"So far north?" Enid looked quite perplexed at that information, her wide, gray eyes blinking slowly.

"Well, that's not sunny or bright. That sounds ghastly this time of year." Clara shivered, sounding and looking every inch the horrified English girl in that moment. It did Graciela's heart good to know that her daughter had assimilated so well.

She was accepted even if Graciela was not. "I do believe my Spanish blood makes me quite unfit for cold climes." She nodded decisively, looking so very mature right then. It was strange to consider that Ela had a baby growing inside her but also a daughter on the cusp of womanhood.

"I'm sure it's quite beautiful in the winter," Graciela countered, knowing very well that the last thought on Marcus's mind had been the inhospitable weather of where he was escaping. He could have very well frozen on his journey north and his demise would be all because of her. Apparently, remaining in Town so close in proximity to Graciela and Colin had been an intolerable notion. No, Marcus's foremost thought had been removing himself from both of them.

"More like quite *freezing*," Enid corrected. "Which is unusual. Marcus was never one to enjoy the bluster of winter." Again, that perplexed look came over Enid's face. She was too clever to not wonder at the unusualness of her brother's abrupt departure.

Compelled to offer some explanation, she proposed the one Colin used. "You must admit he has not been himself since the accident."

"Hm," was Enid's only reply to that.

Thinking back on that conversation now, Graciela hoped Enid wouldn't think her sudden need for departure tomorrow too strange. The girl was by far too shrewd.

Graciela knew they wouldn't want to go, but she couldn't very well leave them behind. They would all go. Fresh air. Away from prying eyes. Distance from Colin. It would serve her well and clear her head so she could decide the right thing to do.

She wouldn't have too much time to reach that decision. She would be visibly increasing soon.

Once in the country, all would resolve itself. She believed that. She had to. It was the only thing she could cling to right now.

She placed a couple stockings in her trunk, certain that Minnie would be appalled at her technique and likely redo all her efforts behind her back.

"Were you planning on telling me? Ever?"

Her heart leapt into her throat at the voice.

She whirled around to find Colin standing there, the doors to her balcony cracked open behind him, letting in a frigid breeze she hadn't noticed until that moment.

"You can't keep doing this." She gulped a breath and struggled to steady her pounding heart.

"Doing what?" He arched a single eyebrow.

"Sneaking into my room," she accused.

"It won't be a problem in the future, because we will be sharing a room. As husband and wife."

His words shot a dangerous thrill through her that she quickly squashed. From the way he was glowering at her, this wasn't a proposal tangled up with professions of love.

"Dios mío, what in heavens are you talking about?"

"Lady Talbot came to visit me tonight."

"Oh," she breathed, cold washing over her as realization took hold. Mary Rebecca had *not* done this to her. She was her friend. How could she have gone behind Graciela's back and told him?

"Don't blame her. She was being sensible. Unlike you." He waved at her half-packed luggage. "Think you can run from this . . . from me? Do you find the notion of binding yourself to me in a permanent fashion so reprehensible?" His gaze flicked down, lingering briefly on her stomach.

She glanced guiltily at her trunks, seeing herself in his eyes at that moment. As a deceiver. She didn't like that image of herself very much and felt immediately compelled to deny it. To try to explain. "I felt it best if I removed myself from Town. I wasn't running away. I can hardly do that. I just needed time and space away."

"From me."

She inclined her head slightly. Suddenly it felt hard to breathe. "I did not say that."

"You didn't have to." His lips twisted into a sneer and he advanced on her, stalked really, backing her up until she dropped down on the bench positioned at the foot of her bed. She craned her neck to look up at him. "I'll tell you what is happening. You're not leaving Town."

She lifted her chin, resenting his tone. Right or wrong, she didn't appreciate any man telling her what to do.

He continued, "Tomorrow I will see about posting an engagement announcement and then we will sit Clara and Enid down and explain that we're to be married."

"An engagement announcement?" He made it sound so simple.

"Yes, best to have it put out there quickly. There will be some talk—"

"Some?" How could he be so cavalier? "There will be a scandal," she corrected.

He shrugged. "If we post an announcement, we will be treating this as though there is no shame in it and it's the most normal thing in the world."

"It's not . . . normal." And everyone would think so. She knew how cruel British Society could be. She'd endured it for years. She expelled a breath. "Colin, we cannot—"

He squatted suddenly before her, seizing her hands in his. "It's done. You're with child. You're carrying *my* child. We cannot *not* marry."

She read the unyielding resolve in his eyes. He was here and ready to do the right thing. *Demanding* that they do the right thing.

His pale blue eyes drilled into hers. Her shoulders sagged under the weight of that stare. "Colin, this isn't what you wanted. We don't—" She stopped and swallowed. "You don't love me. I'm not the bride you wanted."

His jaw tensed, a muscle feathering the taut flesh. "But you're the bride I'm going to have."

She flinched. He didn't contradict her. There was no profession of love or tender feelings. That connection she had felt to him withered and twisted into something misshapen, something that didn't feel good or beautiful.

"Tomorrow," he stated, his gaze holding hers, waiting for her agreement.

After a long moment, she nodded her assent,

not that he was asking for it. Denying him, at this point, seemed foolishness. She didn't have the will or strength. In fact, she felt very empty inside. What did it matter if he failed to love her? What ton marriage was based on such tender sentiment? When had she ever had that?

Except she was long past the days of being a green girl who endured an arranged marriage and then donned a false face for the world. She was her own woman now. She had earned the right to make her own decisions. She had vowed that if she ever married again, it would be for love.

And yet here she was.

But your choices led to this.

Still, that didn't stop the hollow feeling from spreading through her as he turned and left the way he had arrived, his strides carrying him away from her as though he couldn't escape the sight of her soon enough.

She gave her head a slight shake. She was to wed Colin. That thought—that reality—struck her as surreal. As though it were someone else's thought. Another woman should be thinking it. A fresh-faced debutante. Not her.

Graciela caught sight of her reflection in the cheval mirror. She stared back at herself, valiantly trying to pretend as though all of this were normal—as though carrying Colin's child and marrying him were not some absurd bit of fiction one would read in a novel. She shook her head and was again swept with another eerie feeling that this wasn't happening to her. It was a difficult thing to accept that Colin was marrying her. She prayed he wouldn't later regret it.

Chapter 21

True to his word, Colin arrived promptly the next morning as they were breakfasting. Graciela looked up as he was led into the dining room, her pulse spiking at the sight of him.

Clara exclaimed happily at the sight of him. The puppy yipped and took off from under the table, where she was patrolling for lost food.

Colin bent and scratched the dog behind the ears, murmuring at her in a soft voice.

Colin straightened. The puppy continued to dance around him, still not satisfied and hungry for more attention.

Enid smiled in greeting. "Join us, my lord." She waved at the empty seat beside her.

"Thank you." He took his place beside her stepdaughter, sitting tall and erect in his chair. His gaze lifted to Graciela's as a servant appeared and set a plate before him. He gave her the barest nod. She returned the nod, even feeling shaky as a leaf inside.

She raised her cup of steaming tea to her lips and sipped delicately.

Colin tore off a piece of toast and popped it into his mouth, chewing as he considered all of them. He was still angry with her. She sensed it immediately from his stiff movements. It only made the knot in her stomach twist tighter.

Clara prattled on and Graciela listened with half an ear right up until the point of her daughter suggesting they visit Lord Needling's daughters, of all people. She stifled a shudder.

Clara sent Colin a coy look amid a giggle. "I do believe Honoria's older sister, Forsythia, quite fancies you, Strickland. Last time I saw her, she peppered me with questions about you."

"Lord Needling's daughters are all very accomplished and eligible ladies," he said evenly. Graciela recognized the cautiousness of his tone. He shifted in his chair. His blue eyes communicated silently that he wasn't enjoying the topic of conversation.

She sent him the slightest nod as she reached

for the blackberry jam, hoping to convey that she didn't care for it either.

Clara made a humming noise in her throat, her eyes glinting. "So the rumors are true, then? You are in the market for a bride, Strickland."

Graciela almost choked on her tea. She lifted her napkin to her lips, smothering the sound.

Enid glanced at her curiously before looking back at Colin. A pregnant pause fell as they awaited his response—and whilst she prayed for some manner of intervention from this wholly awkward scene.

One corner of his mouth lifted as though he were amused. "Yes, Clara. Yes, it is the truth. I've decided to marry."

Needles of heat attacked Graciela's face. The irony wasn't lost on her. She and Colin were about to confess their impending marriage while Clara intimated that Colin should bind himself in matrimony to an heiress barely out of the schoolroom. It was no small bit of absurdity.

"Ah." Clara nodded knowingly. "I thought as much."

Enid cleared her throat and arched her elegant neck. "Well, this is grand news. We're very happy for you, Colin. You've chosen the young lady already, then?"

"It's Forsythia, yes? I am right. Tell me I am." Clara grinned, clearly proud of her skills of deductive reasoning.

Enid started scooping sugar into her tea with rather intent focus, as though she could not bring herself to look at Colin just then. "Congratulations, Colin. She is a very fortunate young lady."

His chair creaked as he leaned forward. "Forsythia may very well be a fortunate young lady, for I am not offering marriage to the girl."

"You're not?" Clara looked visibly confused.

"You're not?" Enid echoed, lifting her gaze from her cup of tea.

Clara continued, "But that's been all the tattle. According to Honoria, even Forsythia expects an offer from you."

He winced. "I'm sorry if she feels that way, but her father is under no such delusion. He knows that no such offer is forthcoming."

Graciela's face burned hotter as she recalled the exact moment that Needling came to understand that no such offer would ever come.

"Oh, this is exciting! Who, then?" Clara pressed, her face brightly eager.

"Clara, do not pry," Enid chided, shooting a beseeching look for help at Graciela. Usually she would have interceded by now and put an end to her daughter's inquisitiveness as it bordered on rudeness. And yet she could not even think what to say. She was too riddled with nerves and anxiousness at what was to come.

Colin, on the other hand, appeared all that was relaxed. Handsome and at ease as he cut into a kipper. "You both are intimately acquainted with my bride-to-be."

"We are!" Clara hopped a little in her seat. She clapped gaily. "Do not keep us in suspense. Tell us, Colin."

Graciela lowered her hands into her lap beneath the table, twisting her napkin around her fingers until they ran numb.

"Very well." Colin nodded a few times as he looked across the stretch of table to where Graciela sat, still as a pillar of marble. He arched an eyebrow at her. He was indeed still angry with her. There may not have been an easy manner in which to do this, but he certainly wasn't taking any pains to make this less difficult.

"Ela," he said, her name part question, part statement.

Enid followed his gaze to Graciela, the smooth skin of her brow knitting in confusion.

At his pronouncement of her name, Clara

glanced at her. "Does Mama know? Oh, Mama, you know! Tell us."

"I—I—" she stammered beneath her daughter's barrage.

"Oh, no fair! Mama, you know." Clara pouted.

"No, it's not that," she weakly interjected.

Colin shook his head. "It's going to come as some surprise to you, but your mother—" He swung his gaze from Clara to Enid. "Ela and I . . . have decided to wed."

The room plunged into silence.

Even her normally chatter-pot daughter fell silent, her entire expression one of frozen shock with the exception of her madly blinking eyes.

"Did you say you're marrying . . . *each other*?" Enid demanded, her stony expression matching her hard tones. Her gaze shot back and forth between them. Gone was the quiet, reserved girl Graciela had come to know. She wasn't sure quite what to expect from this Enid.

Graciela nodded as Colin confirmed the question with a single "Yes."

Enid chose then to find her porridge of great interest.

"The engagement announcement should be posted tomorrow," he added.

"Engagement," Clara echoed, as though she had never heard the word before.

"Yes. Once the announcement is posted and the special license procured, we will wed. I'm thinking a small ceremony. We can travel to the church in the village neighboring my estate. My parents were wed there. It's fitting."

"Mama," Clara exclaimed with a bewildered shake of her head. She stared at Colin. "But she is older than you!"

Graciela winced.

"Yes, by a few years," Colin calmly agreed.

Clara digested that, looking from one to the other of them now. "I—I had no idea you were even courting."

Courting? Her daughter was so sweetly innocent.

This was the difficult part. Lying to her daughter. Telling her daughter their marriage would be a love match when she knew it was not . . . when a love match was everything she had hoped for Clara to have for herself someday.

Enid had gone quiet. She watched Graciela and Colin with narrowing eyes. Graciela swallowed against the lump in her throat. Enid had been just a girl when Graciela married her father. She had not been easy to win over, but they had entered a respectful accord over the last several years. Even with things harmonious between them, Graciela had always felt guarded . . . as though the fragile peace between them could be shattered far too easily. As though that might happen right now.

She twisted her fingers harder in her lap, wondering, as difficult as imparting this news was, how would she soon explain her condition to Clara and Enid? It would become apparent before too long. A hot wave of mortification washed over her. Eventually they would know the truth behind this marriage. She wouldn't even be able to claim it was a love match at that point.

"We've always held each other in great esteem and fondness," she managed to get out. That, at any rate, was not a lie. At least it had been true before. Staring into Colin's distant gaze, she wasn't so certain what was true anymore. Still, the words rang hollow.

"Fondness?" Clara stared at her as though she had sprouted two heads.

She fidgeted in her seat. For all of her daughter's youth, she was no fool, and fondness and esteem resonated lamely as far as motivations went for Graciela to remarry. Even if the groom in question was so handsome he made a woman's teeth ache.

"I love your mother."

Her gaze flew to Colin. He stared back at her, his face impassive. The blunt declaration made her breath catch. Of course, he was lying. They were just words to make their union more believable.

"Oh," Clara breathed, pressing her hands together over her heart, looking clearly moved.

Sudden laughter broke the spell.

Graciela tracked the source. Enid tossed her head back, her slight shoulders shaking.

"Enid?" Clara frowned.

After some moments, Enid caught her breath and sobered enough to ask, "Are you serious?"

Graciela shared an uncertain look with Colin before nodding.

Enid flattened her palms on the surface of the table and pushed to her feet almost violently, sending her chair clattering to the floor. "Unbelievable." Her gaze snapped from Graciela to Colin and back again. "First you take my father and now this." Her eyes, usually a quiet, smoky gray, stabbed Graciela with hot accusation. She pointed at Colin. "Now him. You could have any man you wanted, but you had to have Colin?"

Graciela blinked, her stomach sinking. She cast a quick glance at Colin. His face reflected the same bafflement she felt. Enid was acting as though she had a yen for Colin. But it couldn't be. She was close to thirty years old. A self-proclaimed spinster. Certainly if she cared for Colin, she would have revealed it at some point over the years.

"Enid," she began, unsure what to say.

"No!" Enid held up a hand, palm out. "Don't."

"I didn't realize . . ." Graciela shook her head, her face burning with embarrassment. "I—I didn't know—"

"At this point, you're an expert at taking everything in my life."

"Enid," Colin said, his voice gently reproving.

It was Enid's turn to shake her head. She turned her gaze on Colin then. "No. I can't hear anything from you right now. I just can't . . . not this."

That said, she whirled on her heels and stormed from the room. Silence fell as they stared after her. Graciela noticed she was breathing heavily and worked to calm herself.

"Well," Clara finally said with a heavy exhale. She smiled weakly at both of them. "I'm so happy for you both."

Chapter 22

Colin stayed a little over an hour before he took his leave with the promise to return for dinner. He had a great many tasks to do if he and Ela were to wed posthaste. And he had every intention that they wed posthaste.

Clara beamed, clearly thrilled that he would be back again. Ela, on the other hand, did not look so happy.

Clara watched closely as he leaned down to kiss the back of Ela's hand.

At the last minute he changed his mind and pressed a quick kiss to her lips. They were affianced, after all. The familiar taste of her washed over him, and he was hard-pressed not to let his mouth linger on her.

She gasped, her gaze swerving to her daughter as color flooded Ela's face. It was a welcome sight. Ever since he'd crept into her bedchamber and informed her of their impending nuptials, she had looked pale. After Enid's reaction she'd gone from pale to bloodless. It roused his protective instincts. She was carrying his child. He wanted her well. Happy and healthy. He needed to forget his anger with her. They should begin their marriage on a peaceful note. He needed to forgive the fact that she'd intended to run away and keep her pregnancy a secret . . . at least for a time.

He could understand that she had been panicked and uncertain. They had come together with no promises or expectations.

Now when they came together, it would be forever. A deep sense of fulfillment curled through him that he shied from examining too closely. He'd always cared about Ela. And he had always hungered for her . . . He admitted that now. She satisfied him in bed as no woman before. That was all that mattered. That was enough. More than enough.

Clara giggled as he lifted his lips from Ela.

Ela's eyes fixed on him, her large dark irises staring at him so solemnly, still full of doubt.

"Everything will be fine," he whispered for her ears alone before fully pulling away, knowing she was fretting over everything. Marcus. Enid. Clara. *Him.* Their baby.

She nodded once, her gaze darting to Clara, clearly not wanting to discuss the matter in front of her daughter.

"I'll see you this evening," he murmured.

Clara addressed her mother. "Shall I speak to Cook? Have her prepare a special celebratory dinner? We should have a cake at the very least. Perhaps her tartlets, as well."

"That sounds delicious," he said.

"It's a pity Marcus isn't here," Clara added wistfully. "He shall miss the celebration."

Guilt flashed across Ela's face at the mention of Marcus. Colin hated that. Hated that she should feel guilt over anything they had done. He didn't regret one damn thing.

He reached out and brushed a finger down Ela's cheek. Just a quick caress. It was a touch well within the bounds of propriety for an affianced couple and yet sparks ignited at the contact. As always with her, he wanted more than a mere touch. He always wanted more. How had he suppressed this wanting for so long?

"Yes, a pity," he agreed, holding Ela's gaze. "We shall have to celebrate enough to make up for his absence."

The rest of his day passed quickly. He sent word ahead to his housekeeper at his family seat that he and a small party would be arriving soon. He then made arrangements to procure a special license from the archbishop. Lastly, he met with his man of affairs and his barrister, informing them of his upcoming change in marital status.

When he returned to the Autenberry town house, dinner was the celebration that Clara promised. And there was cake.

Enid, however, did not make an appearance. Ela attempted to put on a cheerful mien, but he knew it wounded her that Enid would rather stay in her chamber than join them. After Marcus, it would feel as though her family were falling apart.

Clara played the pianoforte for them in the drawing room after dinner until Graciela called a halt. "Thank you. That was lovely, but the hour has grown late, Clara."

The girl nodded and stood from the bench. "Good night, Mama." She pressed a kiss to Ela's cheek. Straightening, she smiled down at him. "Good night, Colin."

"Good night, Clara." He watched as she left the room, realizing with some astonishment that she would be his stepdaughter. He would have a stake in her future.

Somehow he went from having no family at all to acquiring a wife, a stepdaughter and, in the near future, a child of his own. It was a start—the beginning of the family for which he had always longed.

Suddenly his chest swelled. He'd always felt a little bit hollow inside. A faint ache gnawing at the edges of him. He'd thought it simply a part of his existence. Something he had to live with. He'd never thought it would go away. Until now.

A clock ticked on the mantel, the only sound other than the pop and crackle of the fire in the hearth.

His glance slid Ela's way. She was still worried, her face still pale. She'd picked at her food at dinner.

She was his now. He had to take care of her. It was his task to put the color back in her cheeks. See that she worried less. Ate more.

He rose to his feet and pulled the servant's rope.

"What are you doing?" she asked.

A maid appeared before he could answer. She executed a quick curtsy.

"We'd like a tray. Some sandwiches and biscuits." He sent her a glance. "Milk, too." For some reason that sounded restorative. His nanny had always given him milk before bed, insisting it would make him grow strong.

The maid disappeared even as Ela protested, "I don't need—"

"You hardly ate at dinner. You need nourishment. How else will you be able to function?"

She inhaled and nodded with clear reluctance. "Very well."

Moments passed. "She'll forgive you," he said.

"How can you know that?" She clearly understood that he referenced Enid.

He considered his answer. He'd always viewed Enid as the sister he never had. He'd had no idea she perceived him as a romantic interest. She'd always been buried in her books. He hoped to God she had not been holding out all these years for him. "Because the day will come when she becomes so thoroughly enamored with a man that she will realize that whatever she imagined she felt for me was just that—fanciful imaginings."

Ela chewed her lip, her expression a far leap from relieved.

He knelt in front of her and grasped her hands resting on the arms of her chair. "You will see. She will come to realize her mistake and then all will be mended between the both of you."

"I hope so."

The maid returned then, pushing a cart. He rose to his feet as she positioned the food in front of Ela.

"Thank you, Althea," she murmured. The maid curtsied and departed.

Colin immediately began piling a plate of food for her.

"That's too much," she protested.

"Eat. If not for yourself, then feed our child."

She accepted the plate and dutifully obeyed. He watched, letting her eat one sandwich and a biscuit and drink from her glass of milk. She set her glass down and locked eyes for him. "Satisfied?"

"Yes. Thank you."

"And what of Marcus?" she asked. "Will he, too, come to realize his mistake and all will be mended?" She shook her head. "You can't convince me that our marriage won't break this family."

Colin inhaled, wishing he could tell her that her family would come out intact. "Autenberry is a bit trickier," he admitted.

A shadow fell over her gaze. "He shall always feel wronged by the both us."

He thought of the lad he had grown up with . . . the bond they had shared. It went deep. But then, the wound of Colin bedding his stepmother evidently went deep, too. It wouldn't matter that he married her. It would not alleviate Marcus's sense of betrayal.

"He may be lost to us." He could not pretend otherwise. Ela nodded, looking so forlorn that his gut clenched. "It does no good to fret over it. Get some rest. There's naught to be done. Take heart. You shall have a child. Our child." A pause fell before he went on to add, "Tomorrow I'll be leaving to procure our special license."

"Of course."

"I'll be back the day after tomorrow."

"Travel safely, my lord."

She fixed a smile to her lovely face, but he couldn't help feeling that their union was off to a bad start and for the life of him he didn't know how to make it right.

SHE SLEPT FITFULLY that night. It was hardly the rest that Colin had advised she get. He'd also advised for her to take heart. She wished she could. She wished she could enter this marriage with a full heart, knowing that scandal wasn't about to befall her. Wished that her marriage to Colin wouldn't hurt anyone . . . that *she* wasn't hurting anyone, most notably her family.

Her hand slid to the curve of her stomach. A life grew there. She should be happier than ever. And perhaps she could be if this weren't a forced marriage. If Colin wanted to marry her instead of *having* to.

Chapter 23

He rode for Canterbury as if the hounds of hell were at his heels.

He wouldn't spend three weeks waiting at his estate so that the banns could be read in the parish church. Nor would there be a grand wedding at St. Paul's. That would require great orchestration and time they didn't have. They didn't need the spectacle either. All the ton coming out to see the Dowager Duchess of Autenberry marry, their eyes judging and condemning as they tittered behind their hands. No, thank you. He wouldn't put her through that. A special license was the only option.

A sense of urgency propelled him as he rode

through the night back from Canterbury, special license in hand. The archbishop had been amenable to the request. For a fee, of course. He could have stayed the night in Canterbury. An extra day or two wouldn't have caused any delay that would matter in the scheme of things. And yet something told him to get back to Ela as soon as possible.

He arrived in London a little before dawn. He fell into bed and slept a few hours, knowing he couldn't very well show up at Ela's before dawn lit the sky.

He awoke to the aroma of chicory coffee. His valet was there, extending him a cup.

He reached for the proffered cup. "You're heaven-sent, Donald." He sighed in pleasure at the first taste, letting it rouse him.

Within the hour Colin was almost dressed for the day. Donald was holding out his jacket for him when the doors to his chamber burst open and his grandmother waltzed into his bedchamber. His butler hovered behind her with his eyes brimming with apology.

"M-my lord," Donald sputtered, his typically ashen complexion flushed red. Poor man. First Marcus and now Colin's grandmother. This wasn't good for his self-esteem.

"It's fine." Colin waved the old man back and turned his attention to his grandmother.

He hadn't seen her in years but she had changed very little. When he was a child, she had scared the hell out of him. She wasn't a very big woman and yet she had loomed large with her piled-high silver hair and strident voice.

She still possessed the same silver hair, still wore it piled high atop her head in a style better suited for the drawing rooms of forty years ago.

Her silver-topped cane thudded across the floor as she made her way to the sole wingback chair in the room.

"Grandmother," he greeted, waving his valet off. "How nice to see you."

"Enough with the niceties." She waved a hand as she sank down into the chair.

His lips twitched. As they had not exchanged any niceties at all, he was hard-pressed not to laugh.

"Word of your engagement has reached me."

"Well, seeing as I arranged for the announcement to be in the paper, that isn't a surprise."

She knotted her hands over the head of her cane. "This entire match is unacceptable."

He sighed. "I'm sorry you feel that way."

"This must be undone. You must see that. This

marriage cannot take place." She stretched her neck forward, reminding him of a crane. "She is several years your senior, Colin. Past her prime. It is most unseemly. Are you aware of the talk since the announcement came out? I cannot even hold my head high among my friends."

"Perhaps you need new friends."

"Don't be impertinent with me, lad."

He shook his head. "I know this is difficult for you to understand, but I don't care about the talk."

Her lips pinched, wrinkling around the edges. "Even without the scandal of it all, there is the fact that the Duchess of Autenberry is sterile. She only gave birth to one child—" she held a single gnarly finger aloft "—and as indelicate as the topic is, everyone knows of her miscarriages. You require sons."

"She's with child," he snapped.

Perhaps he shouldn't have indulged her with that bit of truth, but he couldn't help himself. The fact that she would march in here and presume to tell him what he should do—whom he should (or should not) marry—when she had so little involvement with him in the course of his life rubbed him ill.

She digested this with no reaction save a tightening of her fingers on the head of her cane.

"Whether she successfully bears you a son is yet to be seen and, in my opinion, still dubious."

"Then it is a good thing, Grandmother," he said tersely, "that your opinion is not one I seek."

She pulled back and squared her shoulders, ever imposing. Her nostrils flared at the insult dealt. "You may very well be the last of our line to be the Earl of Strickland and perhaps that's just as well."

She stood slowly, wincing as she straightened her frame and slapping his hands away when he stepped forward to assist her. Even several inches shorter than he was, she appeared to look down her nose at him. "You've made me a laughingstock. You are a disgrace to the family name. I always knew it about you." She squinted at him. "I saw it in you when you were just a boy. Your father . . . he saw it, too. It was in your eyes. A weakness of character."

He took a breath and held it in, letting it fill him, desperate for that air to fill up all the little spaces and push out the old, aching hollowness.

"You shall end this betrothal."

"You think you can command me? You've scarcely been in my life all these years—"

"Such impudence! I am still your grandmother and the head of this family—"

"You might be overly ambitious describing us as a family."

Blotches of color broke out on her ashen cheeks. "You should cede to my directives."

He tilted his head back as though considering that possibility. Looking back at her again, he pronounced, "I'm going to have to follow my gut here, but thank you for your interest."

"Stupid, insolent cur!" A steely glint entered her eyes.

He tsked his tongue at her. "Don't excite yourself. It can't be healthy," he advised, mildly concerned as a vein began to throb in her forehead.

"I shall have my way in this," she vowed, her voice quiet for all its hardness.

He snorted at the empty threat. What could she do? He was a grown man. He was not at her mercy.

She whirled around, surprisingly quickly for an individual of her age who required a cane.

Scrubbing a hand along his nape, he stepped back and watched her walk from his room, her cane thunking along the floor, jarring him with every impact.

As much as he did not regret his decision to wed Ela, his grandmother's words reverberated through him in a bitter mantra. *You are a dis-*

grace . . . I always knew it about you. Your father . . . he saw it, too. It was in your eyes. A weakness of character.

He thought of the parents he never knew and wondered if they could see him now. If they would agree with his grandmother's opinion of him, too.

GRACIELA SEALED THE letter she had just finished and rose from her writing desk. Before she moved away completely, her gaze latched on to the newspaper spread out along the side of the desk, her engagement announcement displayed there on page three, bold as you please for the world to see. Her stomach cramped. She supposed Colin was right. They should deliver the news themselves. If they acted secretive and ashamed, malicious tongues would only wag faster.

Letter in hand, she strode from the room to hand it off to one of the doormen so that it might be dispatched. Her fingers pressed down, crinkling the parchment. The words inside had been full of false merriment, conveying the news of her most happy betrothal to Lord Strickland. A choking lump rose in her throat. It was a hard thing to lie to a friend. And as Poppy was married to her late husband's illegitimate son, she felt connected to them. Even if Marcus did not, she marked them both as friends.

She'd felt sorry for Struan Mackenzie before she even met him. His name had been muttered about by Marcus, and even before that Autenberry had mentioned that there was some light-skirt in Scotland claiming he had sired her child. Immediately, Graciela had sensed the alleged light-skirt might be telling the truth. Mostly because by then she knew the manner of man she had wed . . . a man who crushed the women he encountered, turning their dreams to dust and leaving their souls forever besmirched.

When she finally met Struan Mackenzie, the resemblance was undeniable and she felt shamed for all he had suffered at the hands of his father—or rather from the neglect of his father.

She'd decided to send the letter because she knew word would reach them of her engagement to Colin—if it had not already—and they deserved some communication from her over the matter.

She halted at the sight of the hall table. A stack of envelopes sat atop it, all addressed to her. An inordinate amount of post for this time of year, when Parliament was not in session and most everyone was at their country homes. The stack continued to grow every day. Ever since word of her engagement to Strickland had become public, the invitations had flooded through her door. Society matrons who had given her the cold shoulder before now sought her presence at their tables. She wasn't so foolish or naïve to think she had somehow become worthy or of consequence to them. Indeed not. Duchess or no, she had only ever been tolerated. Never embraced into all those fine circles. Never accepted.

"Mama!" Clara skidded into the foyer, the puppy close on her heels. Her daughter waved a note anxiously above her head.

"Clara, what is it?" She placed a hand on Clara's shoulder, stopping her from bowling Graciela over.

"It's Enid," she said, gulping for breath. "I just went into her room. It's unlike her to sleep so late, and she's gone."

Disquiet wiggled through her at this declaration. "What do you mean she's gone?"

"She left this note." She thrust the parchment into Graciela's hands. "None of the servants even saw her. I've asked. She must have left in the night." She pointed at the missive. "She said she's gone north to join Marcus."

"What?" She looked down and quickly scanned

the perfectly penned message. Clara was correct. She had decided to venture to the Black Isle to be with Marcus. Without a companion. Alone. That wiggle of disquiet erupted into full-scale alarm.

She looked back up. "But we are not even certain that's where Marcus went."

"Apparently she is convinced. She will be well, won't she, Mama?" Clara gnawed on her lip, looking intently at Graciela, waiting for reassurance.

She quickly adopted a more cheerful countenance, determined to put her at ease. "Of course, Enid will be fine. I don't know a more resourceful young lady. And even if Marcus isn't there, the house is fully staffed. She will arrive there safely by post and be fine."

Clara nodded, still looking uncertain but not quite so frightened as moments ago.

Blast Enid. She knew her stepdaughter was angry and that she felt betrayed . . . perhaps even heartbroken, but such impulsive behavior was unlike her. She lived within the safety of her books. How would she cope all alone out there? So far from home? Heading into the Highlands of Scotland in the dark of winter?

The puppy whimpered at Clara's feet. Graciela looked down at her. "I think she needs to go outside, Clara."

Clara nodded and lifted the small ball of fur up into her arms.

Graciela watched her go and then turned, heading up the stairs for her chamber. Suddenly she felt very tired.

Chapter 24

He found her napping on her bed.

He'd let himself inside. He was familiar with the house and he wasn't in the mood to see anyone else. Only one person called to him and chased away his emptiness. He was selfish enough to want to avoid everyone else.

After his grandmother left, he'd dropped into the chair she had vacated. He thought about her words. Not so much her predictions about Ela but her judgment of him. She was the only family member he had left and when she saw fit to even see him, it was to tell him what a disgrace he was and that he was somehow fundamentally flawed.

He stood just inside her chamber and leaned his back against her door. Her chest rose and fell gently with silent breaths. The fabric of her gown molded perfectly to her breasts and his gut stirred with emotions other than lust. Although there was a healthy dose of that. There was always that. He removed his jacket and started on the buttons of his waistcoat, deftly popping them free.

She stirred on the bed, sighing and stretching languidly. His cock thickened at the sight. He needed her right now. He needed to peel back her skirts and sink inside her until he didn't know where either one of them began and ended.

Her eyes opened with a flutter of dark lashes as he advanced.

At the movement, her gaze swerved his way. She jolted up on her elbows.

"Wh-what are you doing?" She blinked quickly as if needing to clear her vision. Her dulcet tones stroked the flames of his desire and made him hasten. He skimmed her and the realization that she was his—that she would forever be his—slammed into him with base need, filling him with wonder. *Mine.*

"Removing my clothes," he answered. "Why

don't you do the same?" He dropped his garments on a chair and then pulled his shirt over his head in one motion. His trousers followed next.

Her eyes widened, and she held out a hand, palm face out, where the length of her stretched on the bed. "Wait."

He grinned. "We don't need to wait until the wedding night. We've already done this, remember?"

"Oh, I'm very aware. That's what got us here."

He chuckled and arched an eyebrow. "Are you going to undress yourself or do you want me to do it?"

Her chin shot up, fire in her eyes. She looked so beautiful right then that his chest clenched. "And because we've done this before, I must do whatever you command?"

He inhaled swiftly and advanced two steps before forcing himself to stop, curling and uncurling his hands into fists at his sides. "That's not what I said. That's not what I'm saying . . ."

"Because if you think that's how this marriage is to be—"

He leaned down and silenced her with a kiss.

EXCITEMENT ZIPPED DOWN her spine as Colin came over her, his chest bare, smooth skin stretched tight over firm muscles that beckoned her questing fingers.

Every time they had been together it had been nearly dark. She'd never been alone with him in full light like this before.

He came up for air and she sucked in a breath, shaking her head. "It's highly improper for us—"

"We're past propriety, my soon-to-be wife."

"Soon-to-be," she agreed archly. "I'm not your wife yet."

"Semantics. In my mind, we're already bound to each other."

She inhaled, fighting back the small thrill his words gave her. This marriage was born of necessity. She needn't forget that. She couldn't.

She forced a laugh, but something shaky jumped inside her chest and it sounded false. "Now, Colin. Don't make this out to be more than it is."

One corner of his mouth kicked up a split second before his hand shot out to circle the back of her neck. Her laughter died at the sensation of his fingers on her, pulling her hard to him, trapping her.

All levity fled his expression. His deep voice roughened as he uttered, "You're fond of me. You can try to hide from it, but it's here between us."

His eyes drilled into her, a relentless blue, and she felt her spine start to dissolve, sinking into the bed. "Of course I'm fond of you—"

His head descended and the treacherous thought drifted through her mind, *Yes.*

For a moment, she could hardly move, too overwhelmed at the pressure of his mouth on hers, at his chest crushing into hers, at the full delicious weight of him.

He lifted up slightly to growl at her, his eyes flashing, "Open your mouth to me."

Nodding, she parted her lips and then his mouth was back on hers again.

He brought one hand to hold her face, his thumb beneath her chin, tipping her mouth higher for him.

He kissed her bottom lip, then her top, briefly pulling it between his teeth. She moaned. His mouth slanted over hers, kissing her deeper. He licked along the inside of her mouth. Her hands gripped his shoulders, clinging to him as though she feared he would stop—that this still new and thrilling thing would end. She touched her tongue to his. He made a low sound of approval. She felt it vibrate from his chest to hers.

His arms pulled her closer, mashing her breasts

into his chest—breasts that felt aching and heavy in a way she hadn't known was possible.

He kissed her forever, their mouths never breaking. He held her face with both of his hands like she was the most cherished thing in the world. Desire pumped thick through her blood, pooling at her core. Her hands wandered his arms, his back, reveling in the smooth, strong flesh.

"Too many clothes," he purred against her mouth.

She nodded and made a sound of approval as his fingers worked the buttons free down the front of her bodice. He yanked it open and tugged it down her arms anxiously.

She lifted half up off the bed, eagerly accommodating him. He tossed it to the floor with a smack. He went to work on her stays next. He paused once he had stripped her down to her chemise and sat back, consuming her with his eyes.

Her chest lifted high on ragged breaths as he cupped her breast through the thin fabric and she moaned as his deft fingers stroked her, working skillfully. A sharp cry tore from her as he found her nipple and pinched it between his fingers.

"Colin," she choked, pleading.

He settled his weight between the voluminous folds of her skirt. Her legs fought against the heavy fabric, desperate to be free, desperate for the feel of *him*. She dragged her palms down his back and gripped his backside in an anxious act to pull him closer, to bring him against that most aching part of her.

Something snapped then—a fine thread severed. Everything became frantic and feverish between them. His hands tugged, directing her one way and then another as he shoved her skirts up and bared her from the waist down.

He drew away for a moment to observe her, raking her with eyes that burned, scalding her everywhere they looked. "Colin?" she queried.

His gaze fastened on her. "You're beautiful, Ela." His throat worked as he swallowed. "And you're mine."

He covered her with his body, his smooth firmness sliding against her. She gasped as he slipped down her length, his mouth everywhere—her breasts, her stomach, her hips, then lower. *There.* She clutched fistfuls of his hair, arching up off the bed with a cry, well remembering the wicked things he knew how to do there.

His tongue worked against her, leaving her

writhing on the bed. Her hands grabbed fistfuls of the counterpane, hanging on for dear life.

Then his fingers took the place of his mouth, stroking her, finding that secret, buried spot and rubbing it in swift circles, pinching it, squeezing until unrecognizable sounds erupted from deep within her. He added his mouth and sucked that tiny button between his lips, lightly scoring it with his teeth until she came apart, until she shuddered and cried out, ripples of sensation claiming her.

He came back over her again, his body a hard, wonderful weight.

He held her gaze as he settled between her thighs, nudging them wider. His expression was tender as he stared down at her.

She lifted her hips as he began to push inside her. She closed her eyes, her head falling back, throat arching as she felt him inch in, stretching and filling the aching core of her. There was no part of her that didn't feel claimed and possessed by him. His palms flattened with hers, pinning them above her head.

He drove deep, lodging himself inside her. He held himself still there for a moment, watching her face. She wiggled her hips, experimenting, whimpering as the throb flared to life at her center.

His breath hitched, and he pumped his hips, working in and out of her.

The friction made her gasp and cling tighter to him. He increased the tempo, driving into her faster, harder. She met his thrusts, crying out at every impact, straining against their pinned hands. His fingers tightened around hers, holding fast as their bodies moved against each other.

The pressure in her coiled and tensed until it released in a great burst. A shrill cry spilled loose from her throat as she arched against him. She opened her eyes wide, all the colors in the sunlit room brightening and sharpening.

He released her hands.

Her arms fell limp at her sides. He grabbed her thigh, bringing it up and around his hip, lifting her leg as he drove inside of her several more times until he groaned and spent himself, shuddering his release.

"Ela," he gasped near her ear, rolling to the side. Face-to-face, they panted, neither moving.

Moments passed. Slid into minutes. She knew she should move and dress. Anyone could happen upon them. Clara. A servant. But she was reluctant to abandon this perfect cocoon.

"What's it like?" he asked after a while.

"What's what like?" She angled her head and

stared deeply into the pale blue of his eyes, appreciating their beauty.

His hand reached out and smoothed over her belly. "This. Having a child. Being a parent?"

A smile tugged on her mouth and she exhaled.

"Your smile says it all. I've seen it before. Whenever you look at Clara it's there."

"Being a parent is the single most terrifying thing in life." She thought about this a moment longer, testing it for truth. There were times of her life, in her marriage, when she had felt completely lost. She might have even surrendered to despair in those low moments. But motherhood . . . holding that tiny life in her arms for the first time? And then later, watching this little person grow and take flight from the shelter of her arms? Yes. That was even more terrifying than suffering the worst night she had ever endured with Autenberry.

He grimaced, his hand still stroking her belly tenderly. "That's . . . heartening."

She grinned. "Oh, it's thrilling, too," she added in a whisper, her fingers brushing through his hair, reveling in the rich brown. It felt like silk. It reminded her of a stole her mother wore the few times a year it had been warm enough. Her heart pinched a little, thinking of her mother. Even all these years later, she still missed her.

Almost instantly after uttering her wedding vows to Autenberry, regret had assailed her. It lingered in the years of her marriage, but she had stuffed those feelings away, focusing on other things. Happier things like her daughter. She couldn't help but worry if she would soon regret this, too. Would she regret Colin?

She felt slightly ill at the idea. She had never dreamed of being with someone like him . . . handsome and exciting. She would hate for things to end as they did with her late husband. On the surface it was cool civility . . . but underneath? Dislike and contempt. Cruel words as sharp as knives.

She clung to her smile like it were a slippery thing and refused to believe that could happen. Colin might not love her. He might be marrying her out of duty, but he was no Autenberry. "You're going to be a wonderful father." This much she knew was true.

His own smile disappeared from his face. "How do you know that? I can hardly remember my father. I never knew my mother. I never had anyone parent me. My grandmother—" At the mention of her, he stopped with a cringe.

She covered the hand that caressed her stomach with one of her own. "It's about caring, which you will do. You care about people, Colin. You always have. You care now about this child and she's not even here. You'll care when she's born. You'll care every day for the rest of your life . . . even when you want to strangle her for something foolish she says or does. You won't ever stop caring. You'll love her forever."

"She?" he asked, the humor faint and sleepy in his voice. The sound of that velvet voice made ribbons of heat curl through her. Even after they had just come together, he could arouse her again with so little effort. "You're so certain of the gender."

She felt her smile widen. "I think so. Yes."

He made a show of considering that. "I could like having a daughter. One like her mother."

"If she's lucky, she will have your eyes."

"You have very fine eyes, Ela." He curled an arm around her waist and brought her flush to him. "They're deep and soulful. I could lose myself forever in them."

Something crumbled loose inside her. A part of herself she'd been trying so hard to cling to, to keep safe and shielded from him.

It fell, and she couldn't stop it.

Chapter 25

In her nearly twenty years as the Duchess of Autenberry, Graciela had encountered many a steel-eyed dame of the ton who cared little to naught for her station or the due owed to her rank. She read the condemnation in every line writ upon their faces . . . in the wrinkled pursing of lips and the flare of nostrils. She was no proper Englishwoman deserving of the noble designation. She was well accustomed to such treatment.

And yet sitting across from Colin's grandmother, she felt as though she were an eighteen-year-old girl all over again, intimidated and cowed by ladies of superior breeding and years.

The dowager countess knotted her hands around a steel-headed cane and peered closely at Graciela, stripping away flesh and sinew until Graciela felt certain she were examining her very bones.

She was supposed to be preparing for the journey to Holcome Hall, Colin's family seat. Colin left her yesterday afternoon to attend to some business, instructing her to be ready with Clara midmorning.

When she was first informed she had a guest, she assumed it was Mary Rebecca and her daughters. They planned to join them in a few days' time and attend the wedding in Colin's parish church. When Colin asked if she wanted to invite any friends, Mary Rebecca was the first person to pop into her head. Even though Mary Rebecca had betrayed her confidences and told Colin she was with child, she knew her friend meant well and had acted only for her benefit. Graciela had jotted off a missive inviting her last night. Doubtlessly her friend wanted to quiz her on her upcoming nuptials.

Instead, when she arrived in the drawing room, it was to find the dowager countess waiting for her.

"I never entirely approved of my grandson's

association with young Autenberry," she began. "I set aside my reservations, though, because Autenberry was the heir to a dukedom and I had hoped he would not follow in his father's footsteps. That man was the worst manner of reprobate."

In that they were in accord, but Graciela bit her tongue. She did not sense that the lady wanted to hear from her. Indeed, *she* wanted to be heard, not to listen.

She continued, "Duke or not, he was commonplace. His marriage to you is merely one example to that."

Graciela inhaled, marveling how these dames considered themselves to be so well-bred but then felt free to deliver whatever insults seized them.

"You're past your prime," Lady Strickland went on to add. "But fetching enough. Good bones." Her gaze skimmed over her as though she were assessing horseflesh. Graciela held her chin high and suffered the lady's scrutiny. "Ample bosom."

She inhaled a stinging breath.

"All things that shall disappear in the coming years and then what will my grandson be left with? He shall still be in his prime whilst you shall be a woman past her peak, unable to do the one thing God put you on earth for."

"And that is?"

She blinked at her like that were the most startling of foolish questions. "Why, to provide your husband with sons."

She grimaced. "Of course. How silly I did not guess."

"But men never consider the future. That falls to us. To the mothers, and in Colin's case, me. It is my duty to keep him on the right path."

"Why is it you have come here, my lady?" Graciela finally asked.

"You have a healthy child."

Again, Graciela was certain she knew that already. "Yes."

"A daughter." The dowager pursed her lips as though this wasn't entirely satisfactory.

"Yes. Clara is upstairs."

She flexed a heavily veined hand and leaned forward more, her neck stretching out crane-like. "Is it true you've lost a babe before? More than once, in fact?"

Graciela sucked in a breath, feeling very much as though she were a child being interrogated for wrongdoing. "It appears you know a great deal about me." She shifted uneasily, wondering what else she knew. Could she possibly know she was already with child? Had Colin told her?

"I've done my research. It's my duty to know the kind of woman my grandson has chosen for himself."

"Understandable," she murmured, feeling suddenly bared and vulnerable in front of this woman.

"You are not the right match for him," she grimly pronounced.

Could this get any more uncomfortable? She glanced around the room as though searching for an escape.

"I understand this must be difficult to accept, my lady." Graciela herself had difficulty accepting it. So much so she'd practically run away before Colin stopped her.

"Do you in fact understand that?" Lady Strickland angled her head, the cap atop her gray hair coming dangerously close to falling. "If that is the case, then you must own that this is an unorthodox match."

After a moment, Graciela nodded.

The lady pressed on. "And yet you persist in moving forward."

Graciela felt as though she were tiptoeing through a maze of thorns. There was no way to avoid a misstep. No way to avoid getting cut.

"You appear an intelligent woman, and you're

certainly no green girl." Again, the unsubtle dig to her age. "Obviously you can see how inadvisable this match is. My grandson is young. He needs heirs. Sons. He not only needs them, he *wants* them. It seems unlikely you can provide him with those."

He wants them. Somehow that affected her more than the notion of him needing them to extend his progeny.

She took a bracing breath. Part of her delighted to know that she carried his babe now, but then another part of her felt sick knowing that this would likely be the only child she could give him and it might very well be a girl. Would he be disappointed? Would he come to regret marrying her? As Autenberry had done?

She pushed aside the negative thought. Worrying would do no good now. There was no choice in the matter. Colin insisted they wed and she had agreed.

The dowager arched an eyebrow, clearly waiting for some manner of response from Graciela.

She had none to give. There was nothing she could say at this time to appease the old dragon. She wasn't about to inform her of her condition. She would not suffer the indignity of admitting to that.

"Have you nothing to say?"

Graciela found her voice. "We are already engaged. The announcement went out and Colin has procured a special license."

The dowager waved a hand dismissively. "Nothing irreparable. Nothing that cannot be undone. You are not wed yet."

She shook her head, the knot of discomfort that had formed from the first moment of this encounter expanding within her chest. "You should really speak to your grandson about this. I've accepted his offer. I will not renege."

She snorted. "I've already done so."

"And what did he say?"

"I'm here, am I not? The stubborn lad seems to feel like he's obligated to wed you." She tensed beneath the dowager's probing stare. "Apparently you've told him you're increasing."

The words hit her like perfectly aimed arrows. From the way the woman spoke—and looked at her—she obviously had her doubts regarding the veracity of this.

"Well?" she demanded almost shrilly. "Is it true?"

She thought she was lying? Graciela inhaled deeply. Oh, why had Colin confided in her? Did he think it necessary to explain why he would want to marry her? "I think you should leave."

Lady Strickland huffed. "You're asking me to leave? Well, I never have been treated so rudely!"

Graciela flexed her neatly folded fingers in her lap. "Have you not? I find that surprising."

Lady Strickland's mouth sagged, resembling a gaping fish's. Graciela rose and moved to open one of the drawing room doors, indicating she should take her leave.

Leaning heavily on her cane, she pushed to her feet and made her way to the door, her cane contacting loudly with the floor in a steady staccato of thumps. Reaching the door, she stopped and glared at Graciela.

"You should free him. Even if you are with child and this is not some desperate ruse, what are the odds you will deliver to fruition and bear him a son? You will ruin his life. Let him go so that he can then go about marrying a more suitable female."

A more *suitable* female. The words stung. Not because she thought anything was wrong with her. Not because she thought she was unsuitable and undeserving.

They stung because Colin did not love her . . .

and loving her was the only thing that would keep him from regretting marrying her in future days.

She glanced out the door. Seeing no servants lurking, she gestured for Lady Strickland to move ahead of her. "I'll show you out."

"You needn't overly tax yourself. You are kicking me out of your home, after all," she sneered.

Ignoring the snide comment, Graciela led her from the room. At the top of the stairs, she took Lady Strickland's cane from her so that she could cling to the railing for support. She motioned for Graciela to go first. "I'm much too slow. Go ahead of me."

Complying, she started to descend just as voices sounded from below. Her gaze searched ahead, spotting Mary Rebecca entering the foyer. The doorman took her cloak and gloves. Graciela's chest lightened a little.

After her audience with Colin's grandmother, Mary Rebecca was a welcome sight. She was more than halfway to the bottom, a few more steps to go, and calling out a greeting just as she felt something collide hard into her from behind.

A gush of breath escaped her. Her fingers flew to the railing, but she was already moving, propelled too far forward. Velocity and gravity were not on her side.

She was going to fall.

Terror lodged in her throat as her fingers slipped against the cold iron of the railing, trying and failing to get a grip. To hang on to something.

Then she was falling.

Screams filled her ears. Her own or Mary Rebecca's, she was not sure.

The steps rushed up to meet her in a blur. Contact. Jarring pain. Blood at lips. A sharp edge jammed into her elbow.

All the air pushed out from her body as she tumbled down the steps and came to a hard, bruising stop on the marble floor of the foyer.

The world spun around her in a dizzying vortex. Moving so swiftly that nausea rose up in her throat.

And then there was nothing. No sound. No color.

But thankfully, no more pain.

Chapter 26

Graciela waded through a fog, her feet like solid blocks of stone. At least that was how it felt. How *she* felt. Her limbs like lead. Her eyes ever peering into a shadowland. Vestiges of figures drifted ahead, darker smudges within the rolling gray, like wisps of smoke impossible to reach or identify.

She called out, her voice tinny and small.

Those dark ribbons twisted and danced on the air, flickering in and out, away and farther away. Teasing ghosts.

She forced her heavy legs to keep going. Keep moving. Searching. Pushing against the dragging weight, against the deepening ache, the widening void inside her.

Colin.

And something more.

There was another reason for the gnawing bleakness, but it was elusive, rubbing at the edges of her mind like rain at a windowpane, fighting to get in.

She reached for whatever it was. For the intangible thing she felt slipping and draining from her body, easing out like fluid from a sieve.

She stretched her arms, hands wide-open, attempting to seize hold of everything she was losing even if her muddled mind was too clouded to understand.

Her heart knew.

COLIN CLUNG TO Ela's cold hand, lifeless at her side. He bowed his head, his forehead dropping beside her, resting on the bed next to her motionless arm, willing her to move. Get up. Talk. Walk. Be his again.

His fingers flexed around her hand, unable to let go of the softness.

He would never let go.

Her breath came in tiny, labored rasps, lifting

her chest. It was the only movement she made, but proof enough that she lived, and that was everything. All that mattered right now, in this moment.

"My lord." A hand brushed his shoulder.

The voice belonged to Lady Talbot. She had been there from the start of this nightmare. She had witnessed it all. Ever since Ela fell. Since she was *pushed*. Bile rose up in his throat.

Ever since Ela had been *pushed*.

The thought shuddered through him and went down his throat like a jagged shard of glass. His own grandmother had done this to her. Because of him. Ultimately, it was because of him that Ela had been hurt. It was a difficult thing to accept. Something he might never be able to accept.

She was to be his wife and bear his child. The one thing in his life he should have done was make certain no harm befell her. And he had failed in that. If he could go back and untouch her, undo everything, including his pursuit of her, he would. Instantly. If it meant she wouldn't be here like this, he would undo it all.

His gaze devoured her, hurt and broken in her bed.

Hurt. Not broken, he corrected. *Not dead.* He gave her hand the slightest squeeze. Not dead.

The physician had been summoned. He'd come and gone after setting Ela's arm in a sling, promising to return first thing in the morning. He believed her wrist to be badly sprained. Thankfully, she had not fallen from too high a perch, nor did it appear her head sustained any injury in the fall. He'd pronounced her lucky and her recovery as promising.

Right now, as Colin stared down at her, it was difficult to feel lucky. Watching her lying there so bruised and battered with her arm tucked to her side, he had never felt so helpless in all his life.

He was still terrified that she might somehow never open her eyes again. That he might never hear her voice again. Knowing all of this could have been avoided if not for his lunatic grandmother only made the bite deeper . . . sharper.

By the time he had arrived, his grandmother was gone. She'd fled and no one had attempted to stop her. Little thought had been given to the old woman in the wake of the damage she had wrought. The household had been in chaos, all care and focus on Ela. As it should have been.

He did not fault any of the staff for letting his grandmother go. He would handle her later. For now he could not think to leave Ela's side.

Besides, there was no place for that old woman to hide. No place where he would not find her.

"You should take a meal," Lady Talbot suggested.

He simply shook his head, not glancing her way. He kept his gaze trained on Ela. She was pale beneath the usual golden hue of her skin. Dark smudges that resembled bruises marred the thin skin beneath her eyes.

Lady Talbot's fingers tightened ever so slightly on his shoulder. "Then rest for a while in another room. You're no good to her dead exhausted."

"I'll rest enough sitting in this chair."

"Strickland—"

He shot a glance over his shoulder. "I'll rest when she's awake. After I hear her voice with my own ears. When I hear her tell me that she's fine."

Lady Talbot stared at him a moment before nodding.

Suddenly Ela lurched up in bed. Clutching her middle, she brought her knees to her chest and bowed over them with a shrill scream that tore through him.

Lady Talbot rushed to Ela, grasping her gently. "Ela!"

Colin reached for her hand, repeating her name as fear gripped him. He'd wanted her awake, but awake and well. Not like this. Not in pain. Ela in pain clawed through him, making him want to howl out his own agony.

Ela tipped over as though a great wind knocked her over on the bed. Lady Talbot leaned over her. "Ela! What is it?"

He climbed upon the bed on the other side of her, surrounding her, yet careful not to jar or cause her further pain. Her wide eyes gazed up at him, glazed with pain. He'd wanted to stare into her open eyes again, but he didn't want to witness such pain in their depths.

Sweat dotted her brow and tiny tendrils of damp hair clung all around her face.

He came over her, wiping the hair back from her forehead carefully, uncertain where she was hurt and not wanting to make anything worse for her. He wanted only to fix her . . . take all her pain inside himself so that she would never suffer again.

"Ela," he crooned. "What is it? What's wrong?"

She shook her head, her glass eyes welling with tears as her gaze fixed on him, grabbing hold of him in a manner that he felt as tangibly as a fist around his heart. "It's happening."

"What's happening, love?" Just then he noticed a wetness beneath his hand where it was propped upon the bed. He lifted his palm off the bed and brought it before his face, his fingers splayed wide, each digit covered in glistening blood.

Her gaze followed to his hand and a twisted, animal whimper escaped her. "Again," she choked before closing her eyes and dropping her head back on the bed.

Lady Talbot gasped and turned toward where the housekeeper hovered near the door. "Send for the midwife. Quickly."

His bloodied hand seemed to glare back at him, the brutal smears of crimson startling on his skin, holding him riveted.

He had not thought of this. His only thought had been for Ela . . . for *her* well-being. Perhaps it should have occurred to him. It was the reason they were getting married, after all. The reason he had told her, at least.

And yet he'd been wrapped up exclusively in Ela. He had not thought of the child. He hadn't thought his fear could get any worse.

He'd been wrong. This was another fear. Their child.

She was losing their baby.

BY THE TIME the midwife arrived, the worst of the pains had stopped.

Ela no longer cried out and her breathing had evened into a steady cadence. Tired, but even and mild.

It was the only reason he agreed to leave her side and step out into the corridor.

He left the room briefly so that Mary Rebecca and the housekeeper could freshen the linens and help her change clothes. He paced a brisk line outside the door, listening for any sounds that floated through the door, dragging his hands through his hair and pulling hard at the strands.

"Colin?"

He looked up at the sound of Clara's voice.

"Clara," he greeted.

"Is she better?"

"She's awake," he answered.

She released a heavy breath as she continued to stare at him. "Who is that woman? The one in there with Mama?"

He stared back at her. It wasn't his place to explain that a midwife was attending to her mother. "She's here to help your mother."

"But you said she woke up. Isn't she well now?"

He studied this girl who so resembled Ela and felt a surge of protectiveness. He wrapped an arm around her and hugged her. "Of course she is."

The door to the chamber opened and Lady

Talbot stuck her head out. "You can come in now." Her gaze flicked to Clara. "Lord Strickland," she clarified as though he needed to be told that the girl shouldn't enter the bedchamber to witness whatever waited within.

He nodded and stepped away from Clara.

She snatched hold of his wrist. "I want to see her. I need to see her." Clara looked at him so resolutely, her chin thrust out defiantly. She suddenly appeared far older than her fourteen years.

Lady Talbot stepped out into the corridor. The door snicked shut after her as she put her arm around Clara's shoulders and gave her a comforting squeeze. "Not just yet, my dear. Let Colin see her first and then you can come in for a short bit. Your mama is very tired and needs her rest."

Lady Talbot's eyes connected with his and she motioned with her hand, indicating he should enter the chamber.

He didn't need to be told twice. He slipped inside the room. Evening had fallen and it was darker than when he last occupied the space. Lantern light suffused the room and Ela was a motionless shape beneath the covers, her dark hair loose, fanned out all around her.

The midwife was closing up her bag. Mrs.

Wakefield stood close by and the somber mood of the room brought him to a halt.

The midwife lifted her gaze to his. Mrs. Wakefield's gaze skittered away . . . a first for that usually direct lady.

He took a hesitant step forward, his gaze seeking Ela on the bed. He said her name softly. "Ela?"

She didn't stir. She was curled on her side, her back to him, almost as though she was closing him out. Not only him. It felt as though she were closing out the world.

The midwife cleared her throat. He looked to her, searching the kind lines of her face for answers. "How is she?" he asked, the words feeling as though they were ripped from somewhere deep inside him. In his mind, he still saw the blood, heard her cries, saw her stricken eyes.

"She will mend."

He breathed a little easier. His gaze darted back to her and he stepped closer to the bed, determined to see her face, to touch her. He stopped right at the edge, noting the stiff line of her shoulders. She didn't appear to invite anyone's touch.

He looked back at the midwife, noting again her grim expression. His stomach clenched, knowing without having to be told—there was more.

Ela would mend. No mention of the baby.

"And?" he prompted. He might already know, but he needed to hear it. He needed to know.

She shook her head forlornly. "I'm sorry. There was a great deal of blood. I've never seen a baby survive this kind of trauma. I can't say for certain yet, of course . . . but I don't see how it is possible."

A cry choked out from Ela then. He eased down beside her and touched her back.

"Please, don't," she rasped.

"I'm sorry, Ela . . . so sorry." He dropped his hand onto the bed, inching toward her arm, hoping that would be more welcome.

She pulled away as though sensing his oncoming touch. "It's not your fault," she said in a small, tired voice. "You and I were never meant to be, Colin. I suppose none of this was."

He stared hard at the back of her.

She continued. "We don't have to pretend anymore or use an innocent child to bind us together." The words felt like rocks striking him, cutting his skin and stroking deep. "I've already suffered one loveless marriage. I pasted the fake smiles on and let lying words of love drip from my lips. I can't do it again."

"Is that what we were doing?" he asked.

"When you found out about the baby and came

to me, you said we must marry. For the baby. For your honor. Well, you don't have to do that anymore." She sniffled. "Just go."

Her words were no more than a whisper, but they cut him nonetheless. She sounded utterly serious. She wanted him gone.

"I'll be just outside if you need me." He turned and started to leave, noticing that the midwife had quickly taken herself away.

Graciela's voice carried from the bed, stopping him. "Don't."

He turned back around. "Don't . . . what?"

"You don't need to wait outside." He heard her inhale a shuddery breath. "I don't want you to stay here at all. Did you not hear her? It's over. None of this should ever have happened. Go and don't come back, Colin."

He took a step toward her. "Ela, don't say anything you don't mean right now."

She rolled to face him. The sight of her hit him like a blow. She was a so pale. Smudges stood out under eyes like bruises on her skin. "You heard her. There's no baby. A child can't survive that much blood loss. The baby is gone. Again." The last word broke off in a sob.

He closed the distance between them and sank down on the edge of the bed, unable to stay away whilst her heart was so clearly breaking. He knew he couldn't undo anything, but he had to go to her. She held up a hand as though to ward him off.

"Don't you understand?" she bit out. "You're free."

"Ela, we're to be married. I have the special license. We have plans . . ."

She raised her head off the pillow, her eyes gleaming with tears as she glared at him. "The only reason you wanted to marry me was because there was a baby. We never pretended it was for any other reason. We can't change our past mistakes but we can stop future ones."

Frustration welled up inside him. She was correct. He'd never provided her any other reason for their marriage. He'd never claimed love or fondness or even lust. He'd been a coward and used the baby as the reason when it had only ever been a convenient excuse to bind himself to Ela forever.

Because he wanted forever with her.

She continued, repeating those words and believing them—an awful reminder of how he had failed, "Now there's no baby. You're free, Colin."

"Ela." He reached for her hand but she pulled it away.

"I'm not marrying you. There's nothing you can say to compel me to."

Through the sheen of tears in her eyes, cold resolution stared back at him. He'd never seen her like this. She wasn't the Ela he knew anymore. So bleak. So stony and distant from him. It was as though she looked straight through him.

"I know what I said, Ela. The baby was only a part of it. I want to marry *you*. I care about you. I want to marry you because I've never wanted a woman more than I want you." There were more words, more truths, hovering on his tongue. He didn't get them out fast enough for her.

"Stop it." She shook her head. "This is pity talking. Or obligation. I don't know and I don't care. Get out."

He opened his mouth to further refute her accusations but then she rolled back on her side, presenting him with her rigid back. She'd been through hell today. And it was his fault.

He released a breath and turned for the door, but then he paused and looked back.

She was still curled on her side with her back to him, her hair pooling like dark ink around her. In his mind he could still envision her bloodless face. He wanted the color back in her skin . . . the life back in her eyes. As much as his chest ached, he knew she hurt even more. He longed to take the hurt from her. And yet he knew he couldn't. He'd respect her wishes for now and let her rest, sleep and recover her strength. But then he'd be back.

He wasn't forgetting about her no matter what she said to him.

When he entered the hall, there was no sign of Mary Rebecca or Clara. He descended the stairs, his hand skimming the railing. For a moment he had a flash of Ela on these very same steps, tumbling to the base. He pressed a hand to his gut, feeling sick. He knew he should be grateful that she was alive and would mend, but his grandmother's actions had not been without a cost. Their child was gone. He and Ela might never have a child.

And as much as losing their child pained him, he didn't care if they ever had another child. He wanted *her*. Not for the sons she could provide him. He'd take a lifetime with her over a marriage to another woman who could provide him a dozen sons.

One thought brought him to a jarring mental halt.

Perhaps she sincerely didn't want to marry him and she had agreed only for the baby.

The front door opened as he reached the bottom of the stairs, still struggling with that sour possibility.

Enid marched inside, carrying a valise.

They both stopped and stared at each other for a moment until a doorman stepped forward to help her from her cloak and take her gloves and valise.

"You came back," he said unnecessarily.

She nodded. "Yes. I might have been hasty and . . . unreasonable in my anger. It was just a shock." She paused and sucked in a breath, hot color flooding her face. "You see, I might have harbored feelings—"

"Shock was understandable," he interrupted, sparing her and himself. He was in no mood for her awkward confession. "And no need to explain further. Truly." *Please.*

She inhaled, looking at him gratefully.

"Your stepmother missed you. She was worried."

She nodded, her expression turning guilty. "I should not have left the way I did. I'm not proud of myself."

He motioned to the stairs. "Nonsense. I'm certain the sight of you will lift her spirits." He stopped a beat. "She met with an accident today."

He cringed saying the words that made light of all that had happened, but he didn't want to alarm Enid.

"An accident? What happened?"

"Enid!" Lady Talbot called from the top of the stairs. "You're home!" She descended the steps quickly. "Ela will be so happy that you've re-turned."

He accepted his cloak from the doorman, Ela's words still ringing in his ears. *Get out. Go and don't come back, Colin.*

"You're leaving?" Lady Talbot met his gaze. Disappointment tinged her voice. He didn't bother explaining that Ela had demanded his departure. Or that he would return.

"She needs her rest," he said, leaving it at that.

He turned and exited the house.

It took him all of five minutes to decide he would be back.

And who would be with him when he returned.

BY THE NEXT day, Graciela felt more like herself again. At least physically. A little sore, but hale enough. Heartbroken, but no longer in pain. Her body no longer suffered. She would live. She was alive—her heart beating even if it felt dead. Crushed.

There would be no baby. There would be no marriage. No Colin. No *them*.

The midwife had checked on her and stated she was pleased at Ela's progress—whatever that meant. Despite her cheerful demeanor, nothing had changed. There could be no baby now. And there was no Colin anymore. Not in her life.

She knew her words to him had been cruel. Grief had made her lash out, but she would not take them back if she could. She spoke only the truth. Ugly, painful truth.

The only reason they had planned to marry was for the baby. That reason was gone. They would not marry now. He was free. She had set him free to live his life. The manner of life for which he was intended. A life that did not include her.

A brief knock at the door sounded. She looked up just as it swung inward and Colin himself entered the room.

Her heart plunged traitorously.

"Colin? What are you doing here?" She propped herself a little higher in the bed.

Mrs. Wakefield stepped around him. "I'm sorry, Your Grace. He insisted on coming up here. I tried to make him wait." Clara hovered just beyond her, her eyes wide and inquiring.

The ache in Graciela's chest intensified. The sight of him here, when she had already let him go, when the wounds were so fresh . . .

"Go, Colin," she said tiredly. "Please. Set your honor and pity and obligation aside and—"

He glanced her up and down, as though assuring himself that she was properly attired. Seemingly satisfied that her dressing gown covered her well enough, he stepped back out into the corridor. She heard a few murmured words and realized he was speaking to someone. One moment later, he was tugging a gentleman she had never seen before into her bedchamber.

She clutched her dressing gown. Mrs. Wakefield squawked and pushed in behind them. Clara followed hot on their heels.

"Ela, this is the Reverend Rothe. He is here to marry us."

The room fell silent. She didn't blink as she stared at Colin. She didn't even look at the reverend.

A boulder-sized lump rose up in her throat. She fought to swallow it.

Colin took halting steps toward the bed. "Ela," he said gently.

"No," she managed to get out. "This is cruel.

You have overstepped." She shot a glance at the reverend. "Stop this. You go too far."

"No." Colin hastened to her bed and sank down on the edge beside her. "Not far enough. I will never go far enough when it concerns you. Shove me away today. Tomorrow. Next year. I will still be here. I will continue to come for you. Unless—" He stopped for a bracing breath. His gaze locked on her, unflinching, searing. "Unless you can look at me and tell me you don't love me. Because I love you, Ela. I love you and likely always have. It's you I want to spend my life with. It will be you or no other."

She ceased to breathe.

Several moments passed and Clara's skirts rustled as she shifted impatiently. "Mama. Say something," she hissed, motioning wildly with her hands.

Graciela moistened her lips and stared into the eyes of the man she loved . . . and wondered if it could be true. If he could love her as she loved him. If she could be so fortunate and so blessed to have found the thing that she had craved all her life and assumed out of reach to her.

"Ela," he whispered. "Say something. Say yes."

Say yes.

She searched his gaze, looking for the pity, the deep-rooted honor and guilt over what his grandmother had done. She looked for evidence for any of those things. Because if she saw any of that, she would know that he did not really love her. She would know why he was here.

She didn't see that, however. In the brilliance of his stare she saw only one thing. She saw love.

She nodded jerkily, a sob welling up in her chest. "You love me," she choked.

He leaned in, pulling her into his arms. Holding her close, he buried his face in her hair and whispered near her ear. "Of course I love you. I adore you and love you and want to spend my life with you."

She wept as he drew back and pressed kisses to her cheeks and lips, uncaring of their audience.

"I love you, my sweet girl."

"I love you, too," she returned.

He nodded, smiling widely. "Then are you ready to get married?"

She glanced at the reverend, who was smiling indulgently. Even Clara appeared weepy as she hugged Mrs. Wakefield. Both of them, in fact, looked teary eyed.

"Yes. Yes, I am."

Still sitting on the bed with her, he turned to face the reverend, wrapping one arm around her. "We're ready."

"Very good." The gentleman smiled and opened the small Bible he held. "Let's begin."

Chapter 27

Months later . . .

"It's simply not done, Colin," Ela managed to get out between clenched teeth. "You're not supposed to be here." It wasn't the first time she had pointed this out to her husband, but it didn't make him budge from her side—and for all her words of protest, she clung to his hand, squeezing all the harder as her stomach painfully tightened and another wave swelled upon her.

"Really, my lord," the midwife seconded. "Her Ladyship is correct. It's really not done. You should not be in here."

"She can be correct in this and I can be wrong."

He shrugged. "But if you think I'm leaving her side, then you're mad." Colin looked at Graciela as he spoke the words evenly and without heat. He winked at her.

She knew she must look a fright. Her hair had long ago come unbound. Tendrils stuck to her clammy cheeks and neck. She had been hours like this, moaning in pain—but he stared at her with the same love in his eyes as on the day they had married. Perhaps even more. She knew she felt more love for him. It grew each day.

He smoothed the sweaty strands of hair back off her forehead. "I'm not leaving your side."

Amid heavy pants, she nodded as though he were in fact waiting on her agreement.

It had been a long road until this moment. The day he had burst in her chamber with the reverend and sworn his love and married her, they had believed their baby lost.

Now they knew, of course. They had been wrong. Miraculously wrong.

The midwife had been mistaken. Despite the initial blood loss, the babe had continued to grow and thrive in her womb. More than thrive. Ela had grown to whale-like proportions.

She readjusted her grip around his hand, lacing their fingers together as though binding them for life. Not an unrealistic description. Ever since they took their vows, they'd been together every day, enjoying each other with an ease and contentment she had never known before. She was happy. Stupidly, deliriously, blissfully happy.

She'd certainly never believed such a fate could be hers, but it was. Nothing had marred her joy all these months. Not even her lingering fear for the baby. As long as she had Colin and the rest of her family, she felt strong. Even when news reached them of his grandmother's death, it made scarcely a ripple. It was as though a door had been forever closed to that wretched day on the stairs. There was only the present and the future and both belonged to them.

At the insistence of the midwife, she had spent her confinement with very little activity. If she wasn't in bed, then Colin carried her to the salon or drawing room. She was only allowed to walk in order to make use of the facilities and bathe herself.

It had been a long confinement. Even though her instinct had been to protest everyone hovering over her all these months, she had swallowed the urge. They only wanted the best for her and the baby. She, too, wanted to avoid all risks.

Finally, the day had arrived. The baby was coming. And she was thrilled to finally meet their child.

She expelled a breath as blinding agony assailed her again, squeezing her swollen belly. She gritted against the pain, but it was no use. A scream escaped. The sound was unlike anything she had ever heard from herself or any living thing.

"That's it," Mrs. Silver crooned. "I can see the head, Your Ladyship. Baby is coming! Baby is almost here."

"Did you hear that, Ela? You're doing brilliantly. You're almost done."

She dropped back on the bed, gasping hard and still clinging to her husband's hand.

"Now listen to me, my lady. I want you to get ready for another mighty push. If it's big enough, this should be the last one."

"You hear that, Ela? One more and you'll be done . . . and we will meet our baby."

No other words could have compelled her to deliver a greater push. Still clasping Colin's hand, she seized hold of her knee and bore down.

The tension slipped from her body in a rush as her baby came into the world squalling loud enough to alert the entire city of London.

She collapsed, sobbing as aftershocks shook her exhausted body.

Her head felt heavy and wobbly on her neck as she tried to lift it for a glimpse of her child for the first time.

"My lady," Mrs. Silver exclaimed as she lifted the baby up in the air. "You have a fine son. Just give me a moment," she murmured as she worked to cut the cord and wrap him in a thin blanket.

"A son," Graciela choked, tears blurring her eyes as she looked at her husband. "Colin . . . you have a son."

"*We* have a son." He kissed her gently, his fingers lightly stroking her hair.

The midwife lowered her son into her arms. She accepted the warm bundle, gasping softly at her first sight of him. She'd known this moment was coming. She'd known she was having a baby, but this all felt like a dream. Something out of reality and far too good to be true.

The tears started all over again as she feasted her gaze on the baby she had been talking to all these months. "Hello there, my little gentleman. I'm your mother." She traced the perfect bow mouth, the soft curve of his brow and the tiny nose. She captured one of his fists, stroking the satiny skin.

She winced as the midwife prodded at her tender areas, working to put her back to rights. Mrs. Wakefield stood beside her, assisting as she had done throughout the birth.

Ela ignored the discomfort, so enamored of the tiny, perfect life in her arms.

Colin leaned down to press a kiss to their son's forehead, just below the downy thatch of brown hair. "He's beautiful." Wonder tinged his voice. "Like his mother."

"He has the look of you." She stroked the line of his tiny eyebrows. "See. Here. In his brows and the shape of his eyes."

She flinched as another wave of pain came over her. It had been a long time since she last gave birth—it felt a lifetime ago—but she knew she was not yet finished with all the messy business. The afterbirth was yet to come. Although she didn't remember that part as being especially uncomfortable. She hissed out a tight breath. Not like this.

She couldn't mask her pain for long, however. No matter how much she wanted to pretend all was well and revel in the beauty of her son. Her breathing hitched, growing more labored.

"Ela?" Colin's gaze flickered over her face, his forehead creasing in concern.

She nodded. "I—I'm fine—" Another flood of pain crashed over her then and she cried out.

"Ela!" He carefully removed the baby from her arms.

"Something isn't right." She gasped and arched back on the bed as pain knifed her lower back. She might not remember everything, but this . . .

It had *not* been like this the last time. Of that she was absolutely certain.

"What is wrong?" Colin demanded of the midwife as he cradled their son. "Is this normal? Is this—"

Ela cried out again. She couldn't help it. She didn't want anyone to fret, but this was as bad as the labor itself. It shouldn't still hurt like this.

She met Colin's eyes. He looked beautiful holding their son, and her heart clenched. Could she be dying? Could she be leaving them both now? Leaving Clara?

The midwife pressed and felt her drum-tight abdomen and then examined between her legs. Ela peered down at her, reading her anxious expression and trying to comprehend what was happening.

"What is it?" Colin demanded, his voice hard and panicked. She'd never heard such a tone from him before.

Their son began to cry, his plaintive wails filling the air over Mrs. Silver's voice as she feverishly spoke to Mrs. Wakefield, her voice too low for Ela to comprehend.

She dropped her head back on the bed, a keening moan ripping from her as the pain in her back spread over her hips to seize hold of her stomach.

Colin called to her between shouting at the midwife and Mrs. Wakefield.

Mrs. Silver lifted up from between her thighs, a perplexing smile on her face that was in direct contrast to the pain and fear that held Graciela hostage. "My lady, it appears your work here is not done."

She raised her head off the bed. "What?"

"You've one more baby to deliver."

Garbled speech escaped Colin, his expression almost comical for all its astonishment.

She looked from his eye-bulging face to the midwife. "You cannot be serious!"

Mrs. Silver nodded. "Indeed I am. I missed the second heartbeat. My apologies, but I should have suspected. You were a little large." She stopped and directed Mrs. Wakefield for more fresh towels and water. The housekeeper quickly turned to the maid standing behind her, sending her to fetch more supplies.

Mrs. Silver continued, "There's also a greater amount of multiples born to women of your age." She shook her head, still grinning madly. "Not sure the reason behind it. I always thought it was God's last gift to women who were unlikely to bear more children . . . or his sense of humor." She chuckled.

Ela shook her own head and moaned, "This cannot be happening. I don't think I can do it again."

"Oh, you can. And you are."

The maid returned with the needed materials.

Ela turned to Colin and reached for his hand. "Colin."

He shook his head as though coming out of a stupor. "Ela." A slow smile spread across his face.

"Here we are," Mrs. Silver proclaimed. "I can see the head."

The head. Another baby.

She struggled around this new reality. All these months she had struggled with the notion that she could even have another child. Now she was having two.

"Can you give me another push, my lady?"

She shook her head, quite exhausted, but then she looked at Colin and saw him holding their son. He nodded encouragingly at her. Her heart swelled with fresh love. She had to do this. She had to bring their remaining family into the world.

She rose up, gripped her knees and pushed.

Her third child was born, howling possibly even louder than the last one she'd just brought into the world.

"Another boy!" Mrs. Silver cried.

Two boys? Two sons? Sobbing in joy, she looked at Colin . . . only to see he was crying, too.

Mrs. Wakefield took the second baby as the midwife tended to Ela. Colin sank down beside her, placing their firstborn son in the cradle of her arm. Soon their second son was placed in her other arm, tucked into her side.

Colin leaned over and pressed gentle kisses on each of their boys before turning and pressing a slow, tear-laced kiss to her lips. "I love you, my beautiful wife."

Epilogue

Three months later . . .

Graciela eased out of the nursery, shutting the door carefully behind her and releasing a sigh at the blessed silence, however short-lived it would be. She had just placed Nicholas down beside his brother for a much-needed nap. Unlike James, who cherished his sleep and could hardly be roused even for a feeding, Nicholas fought it, preferring to stay awake, his wide eyes watching the world as though fearful he might miss something.

Turning, she strolled down the corridor, grateful for the quiet and hoping it lasted long enough for her to catch a moment alone with Colin. She knew she could leave the care of the babies to servants, and while she did often accept their help—sometimes exhaustion demanded it—she was there for the babies as much as possible. She wanted it that way. She had not known a life such as this could be hers and she did not intend to let a moment of it go by unappreciated.

"Ah, my lady, there you are," Minnie called out, rounding the corner. "This letter just arrived for you. It bears the Duke of Autenberry's mark. I knew you would want it at once."

Her heart leapt. She had not heard from her stepson since he discovered the truth of her affair with Colin. She'd sent letters to all their various properties, detailing the news of her marriage, hoping at least one of the missives would reach Marcus.

With a hurried thank you, she eagerly accepted the envelope and tore into it as hope beat hard in her chest.

Colin assured her Marcus would forgive them and come home eventually. She hoped this would be the evidence of that.

Her fingers fumbled as she unfolded the parchment. Her eyes scanned Marcus's bold scrawl. The missive was short. To the point, but no less shocking. Gasping, she let it drop from her fingers. Lifting her skirts, she raced to find Colin, eventually locating him in the library.

He looked up as she burst inside the room.

"Colin," she finally cried breathlessly, coming to a stop. "Marcus sent word."

He rose from behind the desk swiftly and approached, concern knitting his forehead. "Is everything all right? Is he well?"

She nodded and swallowed as she fought for air. "He is. At least I think so. He's coming home."

Colin clasped her arms and squeezed warmly. "There now. That's brilliant news. I told you he would come around."

She shook her head, smiling uncertainly. "He's not coming home alone." She cleared her throat. "He's bringing a woman with him."

"Is he now?" Colin's expression reflected his surprise. "Well. That is . . . interesting."

She nodded, her heart still pounding. "Indeed. He says she's his wife."